Abigail had the most singular urge to touch him,

to slide her palms over the contours of his body and see if he felt as hard as he looked. The idea that Willem Tremain was dangerous gained more substance with every passing moment. Suddenly she felt downright feverish and more light-headed than the time she drank too much of Lars's dandelion wine.

Unable to stop herself, she raised her fingertips to touch the coin hung around his neck, lightly brushing against his warm, moist skin. Every inch of his body went rigid, and he sucked in his breath with a sharp hiss that made her own skin prickle in response.

"*Abigail.*" Her name was spoken in clear, sharp warning. She jerked her hand back in alarm and shifted her gaze to his face. An emotion unlike any she'd ever read there before burned in his eyes. His jaw was clamped so tightly, his cheek muscles were jumping in rhythmic fashion, and his mouth was drawn into an uncompromising line.

She took a step backward. Something wild and raw had glowed in his eyes, something that made her tremble....

Dear Reader,

When Abigail Cooprel suddenly comes face-to-face with a man who is the very image of her adopted son, she realizes that she will do anything to keep her child, even marry a stranger. *Abbie's Child* is the second book from talented newcomer Linda Castle, whose first book, *Fearless Hearts,* was released during our annual March Madness promotion in 1995, to loud acclaim. Don't miss this month's title, and be sure to keep an eye out for her next book, *The Return of Chase Cordell,* coming in December.

Multigenre author Merline Lovelace can make any time period come alive, and in her new release, *Lady of the Upper Kingdom,* she does just that. This dramatic story of forbidden love brings together two strong-willed people as they struggle to overcome the treachery and distrust that exists between their two cultures, the Egyptian and the Greek.

The new Medieval from Catherine Archer, *Velvet Touch,* the sequel to her previous book, *Velvet Bond,* is the bittersweet story of a young nobleman who is sent by his king to arrange a marriage and settle a feud, only to fall in love with the intended bride. And three-time RITA Award winner, contemporary author Cheryl Reavis, is back this month with *The Bartered Bride,* the moving story of a pregnant woman who must swallow her pride and marry her sister's widower, set in Civil War North Carolina.

Whatever your taste in reading, we hope you will enjoy all four Harlequin Historicals, available wherever books are sold.

Sincerely,

Tracy Farrell,
Senior Editor

LINDA CASTLE

ABBIE'S Child

Harlequin Books

TORONTO • NEW YORK • LONDON
AMSTERDAM • PARIS • SYDNEY • HAMBURG
STOCKHOLM • ATHENS • TOKYO • MILAN
MADRID • WARSAW • BUDAPEST • AUCKLAND

ISBN 0-373-28921-9

ABBIE'S CHILD

This edition published by arrangement with Harlequin Books S.A.

Printed in U.S.A.

Books by Linda Castle

Harlequin Historicals

Fearless Hearts #261
Abbie's Child #321

LINDA CASTLE

Linda Castle is the pseudonym of Linda L. Crockett, a third-generation native New Mexican. Linda started writing in March of 1992, and *Abbie's Child* is her second book from Harlequin Historicals.

When not penning novels, Linda divides her time between being a wife, mother and grandmother. She loves speaking, and teaching what she has learned to aspiring writers. Her best advice: write from the heart.

Linda believes one of the greatest benefits she has received from writing historical novels is the mail from readers. She encourages and welcomes comments to be sent to:

Linda Castle
#18, Road 5795
Farmington, NM 87401

Please include an SASE for a reply/bookmark.

To Bill from your adoring wife and mate,
Logan, Brandon, Liann and Bill from Mom,
Matt and Will from Grammy,
Ira, Clay and Vicki from your sister,
Bob and Terrie from your mother-in-law,
Denise from your stepmother,
Babe from your daughter,
Don and Helen from your daughter-in-law,
Steve, Bonnie, Deb and Wendy
from your sister-in-law,
Mandi, from your aunt,
DA, EW, LA, AS, TB, HS, AS, RG, KV, MC, MT, LB,
CB, HW, SE, LC from a friend,
Western Writers of America from a country girl,
Land of Enchantment Romance Authors from a
New Mexico native,
Romance Writers of America from a
hopeless romantic,
Southwest Writers Workshop from
one with ink in her blood,
San Antonio Romance Authors from your
member from out West,
Margaret Marbury from a very grateful writer,
and most of all to the readers who have opened their
hearts to embrace the characters of my imagination,

Thank you.

Prologue

San Juan Mountains, Colorado
1882

Abigail clung to the sheer side of the mountain trail while another pain knifed through her taut belly. Carl was not even cold in his grave before the first agonizing contraction had gripped her. She sucked in gulps of pine-scented cold air and squeezed her eyes shut against the biting pain. When it began to ebb and flow away as the last half dozen before it, she pulled the threadbare plaid woolen shawl snug around her rounded belly and pushed forward. She rubbed her palms over her chilled arms, but felt no warmth from the action.

Night would begin to descend from the pristine snow-covered peaks to settle around her soon. She glanced at her narrow, stone-littered back trail and wondered if she had made a fatal mistake in trying to reach the closest mining camp of Guston. Carl's and her claim had been more isolated than most—better he had said, in case they had a big strike. Now she bit her lip and wondered if she would reach the boomtown before their child was born. If the baby came on the mountain trail at night she knew full well how slim their chances of survival were. She had begged him to take her into Silverton before her pregnancy came to term, but he had laughed and assured her he was capable of birthing their child. So she was now alone, at the end of her pregnancy, and Carl would never see his baby born.

Fear spurred her forward. She doggedly placed one foot in front of the other and tried to ignore the growing terror in the mauve shadows darkening the treacherous path. She was determined that she and her baby would survive.

Abigail found herself thinking of her mother. Long-buried fears and old memories of loss returned to haunt her. She found herself suddenly terrified of dying in childbirth and leaving her child an orphan—as she and her siblings had been.

"Please don't let me die like Ma," she prayed softly. The image of her dying mother's work-worn face, old too soon from bearing children only to see them die in infancy, swam before her eyes. Sweat beaded on her forehead in a clammy sheet as another contraction halted her progress. She sucked in air and placed both palms against the cool, jagged face of the mountain. Abigail leaned into the rock with the force of the pain. Sharp stones cut into her palms.

"Lord, please not here," she moaned as the last tight ache in her abdomen began to recede. "My baby will not live if it is born here." She heard the ragged edge of fear and defeat in her own words. The sound made her jerk up her head in shock. "It will survive. We will survive." Her throat was stiff and tight with determination.

Abigail inhaled and forced herself forward along the precarious mountain trail toward the gold camp of Guston. She had made the trip with Carl before she got too large. She knew it was not too much farther away.

The intensity of her contractions escalated when she topped a small aspen-covered hill where snow still clung in deep hollows and dark, shadowed crevices. The high-pitched roof of a newly built church steeple loomed ahead. She had heard a tale, many months ago upon her arrival, of the Reverend Mr. Davis. Fresh from England, he was determined to bring salvation to the mineral-rich Babylon of Colorado. The Englishman had refused to give up, even when he had been rejected by both the residents of Red Mountain and Ironton. She had dismissed the story as so much folderol, yet the newly constructed spire soared before her, a solid testimony to his perseverance. Abigail prayed the little church would be the salvation of her unborn child.

She grated her teeth against a new onslaught of pain and waddled forward. Her eyes widened in astonishment when her water broke in a great warm gush between her legs. She hastened toward the narrow rough plank door. "I want to live and protect my baby. Please, God, don't let my baby be an orphan."

Abigail braced herself in the unpainted doorway just before another contraction began. She slapped her palms flat against the doorjamb and gripped the newly milled wood so hard her knuckles turned white. Suddenly, thank God, the door opened. Abigail found herself looking into a pair of pale blue eyes hooded by heavy brows the color of hard winter frost. The old fellow's ruddy complexion and leathery skin marked him as a man who spent most of his time outdoors. He didn't look much like her idea of how an English minister would look.

"Mr. Davis?" she questioned doubtfully between pains. Abigail had heard that the preacher was a much younger man. She doubted this was the Reverend Mr. Davis at all. Before she could form another question, though, she felt the muscles of her back pinch while the pain snaked around her abdomen.

She watched the old face screw into crinkles of confusion, then the next contraction closed around her belly and removed all questions from her mind. When she gasped and clung ever tighter to the door, his eyes dropped to her belly and understanding appeared to blast across his bewildered face.

Hands more rough and gnarled than mountain stone whisked her off her feet. A shabby booted foot deftly slammed the door behind them. One kerosene lamp drove back a little of the darkness inside the church. Abigail found herself laid on a church pew and her skirts being shoved up around her damp thighs. She cringed with embarrassment for half a heartbeat, but then another pain came and the urge to push wiped any such maidenly concerns from her mind.

"Please help my baby." She clamped her teeth together with a painful click.

The old man looked at her with compassion and embarrassment flooding his face. Then he bowed his head. She felt her drenched pantalets being torn from her body. Another pain knifed through her lower back and down her groin. Then there was a warm bulk between her thighs. One last instinctual need to push surged through her, then she slumped back. By the time she raised up on her elbows, the old man was swathing something in his coat and bustling from beside the pew. He disappeared through a narrow door on the far side of the dimly lit room.

Abigail sighed and fell back on the hard, splintery surface in total exhaustion. A wave of contentment folded over her.

Lars looked at the tiny motionless babe wrapped in his coat and felt a lump in his throat. There could be no just reason why fate had capriciously sent two pregnant women to the unfinished church this cold spring day.

He tore off a piece of cloth from his only good shirt and wrapped the lifeless child in it. The woman out there would need an explanation, but how could he provide her with one? He was tongue-tied enough when talking about the weather, or the rising price of supplies at the mercantile. How could he find the proper words to tell the woman her baby daughter was dead? There was no way he could explain to her what had transpired. How could he tell the woman her child died without taking its first breath? He cursed himself silently for being so ill equipped to handle this tragedy, while he prayed for a miracle to save them all.

The lusty wail of a healthy, hungry infant sounded in the silent church. Lars snapped his head around and stared at the crying child in the small wooden box. The poor tyke had been no sooner born than he had become an orphan. He pondered the situation and shook his head at the irony of it all.

A babe without a mother and a mother without a child.

Lars cast a sad glance over the dead woman's body. She lay where she had breathed her last, on the plank of a half-finished church pew. He started to cover her pale bluish face with a blanket when something around her neck caught his eye. He slid his fingers under a slender gold chain and pulled it from her bodice. A strange symbol, like a Chinese dragon rearing on its hind legs, gleamed on the heavy circle of gold.

The woman in the other room called out for her child. Lars shook his head in sadness. The first poor woman had died without even uttering her own name. Now he had no hope of finding the orphaned boy-child's next of kin. Lars had no idea what her name was or where she came from.

The baby began to squall in earnest. The sound of the agitated mother's voice, calling for her dead baby, sent a shiver climbing up Lars's spine. He had to do something.

He closed his eyes and dropped to his knees beside the lifeless woman to say a prayer for her soul. Lars climbed slowly to his feet and shoved the gold necklace deep inside his trouser pocket. He took one last look at the stillborn baby and the dead woman, then he made a bold, desperate decision.

Lars picked up the robust orphan and wrapped him in the blanket he'd found earlier. He knew what he was doing was not right—but what other chance did the child have in a country full of men searching for gold and silver? There was no other choice to be made.

Abigail looked up in relief when the old man approached her. He had his eyes downcast, so she couldn't read the expression in them, but he handled her newborn child as if it were the most fragile and precious thing in the world.

"My baby? Is it all right?" She raised up on her elbows and looked expectantly at the old man's face.

Without a word he thrust the wiggling bundle toward her. She took the squirming baby with trembling hands and pulled back the blanket to take her first look at her babe.

"It's a boy," he said gruffly.

Hot, salty tears of bittersweet joy welled in her eyes. Carl would never know he had a fine, healthy son to carry on his name.

"Matthew. I'm going to call him Matthew," she said softly as she traced a circle on his downy pink cheek with her index finger. A thick, soft cap of pale brown hair lay in curls around his head.

"Hello, Matthew Cooprel. Welcome to the world."

When he puckered his rose-petal lips and unsquinted his eyes to stare up at her, she saw they were the color of a mountain sky. She hugged him close and uttered a prayer of thanks for a healthy baby to love and nurture. She vowed that nothing would ever come between her and this precious child.

Lars felt a sharp pang of guilt each time the woman cooed to the newborn boy. She was so pleased and happy that tears ran in small rivulets down her cheeks. The baby pursed his lips and stared at the woman with blue-eyed contentment. Lars swallowed the lump growing in his throat. The die was cast. Maybe what he was doing wasn't right, but it was the only thing Lars could think of. This little boy deserved a chance, and God in his infinite wisdom had given him one. Lars would simply have to learn to live with the feeling that he had done something dishonest.

While he stared at the woman, another worry gripped him. Who was she? Why was she alone on the mountain? He sighed and realized that he would need to stick around and make certain the woman and the baby were provided for. Lars vowed that the first child he had ever birthed, as long as the boy was in Colorado, would grow up hale and healthy. Perhaps this would assuage a small portion of the guilt already nipping at the corners of his mind.

Lars wondered how he would be able to persuade the lady to allow a perfect stranger to become part of their lives. Whatever it took, he was obligated by guilt and responsibility—he had to do it.

Chapter One

Guston, Colorado
July, 1888

Willem hefted his battered valise and stopped to catch his breath. He looked up at the white-shuttered rooming house, perched a good quarter mile away on the steep hillside, and grimaced.

"Whoever built this place must've been part mountain goat." He sucked in a breath before he trudged on. The July sunshine was finally breaking over the dusky blue summit of the snow-capped peaks surrounding Guston. It filtered down in broken shafts through the thick growth of blue spruce and quaking aspen at the outskirts of the mining town. Willem clenched his teeth and inhaled another gulp of air.

"The air at this height lacks body," he grumbled, and stopped to clear his head. Willem dragged off his cap and looked down at the town. A high mountain breeze ruffled his too-long hair and blew a strand over his eyes. He decided to see if there was a cheap barber available in Guston as soon as he was settled.

Guston was a pretty town, as boomtowns and gold camps went, with well-laid-out lots and thriving businesses. He watched harried activity of construction at the town's border. Wide banners were being stretched between buildings and the harsh sound of an off-key brass band wafted up the steep incline.

"What's the damned occasion?" he mumbled aloud. Whatever it was, he felt a wave of disappointment wash over him. If Moira was in this area, as the Pinkertons believed, she would be harder to ferret out with people milling thicker than fleas on a hound. He slapped the cap back on his head in irritation and resumed his climb up the gravelly slope. The last thing he was interested in was being around a bunch of people celebrating.

He didn't even pause to kick the dirt from his bulky-soled shoes when he reached the boardinghouse. He opened the door wide and stepped inside. The neat-as-a-pin interior and spotless rugs laid atop gleaming wood floors halted him in his tracks. Instantly he backed out to wipe the thick dust from the toes of his shoes on the backs of his trouser legs, but not before the smell of homemade bread enveloped him. His empty belly roared to life.

This was not the usual gold-camp rooming house. Willem stood in a formal parlor, done in shades of Wedgwood blue and cream, while he waited for someone to appear. The steady thunk of a long pendulum in a massive grandfather clock ticked off the minutes while he stood alone. He moved toward a shiny desk along the back wall of the room. A neat hand-lettered sign proclaimed it to be the Registration Desk. Willem noticed the rows of key hooks attached to the wainscoted wall behind it. Only two of them were occupied by numbered room keys. The others were vacant—an indication Otto's opinion of the boardinghouse was shared by other miners. A tiny brass bell sat by another small card that said, Ring For Service. Willem wondered what kind of frowsy old woman ran the place. She had spent considerable time pointing out the obvious by lettering the signs.

He clenched his jaw and grabbed the bell. His wide fingers dwarfed it when he picked it up. The metal clapper had no sooner pealed against the side than he heard rapid footsteps.

"Yes? May I help you?" A woman who was a long way from old or frowsy bustled in, while wiping her flour-covered hands on the front of a worn apron. The smell of cinnamon, apples and baker's yeast drifted with her. Willem grimaced when his empty belly chose that particular moment to fully awaken with a loud, ill-mannered growl.

"I need a place to stay," he grated out.

She fastened blue-green eyes on his face. He had the uncanny feeling she was sizing him up. His three-week growth of beard and dusty clothes would surely make a poor impression—but then, what difference would it make? The merchants in gold camps were interested in a man's money, not his appearance. She puckered her eyebrows for a full minute while she swept him with an appraising gaze. He felt like a bug in a jar.

"Breakfast is at six, supper's at seven. If you wish to have a lunch packed, you provide the tin—fifty cents extra a week. I'll have no cigars, pipes or liquor and I don't abide cussing. I change the sheets each Saturday. We serve dinner in the dining room at one o'clock on Sundays following church services. The room is three dollars a week."

She flipped open a slender, bound book and pushed it toward him. Then she folded her arms, which he could see were lightly freckled below the rolled-up sleeves of her sturdy gray dress, and waited for him to sign.

"The price is highway robbery," he snorted. "I'll not pay it." He folded his own arms at his chest and assumed a stance similar to her own. Will hoped the bluff would work, since he had already inquired at two other rooming houses and found them full.

She shrugged. "Suit yourself." She reached out to close the book. Willem laid his massive hand over her smaller one. Her dark brows met in a surprised scowl.

"Nay," he barked. His breath fanned out over her face and sent a soft strand of pale chestnut hair fluttering down from a crooked bun. He inhaled deeply, and the aroma of clothes starch and clean female filled his nostrils. A wave of memories crashed over him, along with Moira's somewhat vague image. It had been a long time. Willem found himself disgusted by the prospect of having to stay here.

"There'll be no other rooms to have in this town," he snapped.

The woman snatched her hand from under his. "You'll not likely find one as clean or the cooking as wholesome as you'll find here."

"You think a lot of yourself." Will felt his mouth pull into a cynical grimace.

She met his gaze with steady, unblinking eyes, but he sensed she was putting on a brave front. Under her cool gaze he saw a flicker of fear. "I try to be quite honest."

"I'll take the room," he grumbled. Willem picked up the pen from the marble stand and with his thumb flipped open the silver filigree lid on the glass ink bottle. He scrawled his name in haste while he tried to banish the image of anxiety he had seen in the woman's eyes. "You have a banker's heart and a banker's soul, ma'am."

She stared at him, wide-eyed. "I'm sorry you think so. I'm a businesswoman pure and simple. I don't cheat my customers, and I expect them not to cheat me. The rent in advance, if you please." She held out a shaky hand. He saw a dusting of flour in the tracery of fine lines across her palm.

Willem scowled. This woman's miserly ways were going to eat up most of his pocket money. Between her and the Pinkertons he'd be working for Otto Mears until he was too bent and broken to swing a pickax or had vision enough left to light a fuse on a stick of dynamite. He clenched his jaw against the anger and futility that flooded over him.

He dug deep into his pockets. He'd be lucky if he could afford supper after this, much less a haircut. His stomach growled when he placed the coins in her palm. Eating was becoming a luxury—one he indulged in less frequently as his search for Moira stretched on and he'd been compelled to hire the Pinkertons.

She accepted the money and pulled the open ledger toward her to read his name aloud.

"Well, Mr. Willem Tremain, since you're now a paying guest, would you like to sample some of my cooking? You can judge for yourself whether it's worth the price."

He looked at her suspiciously and wondered if he'd have to mortgage his soul for the privilege.

She chuckled. A deep, throaty sound filled his ears. It sent odd sensations careening around his shoulders and down his body. Willem decided the effects of hunger and the thin air at this unholy altitude were addling his judgment.

"It's on the house, Mr. Tremain," she added dryly.

He felt heat flood his face above the thick growth of his beard. She had so easily interpreted his thoughts on the subject it caught him unaware. He coughed and tried to hide his embarrassment.

"I'd like that," he finally managed to grate out.

He looked up at her and saw her swipe at the strand of loose hair near her face. Her hand left a large smudge of flour on her nose. He had the silly urge to reach up and wipe it away, but he stopped short. Nonetheless, he could not tear his eyes away from the blemish on her skin. He unconsciously rubbed the side of his own nose while he studied her face. There was a fine smattering of freckles on her aquiline nose and across her heat-flushed cheeks. He continued to stare while he absently wiped the nonexistent flour from his own face.

"What is it?" Her voice broke the spell he'd woven around himself.

Again he felt fire rise under the three-week stubble along his jaw. "Your—nose," he said haltingly.

"What?" Both eyebrows shot upward toward a heart shaped hairline.

"You...have flour on your nose." He extended his hand toward her face, halted abruptly, then pulled it back. Finally his hand shot out to brush it away. Her eyes widened in shock—or was it fear? Willem realized he'd overstepped the bounds of propriety.

"I'm sorry." He wondered if he was coming undone; this impulsiveness was not like him.

She was looking at him with genuine amazement and perhaps some trepidation.

"Think nothing of it." She shot one more half-suspicious look at him. He could see wariness in the stiff set of her shoulders. "If you want something to eat, come into the kitchen," she said tightly.

Willem bent his tall body to pick up his valise, feeling dazed and bewildered. He was sure it must be a combination of fatigue and hunger.

"Leave it. Nobody will bother it." She waved her hand and indicated he should follow her.

He obediently left his valise, containing his every earthly possession, sitting unguarded on the Chinese patterned rug in front of the desk. Willem followed the swish and sway of the woman's dress into a room of surprisingly large proportions. The smell of spices and yeast sent his empty gut into noisy protest again.

"Here, try one of these." She thrust a chipped china plate, heaped with golden-crusted spirals, toward him. Each roll was larger than his own doubled fist and slathered in butter and honey.

Willem wiped his palm down the front of his trousers and picked one up. He sniffed the rich aroma before he took a bite. The roll melted in his mouth. A blending of sweet cinnamon and the heady, robust taste of yeast bread trickled down the back of his throat.

"Good?" She expectantly raised her brows.

"Mmm." He allowed himself to savor the taste, ignoring the sound of his too-empty stomach demanding more. He'd not had the means to pay the Pinkertons and eat, too, so Willem had done what was most important to his survival. He'd gone without food for two days on his journey to Guston.

"Now that you have sampled my cooking, I suppose I should introduce myself." Their eyes met, and he clearly saw the chill of apprehension in hers.

She was the one who now rubbed her palms across her flour-dusted apron. She thrust her hand toward Willem. He shoved the last piece of roll in his mouth and grasped her clean fingers with his sticky ones.

Abigail craned her neck to look up at him. He was overlarge and lean beneath the rough clothes. His jaw was covered with dark hair only a shade paler than the long strands peeking from under his immigrant's cap. Only his eyes were unusual. They were blue—and held a raw hunger that sent a frisson of apprehension snaking through Abigail. She wasn't sure why, but the man's eyes made a knot in the middle of her stomach.

"I am Abigail Cooprel. The widow Cooprel. Welcome to Guston, Colorado, Mr. Tremain."

Chapter Two

"Pleased to meet you," Willem managed to say around the mouthful of roll. No sooner had he touched her hand than Mrs. Cooprel sucked in a deep breath and snatched it away. He frowned at her undisguised concern, then he wondered why he gave it a second thought, why it should even matter to him.

"Oh, my bread!" She grabbed two thick squares of burlap stuffed to plump proportions and flung open the door of a big black cast-iron stove. A blast of heat filled the kitchen along with the smell of fresh bread. Willem saw beads of sweat appear on her forehead.

"Can I help?" It was a stupid question, but he felt like a slackard, sitting idle while the woman whirled busily around the room.

"If you could put those cooling racks on the table... it would be a great help." She nodded in the direction of three large wire stands leaning against a wall.

"These?" Willem asked as he picked them up. He felt increasingly awkward floundering in the woman's domain.

She pulled a golden-domed loaf as long as his forearm from the darkness of the oven and turned toward him. Willem thought he'd surely died and gone to heaven when the fragrance filled the room. The beast in his belly awakened with a deep growl. Willem groaned and laid the racks on a scrubbed pine table more than ten feet long.

With a deft maneuver of her wrist she dumped the bread out of the hot pan and returned to retrieve another pan from the oven.

"This is where we take our meals," Abigail told him while she lined up a dozen steaming loaves to cool. When she dumped the last loaf on the rack she shoved the oven door closed with a backward kick of her high-buttoned shoe. Then she brought a huge scarred wooden bowl to a thick chopping block in the middle of the kitchen. She removed the flour sack that covered it and dumped out the lump of soft, swollen dough. Her fist hit the fluffy center with a dull *whoosh.*

"Here in the kitchen?" With fascinated interest Willem watched her pound and manipulate the dough.

"Yes. Only Sunday dinner is taken in the dining room. I don't have room for all my tenants in there." She looked up. "Most of the men who room here spend Saturday night and most of Sunday on Blaine Street," she explained with a definite pucker of her brows.

Willem shook his head in confusion. "I'm new in Guston. I don't know of Blaine Street."

"Blaine Street is the sporting section of Guston." Abigail smiled blandly. "Women of easy virtue, gambling and Lord only knows what else are available there. I'm sure you'll find it soon enough."

"I doubt it." Willem had little interest in the topic—or the widow's hasty opinion of his moral beliefs.

He watched her divide the dough into clover-shaped balls and dip them in melted butter. She lined up row after row of ivory dough on a wide metal sheet and popped them into the waiting oven.

"Aren't you a sporting man, Mr. Tremain?" she asked abruptly.

"No, I'm not." Willem told himself the woman needed to ask such questions to assure her own peace of mind, and he tried not to take offense. "You'll not have cause to worry on that account, Mrs. Cooprel. I don't gamble—you'll get your rents on time."

She looked up and studied his face for a long moment. He caught a glint of disquiet, or perhaps it was fright, in her eyes. She dropped heavy lashes to shut out his scrutiny.

"Then you're welcome to have Sunday dinner with us in the dining room," she offered haltingly.

Mrs. Cooprel spread out another section of dough. She spooned cooked apple slices, cinnamon and a generous portion of butter into the center and began to roll up the dough.

Willem leaned against the hand pump and watched her. He didn't know why he lingered here. Maybe it was the warm atmosphere of the kitchen or the homey smells or the fact that his belly was scraping against his backbone that made him wait like a hungry cur needing a handout.

"You are welcome to try more of those." Abigail nodded toward the plump cinnamon rolls in a manner that made him wonder if she had read his mind.

"This is my regular baking day. I always make more than we need." She seemed torn between the urge to feed him and her obvious desire for him to leave.

"Thanks." Willem took another plump roll and relished each delectable bite. The widow was a kind, meddlesome sort, he decided while he ate the roll. He regretted his earlier comment about her greed.

She placed the plank of whatever she had just created into a greased pan. He saw her glance at him curiously from time to time.

"Are you a single man, Mr. Tremain?"

The abrupt question surprised him, but he again told himself the widow would have a need to protect her reputation. He forced himself to treat the question as casually as it had been asked.

"No. I have a wife." He continued to nibble on the roll while he watched her. It might've been his imagination but he could have sworn that the widow Cooprel visibly relaxed when she learned his marital status. That puzzled and intrigued him.

She placed the pan aside and covered it with a clean flour sack. Then she poured coffee into two blue-speckled cups and sat down at the long harvest table.

"Join me?" she asked, with her eyebrows lifting into slender arches. Again Willem had the feeling she had taken more interest in him since she'd learned he was not single—just the opposite of what he would have expected from a widow. Every unmarried female this side of Denver was looking for a husband. Any sort of husband.

Willem stepped away from the hand pump where he'd been leaning and pulled out a chair opposite the widow, then sat down and took a sip of the hot liquid. The coffee was fresh and strong. Exactly the way he liked it and very seldom had.

"After tasting your cooking I imagine you have men lined up at your door with offers of marriage," Willem said wryly.

"I have no desire to remarry." She shoved the cinnamon rolls closer. "It's nice to see a man with a healthy appetite. Makes all the work worthwhile." She sipped her coffee and watched him over the rim of her cup. Will ignored her effort to redirect the conversation.

"Ever? You're a young woman to be making such a permanent decision."

"Perhaps, but I know my own mind." She concentrated on her cup, and he knew the subject was closed.

He searched for a less personal topic to take up the deafening silence in the room. The woman was certainly different. She had a cool reserve about her, and a protective veil seemed to shield her blue eyes.

"You do this every week?" Will told himself he should leave, but he found himself trying to keep the conversation going.

She looked up warily, took a deep breath and nodded.

"Yes. Monday is baking day. Tuesday is cleaning and Wednesday is laundry." She sipped her coffee and flicked a gaze over his road-weary and travel-stained clothes. "I'm sorry I don't do washing for my guests, but there is a fine Chinese laundry right next to the barber and bathhouse on Eureka Street."

Willem chuckled at the none-too-subtle hint. The sound surprised him. He tried to remember how long it had been since he'd heard the sound of his own laughter, but he couldn't recall it.

"Mrs. Cooprel, it has been a while since I had an opportunity to enjoy a bath or clean clothes. I thank you for pointing me in the right direction." He saw himself through her eyes and felt more uncomfortable for it.

"I'm sorry, Mr. Tremain. I only meant—" She ducked her head, and he saw a light wash of color on her cheeks. A long fringe of lashes, sun lightened at the tips, brushed across her high, smooth cheekbones. "I've been here so long I've begun to pick up some peculiarities in my habits. I think it must come from spending so much time in the company of men. Your gender is more open and honest than mine, and sometimes I forget my manners. Please forgive me."

"How long have you been here?" He wondered if she might have been here long enough to know something about Moira.

"My husband brought me to Colorado in 1881." Abigail stiffened.

"Gold?" He took a sip of coffee.

"At first I thought it was, but now when I look back I think Carl had a longing for adventure, not a thirst for gold." She ran her index finger around the rim of the cup.

"How did he die, if you don't mind me asking?" Willem was mentally counting the years in his head. The time could be about right—Moira's trail had taken him in three different directions, but when he hired the Pinkertons a year ago, they managed to track Moira here. Then she vanished without a trace. Looking through the gold camps around Silverton, the Pinkertons had spent every cent Willem could earn. Willem had finally decided to have a look for himself. He could not give up the quest.

"It's been a long time since Carl died. I don't mind talking about it anymore. There was a cave-in at our claim. Carl and the mule were killed instantly." She drained her cup and rose from the chair. "I don't want to be rude, Mr. Tremain, but I have the evening meal to prepare."

She said the words lightly enough but Willem knew very well she wanted him out of her kitchen where she would not feel obliged to entertain him. He brushed crumbs from the cinnamon roll off the front of his woolen shirt and forced himself to smile.

"Thank you for the coffee and rolls. Which room is mine?" he asked when she plunked both their cups into a metal washtub and grabbed the hand pump. The dry, sucking sound of the pump drawing water made an answer impossible for a moment. He waited patiently until water streamed from the spout. When the pan was full she turned to Willem.

"You will be in room number twelve. It's on the third floor. I hope you don't mind the stairs."

"No, that will be just fine." Willem lingered in the doorway for a moment. "There seems to be a lot of activity in town . . . is there something special going on?"

"Yes. We are celebrating Colorado's anniversary of a dozen years of statehood."

"A dozen years?" he asked. "That's an unusual number of years to celebrate."

"We Gustonians never miss any excuse to have a picnic. Summers are short here—we take our pleasures when we can. We have a town band and there will be fireworks this year."

"I see. Thank you for the coffee—and everything, Mrs. Cooprel." Willem turned and left the huge sunny kitchen. He picked up his valise, grabbed the key labeled 12 from the hook on the wall and strode toward the staircase. The news of a shindig did little to lift his flagging spirits.

He gripped the banister with more force than necessary when he thought of how many years he'd been searching in vain for Moira.

If you've learned anything these years, you great fool, have you not at least learned a little patience? He shook his head in amazement at his repeated failings and went in search of his room.

Chapter Three

Willem paused on the second-floor landing, where he was tempted to slump into an inviting rocker by a potted fern. A one-eared ginger tom raised its head and hissed menacingly from the pillowed seat. Will backed off. The old cat yawned, and he saw a missing tooth. The cranky tabby was secure in its ability to defend its territory. Will had no desire to battle the old gladiator for a temporary seat. He turned and trudged up the last flight of stairs. By the time he reached the third floor the idea of going in search of a barber had lost all its appeal. He found the door with a neat, handmade 12 tacked on the middle.

"Mrs. Cooprel's work, I see." Will shook his head. "Is there anything the widow does not put a sign on?" he asked nobody in particular.

Willem unlocked the door. The room was clean and tidy—just what he had expected. A quilted spread in a double wedding ring design brought him up short at the threshold. Memories of Moira stitching a similar one assaulted him. Willem threw his valise on the bed to block out the image. He felt suffocated while he strode to the window, covered with hand-tatted white lace. He pushed the thin fabric aside and forced open the glass. Cool, clean air flooded the room. He inhaled great gulps of it and tried to clear his head of the haunting memories and guilt. Today had brought more forgotten images flitting through his head than the past six years altogether.

Willem leaned out the window and braced his forearms on the sash. Tall mountain pines, close enough to reach out and touch, spread green fronds toward the boardinghouse. A carpet of thick grass and bright clover sprinkled with columbines and daisies blanketed a large area around the house. Taut wires strung between railroad ties formed a long clothesline at one end of the verdant lawn. He could hear the noisy birds cackling inside a sturdy covered chicken coop on the other side. He looked west and saw a neat, well-ordered vegetable patch surrounded by a stake fence.

"I bet the deer and elk love the widow's vegetables," Willem muttered. A dish-faced Jersey cow with great solemn brown eyes looked up at him while she chewed her cud.

He scanned the grounds and located the privy. Around the side, toward a wraparound porch, a tall, fire-engine-red water pump had been installed above a trough fashioned from a massive hollowed-out tree trunk.

It had been long, bleak years since Willem had enjoyed the trappings of such ordered domesticity. The picturesque setting sent an arrow of self-condemnation and reproach shooting through him. He turned away from the window, unable to look at any more.

He shoved the valise to the floor and flopped onto the bed. The springs creaked under his weight while he adjusted his tall frame. The lumpy, narrow mattress felt as soft as a feather bed compared to the hard straw cots he'd become accustomed to since hiring the Pinkertons. He yawned and wished for a single night of peaceful sleep. As quickly, he cursed himself for the stupid fancy. Willem knew the ghosts from his past would never leave him in peace—and furthermore he knew he didn't deserve any.

* * *

Abigail popped the last of the dinner rolls into the hot oven and rubbed her hand over her sweat-dampened forehead. She was glad to see baking day nearly finished. The heavy coins in her pocket jingled and she found herself thinking about her newest boarder. She looked down at her own fingers and saw them trembling.

Is this how it will always be? she asked herself. *Will I constantly be timid and afraid when a stranger comes to rent a room?*

She thought back to the gray day of last winter, when Lars had forever changed her life—for the second time. He had come to her with a story so fantastic that at first she thought he was spinning a yarn for her amusement. But as the tears welled in the old man's eyes, she finally faced the tiny questions that had forever nagged at her about Matthew. She forced herself to acknowledge what she knew was true.

Matthew was not her child. Not the child of her body. Abigail felt something on her cheek and wiped at it. Her fingers came away wet. She was crying again—crying for the daughter she had never known, crying for the woman who had died giving Matthew life, crying for herself.

She sniffed and squared her shoulders. There was no reason to be in such a state, she knew. Years had passed with no long-lost relative coming to claim Matthew. Why should any of that change? Yet, now each time some new boarder knocked at the door there was a moment of panic, a moment when Abigail knew today would be the day she would lose her child.

She sighed and tried to calm her nerves. Maybe she would feel better if Lars had not disappeared like a will-o'-the-wisp right after he'd confessed. She had been expecting him home any day. Surely he would not disappoint Matthew, they had attended every picnic celebration together since Matt was old enough to walk.

Abigail busied herself washing up the cups she and Mr. Tremain had used. Images of her new boarder swam before her eyes. He made her uneasy. His dark, probing eyes and manner sent shivers of dread up her spine. But why? Mr. Tremain said he had a wife, and if Abigail had inquired further, he probably would have told her he had a brood of dark-haired children, as well. He was just another man looking for a clean bed and a hot meal. There was no reason in the world this man should be any different than the others who had rented from her in six years.

She took a deep, calming breath and vowed to keep her imagination under tighter rein. Matthew was not the child of her body but he was the child of her heart, and nobody was going to show up out of the blue and take him from her. She simply had to go on as she had in the past and things would be just fine.

"Still, I'm glad that one's got a wife," she muttered while she rinsed the soap from the cups.

He had a way of looking at her that made tiny shivers run over her arms. She realized it was probably more her imagination than anything else, but Mr. Willem Tremain was different than other miners somehow—dark, lonely, driven in some way.

He frightened her. She shook her head and told herself she was just feeling gloomy. Matthew had been gone all day fishing and she was feeling his absence. She smiled and thought of his bright blue eyes and childish laughter.

Yes, that's all it is. I'm just missing Matthew. She happily went about her chores—but the disturbing image of Willem Tremain's handsome, brooding face never really left her in peace.

Choking darkness and a ton of rock crushing down upon him brought Will awake. He raked his palm over his sweat-beaded face and lay panting. He couldn't remember where he was. Then reality flooded in. He remembered the widow's blue-green eyes. He released the breath he hadn't realized he'd been holding and slid his shoes to the floor.

Willem stretched and comprehended with profound astonishment that he had slept soundly, until just now. He frowned and puzzled over it. Then he decided it was because he'd fallen asleep in the middle of the day. Napping was a luxury a working man rarely indulged in—particularly one who had detectives on his payroll.

He shoved his bulk from the mattress and walked to the washstand. The pitcher was dry. He scowled and caught his reflection in the mirror above the stand. His eyes were hooded by dark lashes and eyebrows. His beard was thick and itched like the devil. He looked meaner than a catamount. It was easy to see why the widow found him so frightening.

He heard laughter and ribald language coming from somewhere in the yard. His curiosity beckoned him to the open window, where he leaned out to see what was going on.

A crowd of rough miners wearing heavier beards than the one he sported were stripped to their long johns at the waist. Their heavy woolen shirts flapped behind them like hen's wings. Willem frowned and watched as a thick bar of soap was passed from one eager hand to the next. Each man put his head under the pump while one of his fellows pumped water over him. In turn they lathered themselves to a foam and repeated the process. Suds and water flowed over the edge of the trough and swirled down the rocky incline toward a flower bed of columbines. Willem was puzzled and intrigued. They appeared to be giving each other a thorough scrubbing at the hand pump. He'd never seen the like in any other gold camp. He decided to go downstairs and take a closer look at the unlikely spectacle.

Willem heard the sounds of pots and pans and Mrs. Cooprel's humming when he crossed the parlor. It sent an odd chill through him. He stepped outside and followed the worn path to the pump. He hooked a thumb in his belt and watched their antics.

"Missus will be mighty upset if we're late, Brawley," a wizened man warned while water dripped from the ends of his drooping mustache.

A mountainous redhead with a beard full of soapsuds nodded solemnly. "Yep. We best hurry along. Besides, ain't this baking day?" His brown eyes twinkled above the froth.

The remark brought hoots of approval from the men and seemed to spur them to frenzied activity. Soap and water spattered Willem in their haste. He jumped back to avoid a complete drenching while he decided this was some more of the widow Cooprel's meddlesome handiwork.

The men rinsed and shook off the excess water like a pack of wet dogs. One or two men looked up and saw Will for the first time. They pulled up their shirts. The popping of several sets of suspenders snapping into place sounded in rapid succession. The tall, red-haired man smoothed back his dripping mane and nodded at Will.

"The widow likes her tenants clean and punctual."

"So I see," Willem quipped. "I'm your new neighbor."

The red-haired miner winked. "Well, unless you boys want to be sucking on the hind teat, I suggest you get a move on."

The group filed into the boardinghouse, leaving Willem and the man called Brawley standing at the pump. Will unbuttoned his shirt and peeled it down to his long johns. The loose shirt, still tucked in to his belt behind, slapped the backs of his thighs while he walked to the pump. He bent at the waist and stuck his unshorn head under the pump. The giant obliged by soaking him in a stream of icy water.

"Thanks for the hand." Willem shivered. He slicked back his hair with one palm and accepted the offered soap to lather his face.

"Don't mention it. I'm Brawley Cummins."

Willem squinted briefly at the man before soap ran into his eyes and blinded him. "Pleased to meet you. I'm Willem Tremain."

"Willem, I hope you don't think I'm rude, but my watch tells me it's seven o'clock. The widow will be dishing up about now."

Before Willem even got his face rinsed off he heard the man tramp off. Abigail Cooprel held amazing influence over these men—or at least, her cooking did.

When Willem walked into the kitchen the room was full of the smell of wholesome food, strong lye soap, damp wool and miners. He looked around the table and saw the same men who'd been making rowdy jokes sitting demurely while Abigail Cooprel piled food on each of their plates. She smiled and offered a word to each man by name, which brought bouts of mumbling shyness and crimson cheeks to most of them. He stood in the doorway and watched, bemused by the change the woman wrought in the men who only minutes ago had been louder than braying mules.

Abigail Cooprel looked up and saw Willem watching her. Her body stiffened and she nodded. "Mr. Willem Tremain, these are the rest of my boarders." There was a baritone murmur that rippled through the room before respectful silence fell like a stone at his feet.

"Do you have a preference of where I sit, Mrs. Cooprel?" Willem asked.

"That one is free." She nodded in the direction of one empty chair at the far end of the table. Willem made his way around and sat down. He waited while she progressed from one plate to the next, until she finally reached him.

"Never found a barber, I see." She cocked an eyebrow and honored him with a sunny grin. He could see no malice in her face, only good-natured humor. It did strike him as odd that she was much friendlier and relaxed in the company of these miners than she'd been earlier with him alone. Then he realized that she probably felt safe by virtue of numbers.

"Actually, the bed looked too good to pass up. I fell asleep." He tried to return her grin but found himself oddly distracted by the clean, womanly scent of her standing so near him.

"Does anyone have the time?" Mrs. Cooprel looked from one burly face to the next.

Brawley Cummins stood and pulled his watch from his pant pocket. Using his thumbnail, he snapped open the face. "It is four minutes past seven, Missus."

Willem saw the men turn to stare expectantly at the back door. Each one looked for the world like a small boy waiting for Father Christmas to arrive.

"Matthew is late, again," Mrs. Cooprel said with a sigh. She sat down in one of the two remaining empty chairs. They were at the opposite end of the table, as far from Willem as possible. After a momentary pause she began to serve herself.

Willem cast a quick glance around the table and picked up a fat brown dinner roll. Ten men turned to stare at him in stupefied horror.

Mrs. Cooprel smiled patiently. "We say grace, Mr. Tremain."

He dropped the bread as if it had burned him. For the life of him, he couldn't prevent the advance of heat across his face. He watched the miners duck their heads, and he did likewise. What was it about this widow that made a man feel like a snot-nosed kid? He felt as if he'd stepped into some sort of bottomless pit where his old life flashed by like a runaway locomotive. Abigail's clear voice invoked a blessing upon the men and her home, while he tried to tamp down his embarrassment.

Willem mumbled a hasty "Amen" just as the door opened behind him. Cool air rushed in. Will turned in his chair to see a panting boy, barefoot and encased from head to toe in loamy mud. The bedraggled child dropped a fishing pole at the back door and stuck a battered, shapeless hat on a peg halfway up the wall.

"Matthew, you are late." Mrs. Cooprel fastened a stern look on the boy. Willem almost squirmed in his own chair. He felt an instant kinship with the child. Only moments ago he had felt the same icy sting of disapproval, he thought.

"I know, Mama. I'm sorry. But I stopped to get these for you." Matthew thrust a wilting bouquet of purple columbines and crushed daisies toward Abigail. "And I caught these." He proudly held up a piece of twine holding two glistening rainbow trout. The widow's face melted into a beaming smile. She accepted the flowers with mist-filled eyes.

"Oh, Matthew, these are truly fine." She raised her head and her eyes swept the table. "Aren't they fine, gentlemen?"

Willem found himself wearing a grin. Damned if he could figure out how he'd got pulled into this drama and why he wasn't wolfing down the savory meat, potatoes and carrots on his plate, but he sat there watching the little boy with rapt attention. While he stared at the dirty-faced boy he painfully acknowledged his own deep, abiding hunger to know his child.

"I'll get these into a jar of water and put them on the table for us all to look at. Now you go wash up." Abigail's voice had the mellow quality of a mother cat purring to its kitten while she rose from the table.

The child nodded his untidy head and scampered off, dropping the fish to the floor on his way. Abigail stared at them as if a gold nugget had just been deposited at her feet.

"Don't you bother. I'll get them, Missus." Brawley scooted his chair out and stood.

Mrs. Cooprel looked at him absently and smiled. Her face was almost angelic in its maternal happiness.

"Thank you, Brawley." She turned and went to the cupboard by the water pump. She finally found a jar to her liking and filled it with water before she arranged the flowers in its mouth. They were wilted and broken, and dirt still clung to the roots in clumps, but she treated the gift as if it were the dandiest bouquet of posies a woman ever received. She placed them in the center of the long table and sighed contentedly.

"The lad needs a man's firm hand but he's comin' along.... He even cleaned the fish himself this time, ma'am. I told him he should do that last week. Guess he's finally listenin'." Brawley put the fish in a pan of water.

If the widow noticed the man's remark she gave no indication. When she was settled back in her chair one of the men at the table took a bite—finally—and Willem seized the opportunity to spear a plump chunk of meat. He popped it into his mouth and savored the taste of venison.

The patter of running feet announced Matthew's return. The boy darted in, still buttoning a clean shirt. His wet hair lay in curly waves around his wide forehead. Willem felt his jaw go slack. His fork froze in midair while he stared.

"Now you look like my little boy and not some ragamuffin." She rubbed her fingers through the child's clean, wet hair. When she patted the empty chair next to her own the boy plopped down. Several of the miners complimented him on the size of his fish. The child took it all with reserved humility.

"Who is this young man?" Will's voice sounded hollow and stiff.

Abigail looked up and smiled proudly. "This is my son, Matthew Cooprel."

Willem felt a tightness in his chest when Matthew turned and smiled at him. His eyes were a piercing sky blue—they made Will's gut twist with pain for the child he longed to find.

"Matthew, this is our newest boarder, Mr. Willem Tremain."

Chapter Four

Willem blinked and forced himself to nod at Matthew in greeting. The boy smiled politely before he turned his attention to the food Abigail was piling on his plate. Matthew occupied himself answering his mother's many questions about his fish. The rest of the men had lapsed into their own private conversations, leaving Willem to his own company. He found himself straining to hear the widow and her boy.

"How did you land such big fish, darling?" Willem saw the veil of reserve evaporate from her eyes. Mrs. Cooprel laughed, and for the first time he saw the real woman beneath the cool shell.

"Mama, you should've seen it." Matthew paused long enough to shove some food into his mouth. He chased it with a gulp of milk. He wiped the white mustache with his napkin before he continued in a rush of words. "One was so big it pulled me down the bank!"

Abigail smiled indulgently and raised one eyebrow, but she didn't comment. She watched Matthew from under her thick fringe of lashes. The boy frowned and wrinkled his nose, obviously considering some weighty problem.

"Well, he almost pulled me in. I did slip and fall in the mud while I was trying to get him out of the water," Matthew admitted sheepishly.

They both laughed. Willem felt his chest constrict. No matter how much he might wish for this bright, healthy child to somehow be his own, he knew he was not—and it cut him to the marrow.

Willem ducked his head and tried to quell the overwhelming depression filling his insides. It had been foolish of him to hope, after all these years, that he could walk into Guston and miraculously find the child he'd never even seen—a child the Pinkerton men had not been able to locate in over a year, even though they had used all their resources and every cent Will could supply to them. He snorted at his cockeyed thinking and tore a piece of bread apart.

Seeing Mrs. Cooprel with her son made him realize how deep his feeling of loss ran. Willem found himself wondering how many similar conversations he had missed out on over the past six years. He shoved another forkful of food into his mouth, but it had lost all its flavor. Willem brooded silently and scolded himself for his foolishness. Matthew laughed and Will raised his head. He watched Abigail and her son while the pain of old scars and lingering regret gripped him in an ever-tightening fist.

Matthew was a fine-knit lad. Wild brown curls framed a face tanned and lightly freckled. He had a glow of health and happiness and blue eyes that twinkled with mischief each time the child answered a curious miner's question. It was easy to see he was well liked by them all, but it appeared to Will that the boy kept himself somewhat apart from them. Brawley Cummins tried to draw Matthew into conversation several times, only to receive short "yes" or "no" answers.

Willem brooded in silence. He felt distanced from the group of men at the table. Certainly not the first time he'd experienced such a feeling of isolation; he'd spent most of his adult life alone, particularly since Moira had left him. But seeing Matthew Cooprel brought his loneliness into crystalline perspective. It was like watching the widow and her small son from behind a pane of window glass. He could see glowing family happiness, witness its magic, but he could never touch it. The unhealed ache in his soul began to bleed like a fresh wound. He didn't think he could stand to watch the blissful scene another minute without crying out in agony.

Willem stood so suddenly the legs of his chair scraped harshly against the wooden floor. Twelve pairs of eyes locked on him in question.

"Excuse me," he grated out. Willem heard restrained anger and pain in his own voice. He forced himself to fold his napkin into a neat square before he strode from the room.

"Do you think we said something wrong?" Abigail asked softly when she heard his heavy tread on the stairs.

"Willem Tremain!" Mac Jordan exclaimed so loudly every head snapped around in his direction.

Brawley frowned. "What in tarnation are you shoutin' about? The man's not here anymore, dunderhead." He glanced at Abigail and shook his head. Mac rolled his eyes at Brawley and wiped the napkin across his bushy, sun-streaked beard.

"I know that. I knew I'd heard the name before.... I've been sitting here trying to place it. Now I know why it seemed so familiar. You know who that man is?" Mac swept the miners' faces with an excited glance. They shook their heads and waited for the explanation.

"That's Willem Tremain—the Black Irish." Mac leaned back in his chair, eminently satisfied with his knowledge. The miners murmured among themselves. Abigail saw them glance toward the doorway, where Willem had so recently departed, with something like awe and respect shining in their eyes.

"Who or what is the Black Irish?" Abigail asked. She frequently found the miners' conversations difficult to fathom, and this time was no exception.

"He's a bloody damned celebrity," Tom Cuthbert blurted out. "Sorry, ma'am." He apologized hastily when she gave him a scathing glance. If Matthew noticed the profanity he did not acknowledge it, thank goodness. Lately she'd been worrying more and more that he would pick up the rough manners and profane speech so common in Guston. She told herself it was silly to fret, but a part of her wondered if leaving wouldn't be the best thing, especially since Lars had revealed the secret of Matthew's parentage. She shook the thought from her mind and forced herself to listen to Tom.

"Tell me," Abigail demanded. She rose from her chair and brought the large speckled coffeepot to the table. Each man filled his cup before he passed it along to the next waiting pair of hands. Tom paused until she was seated again.

"I heard about him when I was in Leadville. He's a wizard with explosives and fearless as a grizzly, they say. The Black Irish can blow the face off a mountainside and find gold or silver or even copper without breaking a hard sweat." His voice rang with admiration. "Or so I hear." Tom took a sip of hot coffee.

"He can single-jack all day without tiring, but I heard he won't go down hole for love nor money," Skipper McClain said dryly. Several other men nodded and murmured in agreement.

"Why is that?" Abigail found her curiosity whetted. It was interesting that her boarders seemed to be very well versed on the man they called the Black Irish, yet none of them had any firsthand information.

"There's more'n one story about why he hates underground. One tale is that he killed a man down hole," Skipper said.

Abigail shifted nervously. There was something about Willem Tremain that made the hair on her arms stand on end and her mouth go dry.

"Do you believe that?" she heard herself asking. She had seen many men come and go and fancied herself to be a better judge of character than to have taken a killer into her house—or so she hoped. She told herself this latest case of nerves was simply a delayed reaction to the truth about Matthew.

Skipper shrugged his wiry shoulders. He fingered his long mustache thoughtfully. "I heard he went down-hole skunked from a night with bawdy women, and botched a blast."

"Yep—killed an entire crew," Snap Jackson supplied authoritatively.

Abigail sipped her coffee and wondered which story might be true. There *was* something unsettling about the man.

"All I've heard, Missus, is that the man works like twelve devils and is always broke as a Methodist parson. The story I hear is that he's never been seen in the company of—" Skipper McClain rubbed his bushy eyebrows thoughtfully and glanced at Matthew "—of women of easy virtue, and he takes risks with dynamite no sane man would."

"I heard there's only one man alive that knows the truth about the Black Irish and what happened—Sennen Mulgrew," Mac Jordan said.

"Didn't he die back in seventy-nine?" Snap asked.

"Naw, he's still alive, and the story I heard is that only he and the Black Irish came out of that hole you all been talking about. Yep, the only man, 'sides the Irish himself, that knows the truth is Sennen Mulgrew." Mac nodded and rubbed his long mustache thoughtfully. A pensive silence settled around the table.

Abigail saw her son sneak a sideways glance toward the men. He squirmed in his seat and she realized he'd been soaking up every word of gossip about her tenant. She felt a wash of shame.

"Well, I suppose whatever the truth, the man's past is his own business," Abigail said. There were nods of agreement around the table. Matthew smiled at her before he wiped his milk mustache.

"How about some apple pie?" She tousled his thick hair. He nodded. Abigail glanced around the table and saw the men grinning beneath their thick covering of facial hair. There was little difference between the gleam in their eyes or Matthew's. The offer of dessert brought the same enthusiasm from them, whether they were six or sixty. She shook her head in amazement. There were times when she felt like the mother of ten overgrown street urchins and not the mother of one small child.

By the time she brought three fat pies to the table, it had been cleared and the plates were in a tub of water. Matthew's brows pinched together in a frown and he worried his bottom lip.

"Mama?"

"Yes?" He glanced at the men before he continued. She knew Matthew hated to bring up anything he considered remotely private in front of the miners. He took a deep breath and focused on her face. She knew he was doing his best to shut the men out of his mind.

"Do you suppose Mr. Tremain is lonely up there?" Matthew rolled his eyes toward the ceiling above his head.

"I don't know, honey. Why do you ask?" Abigail studied her son with wonder. He was one surprise after another and she thanked God every day for such a remarkable child. If he was concerned enough to bring up the topic in front of the men, and perhaps risk a ribbing, it must be weighing heavily on him.

"If I was up there all alone and everyone else was down here laughing and talking, I think I would be lonely," Matthew explained.

A snort from Brawley made Abigail's jaw clench in annoyance. The man was beginning to rankle with his unwanted interference. If he had not been one of her regulars, coming season after season since she first opened the boardinghouse, she would have been fearful of his interest in Matthew. But she gathered his motives were directed not at Matthew but at her. She hoped he would soon realize she had no interest in him as a stepfather for Matthew and certainly not as a husband for herself. Abigail's heart overflowed with love for Matthew alone. She had no room in her life for anyone else—not now, not ever.

"What would you like to do about Mr. Tremain?"

"If it was me up there, I'd like it a lot if someone brought me some pie." Matthew swallowed hard. Abigail knew he was asking for her permission.

"Then perhaps you should," she was surprised to hear herself say.

"Even though it's against the rules to have food in the rooms?" The boy's eyes widened in wonder.

"I think we can bend the rules a bit this time—since you feel so strongly about it." She looked up at the miners. They were all wearing puzzled expressions but they remained silent.

"I'd like that." Matthew finished his milk, wiped his mouth and stood. Abigail cut a generous portion of pie and poured a fresh cup of coffee.

"Can you manage?" she asked. The boy balanced a plate in one small hand and the hot brew in the other. He looked up at her with exasperation written across his young face.

"Mama, I'm not a baby anymore."

"Oh, I'm sorry." She smiled behind her hand and resisted the urge to deposit a kiss on his head. He had recently, in his most serious fashion, asked her to refrain from doing things like kissing him in front of the men. He said it made him feel like a baby—and the miners were not reserved about teasing him. It was the only area where she could exert no proper influence over the rowdy men. Abigail watched Matthew's straight back disappear through the doorway.

"He's growing into a fine boy, Missus," Snap said softly.

"Yes, he is," Abigail agreed.

Willem had lit the lamp on the small chest in his room. Now he stood like a statue, unable to move. He kept telling himself the new sensations he was experiencing were the result of too little rest and food, but he was beginning to wonder.

One moment he ached with longing for a son like Matthew Cooprel, and then he felt so annoyed that he couldn't remain in the same room with the boy. His actions and feelings were at odds with each other. He ran his hand through his long hair and worried he might be coming apart at the seams. A soft tapping at the bottom of his door brought his head up with a snap.

"Who is it?" he growled.

"Matthew Cooprel, sir," a small voice on the other side announced.

Willem felt the vise around his heart tighten. He crossed the room and opened the door. The boy was holding a piece of pie big enough to feed three people and a steaming cup of coffee. He grinned when he realized the boy had knocked with his bare foot.

"I brought you something." Matthew craned his neck to look up into Willem's face.

When he took the hot coffee from him Willem tried not to grin at the serious expression on Matthew's face. A part of him wanted to make the child laugh again, to hear the sound. He saw relief soften the freckled features when he liberated the boy from the burden of the pie plate.

"What is this? Apple pie?" Willem held the golden wedge under his nose while he inhaled with great relish. It was a bittersweet triumph when the boy's face broke into a pleased grin.

"I thought you might be lonely," Matthew said honestly.

His innocent words sent a shaft of cold iron plunging through Willem's chest. God, yes, he was lonely—bitterly lonely. So lonely he couldn't even sit at the table and eat while the widow and her son talked. He finally admitted that was why he had behaved so strangely since he'd walked into this place. The sights, sounds and smells of this home had awakened things inside him, hungry hurting things he had forced to lie dormant for over six years.

"That was real kind of you, Matthew." Will heard the husky catch in his words. "Would you like to sit with me awhile?"

Matthew nodded and launched his body toward the narrow bed. He landed in the middle with a plop. The springs groaned, while the covers disengaged themselves around the edges and furled upward toward the middle. He sat cross-legged and stared like an eager pup at Willem. Will folded himself into the solitary chair and put the coffee on the wooden chest beside him. He cut a forkful of pie.

"I have a loose tooth—do you wanna see?" Matthew asked.

Willem blinked and looked at the boy. He felt an odd ripple of emotion while the child seared him with his clear blue eyes. The small body in the center of the narrow bed resonated with life and energy. Willem couldn't help but grin at the child's generous offer.

"Sure." Willem had to bend nearly double to be able to lean close enough to Matthew. The boy smelled of milk, clean clothes and fresh air. The scent brought desolate hunger racing through Willem's belly again while he stared at Matthew's perfect, small teeth.

Matthew stuck a finger in his mouth. By really concentrating Willem detected the almost imperceptible movement of the front tooth in question.

"Thee?" Matthew asked with his finger still between his lips.

Willem leaned back in his chair and tried to keep from laughing aloud. "Yes, I see." He found himself relaxing a bit. "It should be coming out soon."

Matthew seemed inordinately pleased with Willem's assessment. The boy grinned wider and wiped his moist finger across his pant leg.

"Uncle Lars says when you lose all your baby teeth you're not a baby anymore."

"Are you in a hurry to grow up?" Willem finally popped the thick bite of pie in his mouth. It was delicious. He enjoyed a feast for all his senses as dark corners of his shuttered mind awakened. It was nice to have Matthew tell him about things that mattered to little boys. He found himself wondering if his own son or daughter felt this way about pie and loose teeth and growing up.

"Oh, yes. I want to grow up and be a miner—just like my papa was."

Willem frowned and sipped some coffee. Matthew's words sent the hair on the back of his neck bristling. The child was a comfort but at the same time he made Will strangely uneasy. He realized with a jolt that he felt a strange sensitivity and awareness to the boy—an odd connection of some sort—but he dismissed it as more of his bleak desire to find his own child.

"Has your mama told you stories about your papa?" Willem heard himself ask.

"Lots. He was a miner but he died before I was born." Matthew did a small half bounce on the bed and stared at Willem with round bright eyes. Intelligence and too much natural curiosity burned in those crystal blue depths.

"Are you really the Black Irish?" Matthew blurted out.

Willem felt the hot coffee and pie halt halfway down his gullet. The darkness of old scars and bitter memories crept toward him.

"You don't look black to me," Matthew added helpfully while he squinted at Will's face. His child's voice and candor drove a small part of the gloom from Willem's tortured mind.

"Nor am I Irish," Will quipped dryly. He found himself smiling, even though he hated that name as much as he hated what it represented in his haunted past.

"Well, are you him? Why do they call you that?" The boy stared at Willem and frowned.

"Some fool gave me the name a long time ago. I don't think he knew Welsh and Irish are not the same," Willem mused.

"Couldn't he see you weren't black? Was something wrong with his eyes? Maybe he'd been hurt and couldn't see real good." The boy tilted his head and peered up at Willem for a long time. Then he crinkled his nose and bounced again. "Nope, you're not black at all."

Willem laughed aloud. The child's logic followed a path straight as a lodestone to the truth.

"He called me black because of my black rages and devil's temper, Matthew. I did terrible things when I was angry. I frightened people. I made a promise I would never raise my voice in anger again, but it was too late to change some bad things that had already happened." Willem had never admitted that to anyone before. It was a strange feeling to say it aloud.

"Oh." The boy accepted the answer without question. He sat quietly, fidgeting only every other minute while Willem finished the pie and drank the coffee. Then he bounded off the bed to pick up the empty plate and cup.

"I'll take those to Mama," the boy said. "Mama has a rule that nobody eats in their room, but she let me bring this up. I like you, Mr. Tremain. You are going to be my friend," Matthew declared before he scampered out the door and down the stairs.

Willem found himself grasping the doorjamb for support for several minutes after Matthew left. He hadn't been a friend to anyone—not even himself—for a very long while.

Chapter Five

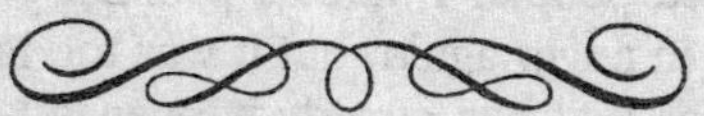

Willem woke to the heavy tread of work boots descending the stairs. He had slept fitfully, visited by his long-dead companions and the black dread that enveloped him each night. He dressed by the pale light of dawn and left his room.

Before he had passed the one-eared ginger tom stretched out on the second floor landing, the smell of home cooking had his mouth watering. When he entered the kitchen he found piles of fluffy flapjacks, small crocks of fresh butter and urns of syrup lined up on the enormous table. Stacks of steaming biscuits waited beside a huge blue crock bowl of thick, rich, cream gravy. Fat patties of fried sausage and thick slices of bacon covered a blue patterned platter. The smell of newly ground coffee beans lingered in the air. His empty belly growled like a roused bear.

"Good morning," Mrs. Cooprel said. "How was your first night?" She was filling lunch tins with crocks and jars and gingham-cloth-covered things, which whetted Will's appetite even more than the sight of her bountiful breakfast table.

"Passable." He felt an odd tingle up his back.

She turned to him with her eyebrows pinched together. From her concerned expression he guessed he had not provided her with the answer she expected. He felt obliged to explain and irritated that her concern could have such a profound effect on him.

"Nothing's wrong with the room, I'm just not much of a sleeper. I wanted to thank you for the pie and coffee last night." Willem found it damned hard to spit out his thanks while her eyes probed his face.

"It was really Matthew's idea," she said tightly. "He seems to like you." Willem heard undisguised disapproval in her voice before she turned and began to whisk around the room like a butterfly in a flower garden. She managed to juggle several tasks at once with no problem. The miners' eyes followed her movements. It was plain they all thought Mrs. Cooprel sat somewhere near the left hand of God.

"Matthew is a bright boy," Willem said for no reason he could think of.

"Yes, he is." Mrs. Cooprel turned her full attention back to filling the lunch pails, so Will looked for an empty chair. The same chair he had occupied last night was vacant, so he settled into it and poured himself coffee. He saw the men filling their plates and wondered if the formality of grace would be repeated at breakfast. He helped himself to biscuits and gravy while he observed the group. Not wishing to embarrass himself with another social blunder, he waited until he saw Snap and Brawley each shove a forkful of syrup-covered flapjacks into their mouths before he picked up his own fork and began to eat.

Abigail rubbed her hands on her apron and sighed. "There they are, gentlemen." She nodded toward the shiny tins lined up on a long plank against one wall. She poured herself a mug of coffee and sat down.

"Matthew is a slugabed this mornin'," Brawley commented with a grunt.

Mrs. Cooprel's face took on the same expressionless quality Willem had witnessed last night. He was curious about the woman and knew he shouldn't be. His thoughts should be only of Moira and his child.

"He was worn out, Brawley," she said tightly. "A growing boy needs his rest."

"Missus." Brawley's voice cracked. He frowned at the sniggers erupting down the length of the table and gulped some coffee. Abigail ducked her head and Willem could've sworn she was giggling. Brawley cleared his throat and tried again. "I was wondering if you and the lad would consider sharin' lunch with me at the picnic? I could partner up with the boy for the games—that way he'd be sure to win this year." Brawley gulped more coffee when he finished, as if speaking had made his mouth go dry.

Willem saw the other men at the table look up. Each face was slack-jawed with suspense, or maybe it was alarm—he didn't know which. Abigail flicked a quick glance over them from under her long fringe of lashes. Willem was sure he saw her frown when she looked back at Brawley.

"That's very kind of you, Brawley, but I've already made other plans."

If she had hit him with a skillet the man couldn't have looked more stricken. His great, wide shoulders seemed to slump.

"I see," Brawley said. A wash of red crept up his face from beneath his beard and climbed until it met his fiery hair.

"I'm expecting Lars to be back by then. You'll have to ask Matthew about the games yourself, but I expect he'll want to be Lars's partner again this year." Abigail smiled and began to fill a plate for herself. Willem saw the light twinkle in her aquamarine eyes. Every bearded face along the table flowered into a smug smile of satisfaction—except for Brawley.

Willem was beginning to figure out the widow. She made sure she kept herself surrounded by many men and no one single man. He could see it was a constant source of irritation to Brawley.

Willem frowned. He felt his curiosity whetted about the mysterious Lars. Matthew's face had softened with affection when he'd spoken of his uncle the night before.

"The sun is climbing. I best be off to the Bonnet. Thanks for the grub, Missus." Snap Jackson stood and pulled on his shapeless hat. One by one the men rose and trooped from the kitchen. Only Brawley and Will remained. After a few minutes Brawley shot Willem a dark glance before he, too, grabbed his hat.

"Some of us have a job to be at," he snarled before he left the kitchen. Willem heard the front door close with a thud.

"It appears you and I are the only ones who don't have to be someplace special, Mrs. Cooprel," Willem said across the long expanse of table. He saw color creep into her cheeks and knew he'd found the right of it. She was a woman who could hold her own in a crowd of the roughest men, but alone with only one man she was shy and uncertain of herself.

"Yes—yes, we do," she choked out. "But Matthew is upstairs." A shadow of fear flitted through her eyes.

Willem sipped his coffee slowly and watched her. She was chewing her food as if it was made of sand. He found it ironic that he should bother her, when all she had to do was look at him with those aqua eyes and he felt the foundation shift beneath his feet. Willem chided himself for thinking foolish thoughts and forced himself to leave her company.

"Please tell Matthew goodbye for me and thank him again for the pie—and the good company."

"Yes—yes, I will."

From her chair she met his gaze, and he felt something powerful leap to life inside his chest. It was similar to the feeling he'd had when Matthew had come to his room last night, only this was primal and strong in a hot, dark way.

"Are you looking for work, Mr. Tremain?" she asked softly while he stared at her over the half-empty platters of food.

"No, I've already got a job. They're not expecting me until tomorrow but I think I'll let Otto know I made it." He frowned and wondered why he was telling her his whole life's story.

"Otto Mears?" Her eyes followed him when he rose from the table. He didn't want to leave her, even though he found her company confusing and almost painful.

"Yes. I worked for him some years back when he was putting through the toll road to Silverton." Willem felt the darkness rolling forward from the edge of his memories. That had been before Moira left, before sadness claimed their lives.

"You must be very good at what you do if you work for Mr. Mears."

Willem shrugged. He never considered himself to be any great hand at anything special. His expertise with dynamite and powder was more an act of God and his Welsh mining heritage than any degree of skill on his part. "I never thought much about it."

Mrs. Cooprel frowned before she looked away. He could feel the tension in the room. "I'll give Matthew your message, Mr. Tremain. Have a pleasant day."

Willem dodged the mule train and jumped out of the way as a twelve-foot length of rail iron nearly crushed his foot. He'd been negotiating a swarm of men, endless lengths of track and teams of surly pack animals for thirty minutes, and he still had not found Otto Mears. He'd heard the man was looking for able-bodied men to help get the train from Silverton to Red Mountain, Guston and Ironton before the first snow, but he was shocked to see the multitude clinging to the treacherous mountainside. He finally found a battered tent and stepped up to the opening.

"Hello, inside," Will called.

"Vhat you vant?" a harsh voice snapped from inside the canvas.

"Hello, Otto." Willem stood back and folded his hands across his chest while he waited for Otto to emerge.

"Vhat?" A small man poked his head out from under the flap and glared up at Willem. Recognition washed slowly across the wiry man's sharp features. "So, is you. Vhen you git here?" He talked rapidly while he emerged from the tent.

"Yesterday. How are you, Otto?" Willem extended his hand and watched a smile begin in the man's eyes and slowly descend until it finally reached Otto's lips.

"I am goot. Now you are here you can move dat." Otto pointed disgustedly at a rugged outcrop of rock in the direct path of an advancing ribbon of creosote-soaked ties and parallel iron.

"What's the matter, Otto, pick and shovel not fast enough for you?"

Otto lapsed into a string of words in his native tongue. "You make joke," he finally said with a frown. He jabbed Willem in the ribs and winked. "You still got the knack?"

"Explosives, you mean?" Willem shrugged. "I can move the rock for you."

"Vhat kind of explosives you use for dat?" Otto stood back and squinted his eyes.

"Dynamite placed in the right spot should bring it down smooth."

"Damn, Black Irish, you nefer change, by Sheminie! I guess you don't vant no drink, either?"

Willem shook his head.

"Goot. I don't haf nothing for you, anyvay. Vhy you got dat brush on your face?"

"Broke."

"Got damn, Black Irish—you should be richer dan dat damn Midas. You don't gamble or drink. Haf you got yourself a fancy voman? Is dat vhere your money goes?"

"No." Willem shrugged.

"Den vhy are you alvays broke? Here—go to town, find a sheepshearer to take care of dat hair." Otto dug deep into his pocket and pulled out some crumpled bills.

"No, I'll wait until payday." Will held up his hand to refuse the money.

"The hell you vill. I don't vant my men being blown up vhen the vind blows dat mane in your damn eyes." Otto grabbed Willem's hand and thrust the money into it.

"I see you're as bossy as ever, Otto," Willem said, and shoved the money into his faded trouser pocket.

"Yah. Don't you be forgetting who the boss is. I see you tomorrow?"

"I'll be here in the morning." Willem turned and walked away.

Otto watched Willem weave his way through the mules, burros and men wielding eighteen-pound jacks while he wondered about the mysterious Black Irish. He felt a bony hand jab him in his ribs.

"Vhat?" He felt about as patient as a surly badger this morning. "Oh, is you, Lars."

The old man leaned over to spit a mouthful of tobacco juice on the hard rocks at his feet. "Who was that, Otto?"

"Vhat? You don't know the Black Irish?" Otto was incredulous.

"Heard of him. Never met him," Lars admitted.

"Vhy didn't you say you vanted to meet the Black Irish?" Otto demanded. "I vould've introduced you. He'll be back tomorrow. He's going to blow dat damn mountain out of my vay, den ve git dis damn railroad built, by Sheminie."

The barber wrapped a hot, steamy towel around Will's face and patted it several times. Willem closed his eyes and allowed his ears to focus on the sounds of the bustling activity in the street outside the barber shop. He felt good after the bath, and it was a real treat to be getting his whiskers sheared. He had never tried to grow a beard in earnest, and this experience of having one had not changed his view about doing so. "How's that feel?" The barber's voice drifted to Will through layers of towel swathed over his face.

"Fine." Willem thought his own reply sounded like a muffled grunt but the barber seemed to understand.

"Good. Just relax while those whiskers soften up a bit."

Will's chair suddenly spun around. The darkness and rotation brought a moment of panic. Willem felt his heart thud painfully in his chest while he grew more disoriented. He had the sensation of the floor buckling beneath his chair. He envisioned a great dark chasm opening up. Suddenly the hot towel was whipped from his face. The horrible falling sensation disappeared. Will sucked in a deep breath and gripped the arms of the barber chair while he waited for his pulse to return to normal.

"What do you want? Clean shave, mustache? Muttonchops are real popular with the local businessmen," the barber suggested to Willem.

"Take it down to the hide," Willem said when he could speak normally again.

"You're the boss." The barber grabbed a shaving cup and worked up a thick lather with a bristle brush. He swabbed

Will's face with all the finesse of a drunken house painter. When he gave the chair another spin, Willem saw a reflection of his froth-covered image go whirling by in the big tilted mirror on the wall. He looked like a rabid dog, all covered in foam. He nearly chuckled out loud at the ridiculous sight of himself.

When the straight edge whisked over his jaw, Willem held his breath and his humor faded away. He never had learned to act casual with a man brandishing a sharp razor at his throat. He sat stiff as a poker while the barber took swipe after swipe. Finally the man pinched Will's nostrils together and took one quick stroke under his nose. He toweled Willem off and splashed a handful of what felt like horse liniment across his tingling cheeks.

"Holy Moses!" Willem sucked in his breath. "What the blue blazes is that?" He leapt from the barber chair.

"Bay rum, sir," the barber replied cheerfully. He took a step back and regarded Willem with a smile.

"Makes me smell like a damned French whore." Willem dug into his pocket and paid the man.

Will stepped out into the street and watched the marching band stomp toward him. The sound of their pitiful playing grated on his nerves. He decided to get as far away from the caterwauling as possible, and set off at a good clip in the opposite direction, not caring where it would lead him as long as it was quiet. Willem walked until he could no longer hear the skrill of horns or thump of the drum. He looked overhead and spotted a street sign.

"So this is Blaine Street." Willem knew the Pinkertons had checked every brothel between Animas City and Denver looking for Moira. He also knew they'd never find her in a bawdy house. Moira had barely tolerated his attentions. No, she would not have sold her body to men. Still, he'd never given up hope that he might someday turn a corner and simply find her standing there. After so many rebuffs, he had stopped wanting her years ago, but he could not put aside feelings about the mother of his child or his convictions about the sanctity of marriage. It ate at him day and night. And finally, finding his child and bringing it up properly—in a home with both mother and father—had become his obsession.

The image of Matthew Cooprel's face swam before his eyes. The boy was the kind of son any man would be proud to call his own. Willem stood there staring blankly at the sign while a new thought dawned. What if Moira had given the baby to someone else to raise? A cold chill raced up his back at the thought. She had been so young, and he had frightened her with his black temper. Maybe she had run away out of fear and fostered the baby out. The new and disturbing suspicion would have to be explored. If she had done that and left the area, it would account for the Pinkerton's inability to find her. He'd have to talk it over with Paxton Kane when he arrived on Monday.

Willem looked up and down the notorious street and read a collection of hand-painted windows. Mulligan's Saloon, Petrie's Emporium and Silvio's Billiard Parlor caught his eye. A heavy hand clamped onto his shoulder, and Will spun around.

"Taking in the local sights?" Snap Jackson asked with a grin.

"Sort of," Willem replied.

"Whoa—somebody sure enough skinned you." Snap gestured at Willem's lack of beard and shorter hair and chuckled derisively. "I'm heading over to Silvio's for a beer and a game of billiards. Want to join me?"

Beer didn't interest Will and he'd never taken the precious time to learn billiards, but Snap seemed to know his way around pretty well. Perhaps he might stumble on some bit of news about Moira.

"Sure, why not?" Will fell into step beside the man.

The inside of Silvio's was like every other beer hall Willem had ever seen—dark and musty with a lingering smell of stale tobacco and unwashed bodies. His stomach roiled while a new wash of unpleasant memories gained momentum. Snap ordered a mug and offered Willem one.

"No, thanks." Willem held up his hand.

Snap shrugged and moved toward the billiard table. The green felt cover was fading in the middle and the laced leather pouches under the holes needed to be retied, but Snap grabbed a cue stick and set his beer aside without hesitation.

"Rack them up, Will."

"I never learned to play. I'll just watch if you don't mind." Willem leaned against a nearby wall and crossed his arms at his chest.

"Whatever you say." Snap leaned his wiry torso over the edge of the table, tented his fingers on the felt and proceeded to pop the painted ivory balls into the holes. Willem had to admire the man's finesse.

"Snap, have you been here long?" he asked when the man paused for a gulp of beer.

"Seems like forever." He wiped beer foam from his mouth. "I come and go with the thaw and the freeze."

"You spend much time down here, on Blaine Street, I mean?"

Snap frowned and set his beer down. "About as much as most men. You got a reason for asking?"

Willem felt like a fool asking personal questions of a stranger. He wasn't any good at this. Paxton had told him he didn't know how to ask questions, and now he saw it was true.

"I'm looking for a woman," Willem said flatly.

"Just open your mouth and yell. This is the place for it."

"No, I mean a particular woman. She has red hair and pale blue eyes, a little slip of a thing." Willem heard the catch in his throat when he described her.

"Does this particular woman have a name?" Snap leaned on his billiard stick.

"Moira—Moira Tremain." Willem was surprised at how much pain it caused him to say her name after all this time, after all these years.

"Your sister?"

"No. She's my wife."

Chapter Six

Willem walked aimlessly while he thought of Moira. She had been a pretty vixen of a girl—impulsive as a wild fox. Her curly flame-colored hair and round blue eyes made it easy for her to wrap him around her pampered little finger. His stomach contorted when he thought of their wedding day. What should've been a happy beginning for the two of them had been strained and tearful.

Willem had always wanted the child they created on their wedding night, and Moira seemed to adjust to the idea. If only he had been less hotheaded, maybe he wouldn't have scared her so. If only there hadn't been all those ridiculous stories about 'the Black Irish' and his deadly temper, if only she hadn't believed them.

If only.

The words echoed in his mind. He'd been less than understanding about her needs, and in the end she had run from him in fear. His lack of sensitivity and her tender years had cost them both dearly. For the first time Willem thought perhaps he wasn't totally responsible for the mess he and Moira had made of their lives. Maybe his beautiful child bride did share a tiny fraction of the blame.

He stopped his soul-searching and found himself standing in front of the widow Cooprel's boardinghouse. Willem wondered why he seemed drawn to this place like iron filings to a magnet.

Perhaps it was the boy.

He shrugged and climbed the stairs to his room for a few hours' rest, too weary to muddle through any more puzzles or memories.

The sound of Matthew's husky laughter woke Willem. He lay across the narrow bed with his forearm thrown over his eyes and allowed the sound to sluice over him. It was like standing under a tight dry roof and listening to sweet spring rain fall around him. It invigorated and refreshed his barren soul.

He stood and went to see what brought the child such happiness. Willem's heart skipped two beats when he peered out the open window.

Abigail and Matthew were playing chase around a row of heavy Chinese rugs strung along a sturdy wire clothesline. Abigail had her hair loose and tied back in an old red kerchief. Willem never had imagined it would be so long. It rippled free down her back in chestnut waves that caught the sun and turned it into a prism of light. She clutched a straw broom in her hands and brandished it like a weapon. Matthew dodged around the protection of the rugs while he laughed at her mock fierceness.

Their antics brought a bittersweet joy to Willem. They were like a couple of otter pups at play. Mrs. Cooprel seemed so young and innocent while she darted and ran across the grass. He recalled her telling him Tuesday was her cleaning day. She must've been beating the rugs when the boy taunted her into mischief. He sighed and leaned farther out the window, relishing the innocent sight of the widow and her son. But when she suddenly dropped the broom and picked up her skirts to give chase, Willem sucked in his breath. He no longer saw innocence in Abigail Cooprel, but the flesh-and-blood woman beneath.

Her pale feet and slender ankles were bare. She curled her toes into the clover blossoms and thick grass when she paused between sprints. She hitched her skirt higher and laughed when Matthew rolled in the turf.

A hard knot formed inside Will's belly.

Abigail Cooprel had long, coltish legs, smooth, supple and creamy as white satin. Willem felt a jolt of heat blaze through him each time her petticoats and skirt inched higher.

His sex awakened by tiny relentless degrees. His pulse quickened and thrummed deep inside his ears. A slow inferno began in his stomach, then snaked around and twined its way lower on a sizzling journey toward his throbbing groin. He felt his member harden and swell with each dull thump of his quaking heart. His long-denied libido sprang to life while he stared openmouthed at the woman below.

Abigail laughed, and the throaty sound sent Will's long-suppressed passion roaring to life. He groaned and closed his eyes. He'd made a vow to cleave only to Moira. He'd kept that sacred marriage vow without difficulty for nearly seven years. But now he felt an ache so deep and raw and hungry it split him wide open with need for a woman—need for *that* woman running through the meadow grass like a woodland sprite.

What was it about this place that was turning him inside out? What was it about the widow that was making him want to abandon his beliefs, break vows and sunder promises?

Will clenched his jaw and tore himself away from the open window. He couldn't deny the widow's seductive lure—he just couldn't give in to it.

He swore under his breath. Willem kept reminding himself she wasn't very pretty...except for her eyes...and that thick mane of hair...and legs smoother than alabaster. Except for those few attributes she was quite plain. If only he could convince the burning between his legs of it.

Willem paced his room while his blood ran hot and thick in his veins. After long hours of torture, the sound of rough miners' voices finally wafted up the stairs. He felt he could face the widow without making a fool of himself as long as the other miners were around.

Willem splashed cold water on his face and slicked back his hair. He caught sight of himself in the mirror and saw himself anew. A spark of life was in his eyes, an ember that hadn't burned there for years. It had been missing since he'd walked into his empty house and found a note pinned beside the empty cradle. The inner fire of his soul had been numb since his search for Moira and the baby had begun.

He took a deep breath and ran his palm over his short, wet hair. The widow had awakened the man inside him, while Matthew had begun to thaw the broken heart of a long-denied father. Since viewing Abigail earlier, all the parts of his body were waking in the bargain. The realization sent a tiny shiver of astonishment through him.

The sound of Abigail's husky laughter arrested him when he entered the bright kitchen. She had her back to him, but turned and met his gaze when he scraped the legs of his chair across the floor. A strange energy arced across the room between them. Will felt as if his skin was shrinking around his bones. A tight tingling sensation prickled along his scalp. He struggled to master the unfamiliar sensations of pure, white-hot lust surging through him.

He wanted her. Could she see it?

"Mr. Tremain." Abigail swallowed hard. She gripped the bowl in her hands until her fingers turned white. Her blue-green eyes pierced his heart with the look she gave him. "My word, but it's nice to see a man without all that hair covering his face." She blushed.

Willem knew she regretted her words the instant they left her lips. It gave him a warm, fluttering feeling to hear her compliment him. She dropped her eyes and moved toward the table. Why this woman was so determined to keep herself locked away, he couldn't fathom. He found himself pleased that she noticed his appearance and more pleased that she said so. It was an odd thing, this growing need for her to treat him with a little more kindness or interest than she showed the other men in her house. He found himself wondering if each one of them felt the same way he did, and on the heels of the thought came a ripple of envy for those who'd known her longer than himself.

Fantasies of her long legs wrapped around his waist hammered at Will. "I saw you earlier—when you and Matthew were beating rugs." He didn't know why he said it, but there was something powerful gnawing at him, making him push her into a corner. He had a desire to make her aware of the effect she had upon him.

Abigail looked up in wide-eyed amazement. Fear, or something like it, flickered through her eyes. He knew she was remembering her unguarded moments at play with Matthew. "I hope we didn't disturb you," she finally managed to stammer.

"Not at all." Willem felt eyes upon his back. He turned and found the miners staring at him with a mixture of disbelief and downright shock in their eyes. Brawley wore a frown so deep Willem thought the light might leave the room in fear of his black countenance. Only Matthew grinned at Will with something akin to friendship shining in his eyes. It made his stomach twist, the way the boy looked at him.

He glanced up and found the widow staring at him and the boy. Confusion and hostility were written on her face.

Abigail frowned and willed her hands to stop shaking. The man had a way of—unsettling her. She glanced at him and Matthew again. There was something different about Willem Tremain. Even Matthew sensed it—she could see it shining in his eyes. She watched her son admire the man and she felt a pang of something suspiciously like jealousy ripple through her. In all the years she'd run the boardinghouse Matthew had never made the slightest effort to get friendly with a boarder. The way he warmed up to Willem Tremain frightened her. And the way her stomach knotted up when Will's piercing eyes focused on her made the uneasiness worse. This man made her apprehensive in a way she could not understand.

He wasn't tame—he wasn't even house-gentle, not this one. He looked up at her again and she felt a tingling sensation bridge the empty space between them. This one could be dangerous to her in some unfathomable way.... She saw banked fires smoldering in his probing sapphire eyes and knew he was a threat to her happiness.

She had to keep him away from her and Matthew, she had to ignore the way he made her *feel.*

Abigail brought a bowl of potatoes to the table and Will inhaled the scent of lemon oil, fresh air and sunshine clinging to the lopsided bun of hair trying to tumble down her back. The memory of her pale legs pumping rhythmically while she ran made him squirm on the hard wooden chair. She accidentally brushed him with her forearm and he felt a hot zing radiate from the point of contact. He heard her sharp intake of breath before she moved away. She was afraid of him. He could see it in the trembling hands and stiff movements of her slender body.

Mrs. Cooprel sat at the far end of the table and glanced up only once. She was quieter than last night, and he saw her brows crinkled into a tight frown. Brawley leaned over and said something to her and she looked up. Her gaze locked with Will's across the length of the table. She licked her lips, and another wave of heat flowed through his blood. She lowered her lashes and avoided his eyes after that. He wondered if she had any notion of what her tremulous mouth was doing to his insides.

Will brought food to his mouth, chewed and swallowed, but he couldn't have identified the menu if his soul had depended upon it. By the time Abigail brought a still-bubbling peach cobbler to the table, he was in full rut.

Abigail gripped the pan more tightly and told herself to stop acting like a green girl. She realized her uncharacteristic silence was making her unease more obvious each passing moment. She searched her mind for some safe topic to speak to Willem Tremain about.

"I would've cleaned your room today, Mr. Tremain, but when I peeked in you were sleeping," she said tautly when she served him.

Willem met her shy gaze, and the playful woman he'd witnessed earlier shimmered before him, like a half-remembered dream. The thought of Mrs. Cooprel in his bedroom—alone—with him sent a burning lancet of need through his loins. He wished he'd not been asleep when she entered his room.... He quickly chastised himself. After all he was a married man.

"I'm sorry if I inconvenienced you by not letting you know, Mrs. Cooprel. I usually don't fall asleep so easily."

"I—I only mentioned it because I told you about my schedule, Mr. Tremain." A crimson flush climbed her cheeks. "I didn't want you to think I wasn't giving you the service I promised."

Her stammering words sent his temperature rising. She had stumbled over words that made his blood boil with double meaning. He knew she felt his passion, which had to be why she acted so nervous around him. He didn't want to frighten her—never wanted to frighten any woman ever again—yet it was obvious she was afraid. Will searched for some way to make her understand she didn't have to fear him. No matter how desperately he burned for her he would never make a move in her direction. He had promised himself to Moira till death parted them. And even though she had chosen to flee from him, he still believed in those vows.

"Mrs. Cooprel?"

"Yes, Mr. Tremain?" Her voice was soft. She looked at him like a trapped doe before dropping her lashes over eyes gone wide and luminous.

"Would you please call me Will?" He felt the same charged energy surround him and prayed she could not sense it. He fairly rocked from the impact. He watched her bottom lip tremble. When she glanced up at him he caught the alarm in her blue-green eyes.

"If—if you wish." She swallowed hard.

He hoped she would understand he meant her no harm. He would never violate his promise, no matter what. Willem heard her sharp intake of breath. He saw her knuckles blanch while she held the pan of cobbler between them like a wall of protection from his lust. Watching Abigail confirmed his suspicion—she flitted among the men in her house like a little ruby-throated hummingbird, but got close to none of them.

"And may I call you—Abigail?" He stumbled over her name and it left a taste of sweet forbidden fruit in his mouth. He saw her glance once at Matthew's expectant face. Something like pain filled her eyes in that moment.

"Certainly, Mr. Tremain—I mean Willem—that would be only fair," she finally said in a tight voice. She glanced at him one last time, and he was sure he saw resentment and fear controlling every constricted line bracketing her mouth.

He instantly regretted what he'd asked of her. It had not made her fear him less—in fact, it seemed she trembled more—and he could feel the hostility growing between them. Willem sighed in frustration. Instead of worrying about Abigail Cooprel he should be concentrating on finding Moira and his child. He would do well to remember that.

Willem clenched his jaw and cursed himself silently. The woman stirred his blood, but he could never forget the promise he'd made on his wedding day. Abigail Cooprel had no way of knowing it, but she was safer around him than any man jack at her table.

Chapter Seven

Lars stepped out of the Silverton bank and savored the brief respite from the crushing guilt he'd carried since the night of Matthew's birth. He folded up the receipt and put it in his pocket. He would add it to the stash he had acquired over the years. He'd deposited gold dust to Matthew's now sizable account secretly since the boy's birth. He sighed and knew this moment of peace would be a short lull at best, then his conscience would start gnawing at him again. The old man put his battered hat back on his head and crossed Greene Street. The sky was gray with scudding clouds. His joints ached today, a lingering souvenir of the cold months he spent high up on the mountain.

He'd been gone since early spring, scraping the ore out of the stingy rocks. After he had finally found the courage to tell Abigail the truth, he had turned coward again. He had fled into the quiet solitude of the mountains, unable to face Abbie, unable to look into her eyes. Yet he knew he had to go back. She would have questions—questions only he could answer.

Before he left he had not even told her where he had buried her little daughter. A hard lump formed in his throat. He had never been much good at talking to women, and being around Abbie all these years hadn't changed a thing.

Funny how it had all worked out, he thought. He'd been so sure it was right... letting Abigail believe Matthew was her son.

That was his first mistake. He should have told her right off. He realized it when he saw how much fear and hurt appeared in her eyes when he finally did tell her. He had betrayed her with his silence.

Lars rubbed his fingers over the gold disk secreted beneath his shirt. It hung like a millstone about his neck—a tangible reminder of the lie he'd told. He'd done everything he could to insure the boy's future. He'd even built the boardinghouse, and had thought the act might silence the nameless woman's voice—but it hadn't.

That was his second mistake. Finally the dead woman's memory had forced him to tell Abigail what he had done.

He had stayed away longer than usual this time, hoping in some small way to atone for the lie he'd saddled them all with. But deep down inside he knew that gold was not the answer.

His only solace in the whole sorry mess was Matthew. The boy had taken the place of children and grandchildren he never had. He smiled when he thought of the little scamp. He ought to bring him something, a present, something special for a growing boy....

Lars saw men loading up Otto's mule train and he tried to quicken his pace. The effort only made his limp worse, so he slowed down. He was old and the mountain cold never quite left his bones. He shrugged. If they left without him, then so be it, he'd hitch a ride with another group. The men laying track were thick as ants on a hillside.

A mule brayed and Lars jumped sideways to avoid an iron-shod hoof. A dark-haired man with a clean-shaven lantern jaw was lashing an iron section of rail to the protesting animal's side. He looked at the man again and saw with surprise it was the Black Irish, stripped of his beard and long hair. Otto had pointed him out to Lars only the day before. Lars paused to watch him work with the fractious mule. The Irish was exceptionally tall, with great wide shoulders and thick arms. His large hands were steady and his voice low while he crooned soothing words to the ornery beast.

Lars had heard all the dark rumors about the man. He found it hard to believe he was watching the fellow known across the goldfields as a man with a short fuse and a killing anger. This person showed no trace of bad humor; in fact, he was the picture of patience while he finished fastening the heavy burden. Lars had to admit that with his glowing blue eyes and dark hair curling over his thick brows he looked like Lucifer himself risen from perdition. But the man seemed an ordinary sort—certainly not the fire-spitting terror Lars had heard about. A teamster bellowed the command to move. Lars found the last wagon and flopped inside while he wondered what he could give Matthew.

Willem jumped down from the wagon and grabbed the crate of dynamite. He hefted it up on his shoulder and strode to the deserted cliff face. A golden-pelted marmot raised its head from the task of eating and eyed Willem. He had little interest in the man or the dynamite.

"Better find cover." Will's voice sounded too loud in the silence of the mountain. The marmot made a deep grunt to show his displeasure and scurried over the rocky ridge. Willem set the box down and pried open the lid with a short crowbar. He picked up several sticks of dynamite and a roll of fuse.

The rock was cool to the touch when he rubbed his palm over it. There were times, like now, when Will fancied he could feel a heartbeat thrumming deep inside the mountain. He closed his eyes and let the sensation ripple through him.

Yes, if he placed the charge just so, right here, the rock would sheer off cleaner than a slice of the widow's homemade pie. He frowned at the wayward notions and busied himself with chisel and sledge. He single-jacked until he had created a cleft deep enough to hold the charge.

More and more thoughts of Abigail and Matthew crept into his head while he worked. It disturbed him and made him feel as if he was standing over an ant den. He was itchy and restless and confused.

His hands worked automatically. He'd done this so many times he could do it blindfolded. Willem knew by instinct the charge would remove several tons of meddlesome stone from Otto's determined path. He lit the fuse and darted toward shelter behind a large outcropping.

Will ducked his head. He heard the blast and felt the earth shudder. A spray of fine rocks and gravel pelted his arms and shoulders. He squinted through the settling dust. The mountain surface was smooth and straight, just as he knew it would be.

"Otto will be happy...until the next time." Willem chuckled.

Lars crept through the parlor and up the stairs. His room, the one Abigail never rented, was on the third floor. He grimaced when he thought of carrying the weight of the squirming gunnysack that far. While he put one broken-down boot in front of the other, he cursed himself for becoming old and weak. He hobbled up the stairs and chuckled to himself when the sack wiggled and threw him off-balance. The boy would be happier than a whitewashed pig when he saw what was inside.

He opened the door to his room and set the heavy sack down, then breathed a sigh of relief. He placed his hands at the small of his back and stretched. His bones popped in loud protest. When he was upright he grinned in anticipation. He couldn't wait to see the lad's face—he knew he'd be delighted. Now, Abigail might be a different matter altogether....

Abigail stopped plucking feathers from the fat hen the moment she thought she'd heard the front door close. She waited a minute, but no one rang the bell on the desk or called out, so she chalked it up to her imagination. She'd been on tenterhooks since Willem Tremain had moved in—every noise or shadow made her jump out of her skin. She scolded herself for allowing the man to unnerve her, and jerked a handful of pungent feathers from the sodden bird.

She watched Matthew out the kitchen window. He was swinging a pickax that Lars had shortened to accommodate his child's stature, trying to break open a melon-sized geode. She smiled and stopped a moment to observe him. She noticed his trousers no longer reached his boot tops.

"There is nothing left to let out," she muttered in exasperation.

Carl had not been a large man, and she was only slightly over average height. She had often wondered where Matthew got his size and amazing breadth of shoulder. Now she realized with a painful wrenching to her heart that she knew nothing about Matthew's people.

"Some relative must've been a large, robust man," she said softly. A tight lump grew in her throat and she knew she would cry if she continued to think about it.

She rinsed the naked bird in hot water and quickly removed the innards. Then she used her meat cleaver to neatly sever it in half, and then in half again. The water was at a rapid boil when she plopped the pieces in. Chicken and dumplings was Matthew's favorite meal.

Willem Tremain nudged uninvited into Abigail's thoughts again. He frightened her in some inexplicable manner. Since he had called her by name, she'd been finding herself puzzling over him more and more. He was an odd man, one with many closed doors and secrets, one that made her tremble inside. He said he had a wife, something men in gold camps rarely admitted.

Abigail had found herself more curious about Willem Tremain and his absent wife with each passing day. He was not like the other men who lived here. He did not seem the type to put women on pedestals and admire them from afar. Willem Tremain was the kind of man who pulled women down to earth and made them feel things—things better left alone.

Abigail felt as if he were searing her flesh every time he raked those sapphire eyes over her face. There was something threatening about him. There was something hidden in the depths of his eyes she couldn't quite put her finger on.... Or was it her own long-buried emotions she found such a threat?

She and Matthew were safe and happy. They had been content—until Willem Tremain showed up. Now she saw a light and a hunger in her son's eyes and it hurt her deeply. She had begun to think she could not give him everything he needed. She also found her own cocoon of safety being battered by the strange, brooding man. Willem Tremain made her quake inside with hidden longings, the kind of longing that brought grief and pain when she was left alone. Men didn't stay, for if death didn't take them, then rumors of bigger strikes did. Year after year she had seen the men under her roof go, and usually they never came back. Only old Lars had been constant.

She thought back to the night of Matthew's birth. Carl had died, her baby had died. Only by the grace of God had she and Matthew survived. Abigail sighed and swiped at the tears on her cheeks.

The tall clock in the parlor chimed the hour and Abigail shook her head to remove the spell of sad memory. She had been standing over the pot of boiling chicken with a lump of raw dumpling in her hand for long minutes. The miners would be home and expecting a meal all too soon. She clenched her jaw and told herself to forget Willem Tremain and the way her heart fluttered each time he looked at her. She told herself she was Matthew's mother—the only mother he had ever known. There was no way Willem Tremain could come between them.

Nonetheless, he had gotten under her skin. She didn't trust him, but worse, she didn't trust how he made her feel inside. At least summer was almost over. Willem Tremain would be leaving along with all the rest of her boarders. She and Matthew would be alone and safe together when the first hard frost came. Then there would be no men coming to her door and no threat of losing her child.

Willem jumped out of the huge wagon and thanked Fred Valsen for the ride. He slapped his cap against one pant leg and sent a spiral of dust and the smell of cordite swirling into the sunshine around his head. He was looking forward to the refreshing cold-water scrubbing at the pump outside Abigail's boardinghouse. Washing up every day and sitting down to eat was more appealing than he remembered. He slapped the cap back on his hair and rubbed his palm over his jaw. Rock grit raked along his cheeks. He could just imagine what he looked like, caked with rock dust. The only clean spots would be the small rings around his eyes where sweat had cut through the grime. He snorted and laughed at the mental picture he had of himself.

Will looked up and saw smoke wafting from the stovepipe of Abigail's kitchen. He took a deep breath. The smell of something wonderful made him regret not buying a tin so he could pay Abigail to pack him a lunch like she did the other miners. His mouth was watering just thinking about it. The oddity of wishing to pay Abigail more money did not escape him. He told himself he would not find Moira any more quickly if he starved, but still, the niggling worry that he was somehow allowing himself to become more and more preoccupied with Abigail Cooprel would not go away.

He strode to the pump and wondered why nobody else was about. Brawley, Snap, Tom and Mac worked at the Blue Bonnet and Guston mines, many miles closer than where Will was laboring on Otto's railroad. He glanced at the westering sun and knew he'd not come back early. With a shrug he stripped down to bare skin at the waist. He had chosen to shed his long underwear when he bathed in town, and considered himself lucky the vermin hadn't moved in.

He stuck his head under the pump and vigorously worked the handle up and down. A gush of cold water flowed over his shoulders and he sucked in a ragged breath. After a shivering moment he adjusted to the frigid temperature. Willem grabbed the cake of soap and scrubbed his hair and face. He slid the medallion aside and lathered the sweat and dust-streaked hair on his chest. Covered in soap lather, he stuck his body back under the spout and rinsed. His torso tingled pleasantly from the rough scrubbing and icy water. He combed his hair back with his fingers and wiped his palm over his wet jaw. Then he turned to pick up his shirt and discovered it had fallen into a puddle.

"Damn it," he cursed, and picked up the sodden fabric to wring it out.

It was quiet as a church without the other miners around. His shoes crunched on the pebbly walkway, sounding loud as a gold rocker box. He put his hand on the doorknob and was wondering again where the men were when something soft and warm hit him in the chest.

Willem heard Abigail take a quick breath. He snapped his head around in disbelief. She was blinking her eyes and tottering off-balance. He grabbed her shoulders to steady her, and felt her startled breath fan across his dripping chest. It sent a frisson of cool air through the hair on his chest, and chill bumps traced a path around his nipples.

"Abigail," he said. "I'm sorry—are you all right?"

She looked up at his blue eyes, which were lit with forbidden primal fire, and found the air squeezed from her constricted lungs.

"I...yes...yes...I—" She took a deep breath and smelled him, all heady male and clean bare skin. "I'm fine."

She lied. He knew it the moment she said the words.

She could feel his strength, his dark disturbing quality through the thin fabric of her dress where his hands gripped her. She was not all right. She was profoundly *not* all right.

Willem frowned and held himself rigid. She was unnerved by their abrupt contact. In truth, so was he. Her pounding pulse telegraphed through his fingers and up his bare arms. She was soft, supple and inviting. Thoughts raced through his head, dark, forbidden thoughts that made his groin heavy and his breath catch in his throat. She was a woman he could covet, but could never have.

"Mr. Tremain—I mean, Willem, you scared the life out of me," she said in a breathy whisper. "I was coming to see if something was wrong."

"Why would you think something was wrong?" He gazed from her wide eyes to her trembling mouth. Those lips would feel like the petals of a rose, he knew. She would taste of honeyed wine and *life.*

He wanted her. God forgive him—Moira forgive him—he wanted Abigail Cooprel with an intensity he had never experienced even in his randy youth. He tried to tamp down his ardor and noticed with shocked pleasure that he was still holding her shoulders while standing half-inside her front door.

She blinked, and he watched her pupils grow and shrink in size. Her lips parted slightly and she inhaled deeply.

"Nobody came down to dinner. I was worried there might've been an accident at one of the mines."

Her heart was fluttering like a captured moth inside her chest. He could feel it. Each beat sent a message to his own tormented soul. He had to let her go, to get control of himself. He was not a man free to follow the whims of his body. Willem forced himself to acknowledge the bitter truth that he could not have Abigail Cooprel, not now or ever. He had a wife and when he found her they would sort out their lives—if not for themselves, then for the child.

No, Willem had to forget about Abigail Cooprel.

"I'm sure the others will be along shortly. If there had been an accident we would've heard the warning whistle. None of them would miss your cooking." He released her shoulders and forced his palms stiffly to his thighs. His hands ached to touch her again. He watched the roses bloom in her cheeks and felt something powerful burst inside his chest. He didn't want to think about what that feeling might be.

Her wide blue-green eyes and blushing face tugged at him, tempted him. He wanted to take the pins from her hair and see it tumble down around her firm, lean shoulders as it had been the day she'd played with Matthew. He wanted to hold her, just for a while. Willem dared not allow himself to indulge in such fantasies. A moan escaped his clenched jaw.

"Is something wrong?" Her voice quavered a bit. She tilted her head to the side and looked at him just the way Matthew had done. Her eyes were full of compassion and life.

"No. Nothing is wrong. I just need to put my shirt on. I'm taking a chill." His voice was harsh with the lie. He was on fire, blazing with a hot need only Abigail's body could cool.

Her eyes drifted from his face to his neck, and he saw her fully comprehend his half-dressed state. It made him all the more aware of her furtive looks while she tried not to stare at his bare chest. His manhood blazed with turgid heat and there was a hollow gnawing in his belly.

She swallowed hard and blinked. The dark hair on Will's collarbones and chest were wet and running with tiny rivulets of water. They met and merged into small lines as they meandered over bulging hard muscle. Willem Tremain had the body of a man who'd swung an eighteen-pound sledge most of his life. He was broad, hard and all male.

Abigail tried to look away, but she couldn't. She'd nearly forgotten what a man's body looked like. The other miners were always swathed in hair, beards and thick layers of coarse clothing. She had not looked upon a man's body for over six years and she was hungry for the sight.

Willem's body was a lean network of brawn. She stared at him, unable to move or turn away. Abigail found herself mesmerized by his physique and the strange gold disk nestled among the damp curls of soft hair in the middle of his massive chest.

Abigail felt a peculiar heat radiating from her middle. It was so hot, and her heart was beating rapidly. She wondered if perhaps she was ailing.

Willem tensed, and she watched in appreciation when every one of his corded muscles hardened to stone. She had the most singular urge to touch him, to slide her palms over the contours of his body and see if he felt as hard as he looked. The thought startled her more than running into him had. She had not felt such stirring within her since Carl's death. The idea that Willem Tremain was dangerous—a dark, lethal presence in her life—gained more substance. She should be afraid, truly afraid.

"What an odd coin," she managed to stammer.

"It's an old family design." Willem's voice sounded huskier than usual. She surely must be sickening. Abigail felt downright feverish and more light-headed than the time she drank too much of Lars's dandelion wine.

"It's lovely. It looks very old...." She raised her fingertips to touch it. Her nails lightly scraped over the edge of the disk and brushed Will's warm, moist skin. Every inch of his body went rigid. The room became electrified when her fingers touched his chest. He sucked in his breath with a sharp hiss that made her own skin prickle in response.

"Abigail." Her name was spoken in clear, sharp warning.

She jerked her hand back in alarm and snapped her gaze up to his face. Something burned in his eyes unlike any emotion Abigail had ever read there before. Unruly dark curls of wet hair surrounded his stern, smooth cheeks. His jaw was clamped so tightly that his cheek muscles were jumping in rhythmic fashion. His sensuous mouth was drawn into an uncompromising line, and his narrowed eyes held a forbidding glow. She took a step backward in fear of his glowering countenance.

"I'm sorry.... I—I didn't mean...p-please forgive my familiarity..." she stammered. She whirled around and fled to the safety of her kitchen. Something wild and raw had burned in Will's eyes, something that made her tremble with fear.

Willem let his breath out in a long, strained hiss. He closed his eyes and swallowed hard. The hungry beast inside him was awake. It roared ravenously and demanded to be sated. He shuddered while he fought to control his inner yearnings. Her nearness had shown him once again that the physical part of his nature was not as subdued as he had so foolishly believed. Willem had no intention of acting upon his urges, but that didn't make them any less powerful—or painful. Abigail Cooprel ignited a fuse deep within his chest. Willem prayed he'd be man enough to survive the blast when it finally exploded.

"Paxton, I hope you have some news for me." Willem sighed as he headed toward his room. He took the stairs two at a time but could not outrun the lust burning inside his body.

In his room, Willem buttoned the clean shirt and looked in the mirror. He still saw traces of desire smoldering in his own eyes. Abigail had a way about her that was hard to resist. Maybe it was the anxiety in her eyes when she looked at him, or maybe it was seeing both her sides—the one she showed the miners and the secret one he'd glimpsed while she played with Matthew. Whatever it was, it was damned near putting him on his knees.

He heard gruff laughter and realized that some of Abigail's stray flock had come home while he'd been trying to quell the fever in his blood. He reminded himself of Moira. He could never allow himself to be unfaithful to her because he believed in the sanctity of marriage. Willem had never been tempted to spend his time with harlots and tarts who made their living from men's physical needs. It seemed ironic to be drowning in a river of lust over a prim and proper widow lady like Abigail Cooprel. Will sighed and prayed Paxton would be able to tell him something tangible before he made a fool of himself over her.

Chapter Eight

Willem stood in the doorway of the kitchen and felt his jaw go slack. He laid his palm on the doorjamb to steady himself. The sight he beheld was so unbelievable he thought he might be dreaming. But when he glanced at Matthew, he saw the boy's eyes were rounder than a harvest moon and his mouth was hanging open in shock.

A gruff cough snapped Will from his trance. He looked from one shocking face to the next around the entire length of the long table. Every man jack was sporting a face smoother and pinker than a baby's bare bottom. Instead of full-bearded miners, Will was staring at a group of clean-shaven cherubs.

Willem glanced up and caught sight of Abigail across the room. Instead of choking back amused laughter at her tenants' appearance, she was nervous and distracted. Her teeth were worrying her bottom lip, and Will felt hot tension in the way she pointedly avoided meeting his gaze. He absently fingered the medallion beneath his shirt and reprimanded himself for being the cause of her distress. His behavior earlier had been unseemly and now she was embarrassed or terrified—he wasn't sure which. The thought that he had once again scared a woman brought a knot to the pit of his stomach. Willem raked another glance over the heads of her newly shaved and shorn boarders. He wondered if Abigail had even noticed their new hairless faces. If she had, she certainly wasn't letting on. She acted like a skittish mare in blinders while she went about her usual chores in the kitchen. She looked straight ahead, never allowing her eyes to falter right or left—and most particularly, never in Willem's direction.

"Well, I wish somebody would say something," Tom Cuthbert snapped at nobody in particular.

A strange feeling slithered through Will's gut. He was beginning to find the whole scene less amusing with each passing minute. The ten half-tanned, half-pale masculine faces—each one bisected by tender pink skin that had not been touched by sunshine for years—should have sent him into gales of uncontrollable laughter.

It should have, but it didn't.

Willem felt a new disturbing emotion rise above the other vexing feelings he had been experiencing on a daily basis. A dull, throbbing irritation at the miners started to grow and gain force. It surprised Will, but he had to admit he was put out the men would go to such lengths to garner Abigail's notice.

He thought back to her abrupt and soon regretted compliment about his clean-shaven face and knew that was what had brought on the men's new attitude about shaving. He stood there silently considering the situation and wondered why he should care one way or the other about it.

He locked eyes with Brawley, and the hair on his nape bristled. Brawley was half-sick with wanting Abigail Cooprel. It showed in his eyes and in the way he watched the widow. Willem glanced up and caught Abigail watching him. There was a peculiar exposed look in her eyes. It tugged at him, made him want to get near her again, made him remember the way it felt to touch her.

Abigail held Willem's gaze for long minutes even though she knew it was a mistake. She felt as if she were seeing him for the first time. His eyes were narrowed and his expression was fiercer than a mountain thunderhead. She feared him and she trusted him less with each passing day. He wanted something from her...but what? Willem Tremain possessed the fine chiseled looks that could get him any woman he wanted, so Abigail dismissed the possibility that it might be her. She was no great looker, so what else could Willem Tremain possibly want here in her house?

Willem wrenched his gaze from Abigail. If he wasn't careful he'd fall under her spell, and he could not do that. Moira and his child were out there—somewhere. He had commitments to honor—vows that bound him for life.

"Matthew, I have a surprise for you." A booming voice sent Willem whirling around. He'd been so hypnotized by Abigail and the lure of her blue-green eyes that he had not even heard the door in the parlor open or shut.

He turned at the same instant Matthew launched his body off the chair and away from the table. The boy sprinted through the doorway toward the sound of the gravelly voice. Willem stepped aside to avoid being run down by the excited boy.

Abigail stepped behind him. He smelled her, the combination of spices and cleanliness that followed her everywhere. His gut twisted. He hated the way she could tie him into knots with her nearness. Willem told himself not to look at her, not to court temptation, but he did it anyway.

She was wearing a smile the likes of which he'd not seen before. The anxiety in her expression had vanished. It had been replaced by a glow of pure shining affection. His head snapped up to find out what—who—brought that look of happiness to her face.

"When did you return?" Abigail strode forward, oblivious to Will's curiosity. He felt his interest increase a thousandfold when Abigail embraced a tall old miner. A large, lumpy gunnysack wiggled behind the man's back.

"Earlier. You were busy in the kitchen."

"That must've been the noise I heard." She straightened the frayed lapels of his old coat and patted his shoulder.

"Uncle Lars." Matthew grabbed the wiry man's leg and squeezed. Gnarled arthritic fingers stroked the wild brown curls on the boy's head.

Willem continued to watch the trio, his vexation growing each minute. The name Matthew spoke with such feeling brought something very much like envy marching into Will's chest. The old man's eyes skimmed over Willem before he looked down at the boy's happy face. Will saw true fondness sparkling in the crystal blue orbs.

"I have something for you." The man's voice was deep and tinged with an interesting combination of accents. Not true American, but a blend of German, Austrian, Irish and English, he guessed—the common dialect of Colorado mining camps from the West Coast to the Rockies.

"For me?" Matthew's voice cracked with excitement. He released the leg he'd been holding and his body stiffened in anticipation.

"Mmm. I took one look at it and knew you were the perfect person." The old man's knees sounded like seasoned oak splitting when he squatted by the lumpy bag. He began to untie a rope around the top of the gunny sack.

Matthew's bright blue eyes followed each sluggish movement of Lars's gnarled fingers. Will could see it was costing the lad dearly to keep from jumping in and untying the stubborn knot by himself. He was wondering how long Matthew's control could possibly last when the bag abruptly fell open and a tawny form tumbled out.

Then, on Thursday, July 31, at the moment the clock struck seven-thirty, all hell broke loose in Abigail Cooprel's boardinghouse.

A fawn-colored stick of dynamite exploded into the parlor. Abigail moaned, Matthew squealed in pleasure and Lars chuckled as he tottered up off the floor to keep from being mauled by Matthew and the excited animal. Will rubbed his smooth jaw and raised his brows in surprise. Whatever he'd expected, this wasn't it. It was just a whim of fate that placed the one-eared tomcat halfway down the staircase when the dog—at least Willem thought the leggy critter was supposed to be a dog—caught the tabby's scent. The startled cat bristled and bent nearly double in an effort to look big and mean. Unfortunately his narrowed eyes and fluffed-up body did little to impress the excited dog.

"Oh, no," Abigail moaned.

The dog froze for an instant. She turned her black-masked muzzle toward the stairs while she sniffed in great heaving gulps of air. For one eventful moment their eyes locked—amber coals full of indignant fury focused on liquid brown orbs of good-natured mischief. From that moment on, there was no turning back for either of them.

The dog hunkered down in front, the cat arched upward in the middle. The miners all sucked in a suspenseful breath.

Willem watched the hound gather her body into a tight knot of muscle and bone. Her long tail froze in midswing near one bent hock. Silence fell over the room while the battle lines were drawn.

"Look out," Will advised the stunned crowd.

The dog sprang forward and the ginger tom flew straight up in the air. Willem hadn't known an old cat could execute a half twist in midair, but that one did. When the furious tabby hit the floor it let out a long, low yowl that sent shivers up Willem's spine and the dog into a song of excited baying. Then the pup was galvanized into action. She was running full tilt but the patterned Chinese rug under her feet was rapidly piling up behind her like the pleats of a squeeze-box. She increased her pace with long, determined strides. Gangly legs pumped with escalating speed. She soon reached top velocity and her back legs were actually over-reaching the front. The determined pup was finally re-warded by reaching the fringed edge of the rug.

"Stand back." Willem grabbed Abigail's shoulders and pulled her against him as the dog's front paws found pur-chase on the clean wooden floor. The canine shot forward like a cannonball after a yowling streak of orange fur.

"Oh, my house!" Abigail wailed, and stuck her knuck-les in her mouth.

The first casualty of the fray was a tall oak stand with a blue pot full of columbines and wild roses. It crashed to the floor and spread out like a too-ripe melon being dropped from a produce wagon.

The ginger tom avoided the hound, which Willem de-cided was an underweight female Great Dane, by sprinting across the long counter where Abigail usually filled the lunch tins. Clangs of metal hitting the flour echoed with amazing regularity while the cat cleared the work space. His evasive maneuver was working pretty well until the dog got wise and leapt up to join the wide-eyed cat on the narrow wooden plank.

A yowl Willem was sure could be heard in Silverton woke them all from their entranced lethargy and spurred every-one to action. The cat leapt from the plank to the top of the cast-iron stove, but its stay was understandably short. The smell of singed fur filled the kitchen when its tail, blown up like a fat dry pine cone, got too near the hot stovepipe.

"I've had enough of this!" Brawley roared above the din of barking and hissing. He pushed up his sleeves to expose beefy arms covered with coarse red hair.

"I'd be careful if I were you," Willem said just before the behemoth grabbed the cat around the middle with both hands. Brawley's yelp of pain and shock blended with the sound of dog and cat. There was a blur of flesh, orange fur and red plaid shirt. For one frenzied minute man and beast blended. The Dane held back willingly, happy to share her plunder with this human who was game enough to join the contest. Satisfied amusement gleamed in her brown eyes while the man and cat sorted each other out with all the finesse of a hay mower.

When Brawley finally managed to persuade the cat to let *him* go, he was cussing a blue streak and hopping on one booted foot. Willem tried not to laugh when he saw the old mouser had shredded most of Brawley's shirt and a sizable portion of one tender, newly shaved jaw.

"I bet that hurts," Willem sympathized while Brawley made a beeline for the stairs. Will was developing an odd attachment to the one-eared tom.

In the frenzy, Abigail had moved beside him, wiggling with excitement and distress. Each movement sent his pulse pounding erratically. He grated his teeth and scooted away from her a bit, dangerously aware of her soft curves, the way she pressed against him and the earthy smell of her hair. He chewed the inside of his mouth and tried to ignore the effect she had on him. Willem tried to get his mind off Abigail by watching the boy. Matthew was doubled over giggling in the middle of the parlor and Lars was scooting discreetly out of Abigail's sight.

"Oh, do something, Willem," she wailed, and looked up at Willem with aquamarine eyes full of unshed tears. Her face was a picture he'd carry with him always. In that short, emotion-filled instant she branded her name on his heart. Her lips were parted and her eyes, which reminded him for all the world of peacock copper glistening in the mountain mist, beseeched him for help.

At that precise moment Willem wouldn't have denied her anything short of his own life. His last shred of hope for a normal life with Moira died right then. Willem mourned for the loss but knew in his heart that six years of separation had done the killing, not Abigail Cooprel or his growing interest in her.

A sudden loud thud drew his attention back to the fray. He dodged the miners, who were jumping out of the path of flailing claws and slathering jaws, to reach the hand pump.

"Tom." Willem's voice boomed above the din to get the attention of the miner. "When I yell, you open the back door."

The man nodded to show he understood while he kept a watchful eye on the cat. The sound of chairs hitting the floor tracked the cat's progress while the pup chased it under the long, food-laden dinner table.

Willem snagged an empty bucket and filled it with water. Something crashed against the back of his legs and tossed him off-balance. He looked back and saw Skipper McClain, the Dane's latest victim, in a tangle of feet on the floor. The man was cursing worse than Brawley, and Will saw Abigail staring at Tom as if he'd sprouted horns and cloven hooves. Will recovered his balance and picked up the bucket of water with both hands. He waited until the cat made one more pass in front of him, and then he let the dog have it right in the face with the bucketful of cold water. She skidded to a sliding stop, sloshing water over most of the miners in the process.

"Now!" Will yelled.

Tom opened the back door, and the orange streak of fur flew through the opening to safety.

"Close it quick!" Willem shouted, and the door slammed shut.

The stunned, dripping Dane stood spraddle-legged in the middle of Abigail's demolished kitchen. After half a minute of rest she shook vigorously. Her body shivered from nose to tail and soaked down the few humans who hadn't already been drenched or mauled by the chase. Then the dog lolled a ruby tongue out one side of her mouth and trotted over to Matthew. She sat down sedately beside him and looked up at Abigail with brown eyes full of love. One ear was folded backward. The hound was the picture of absolute contentment.

Abigail put her hands on her hips and stomped forward. "You—you—hound from hell!"

"Mama!" Matthew gasped and put his arm protectively around the brute's wet neck. The dog dragged her wide pink tongue along the side of his face in a gesture of happiness. Willem knew right then it was love at first sight between the boy and the Dane.

"You cursed, Mama." Matthew's blue eyes were round with shock and accusation.

"Oh." Abigail slapped her hand over her mouth. Her eyes were wide and luminous. A bright pink blush colored her face around her fingertips.

She darted another pleading glance at Will. She'd never looked prettier or more fragile than she did right now. A wide chasm opened up inside him. He felt something, something odd and poignant, for this woman who was strong and independent, yet looked at him with her imploring eyes like a helpless doe. He tried with all his might to conjure up Moira's image in his mind but he could not. He could not remember the shape of her face or the color of her eyes or being besotted with love for her. It made Willem mourn for things that could never be—not with Moira and not with Abigail Cooprel. He was a man caught between heaven and hell. A man without a wife but a man who was not free.

He knew with an aching sadness that when he found Moira, a part of him would always belong to Abigail.

Chapter Nine

"Lars, how could you?" Abigail wailed into her apron. Willem saw her shoulders quake before he heard a muffled sob of pure frustration. Most of the past half hour had been spent picking up the worst of the wreckage. Willem resisted the temptation to return Matthew's impish grin when the boy caught his eye behind Abigail's rigid back. Instead, he forced himself to take a serious survey of the parlor. The destruction was more comical than tragic. The wet rugs had been hung out, the glass swept up and the floor mopped dry. The clock was still ticking away the minutes with regularity. There wasn't really anything permanently damaged.

Will wanted to ease the tension in the room, wanted to erase the misery and anger from Abigail's face. He wanted to fold her into his arms and stroke her head. He wanted to reassure her and tell her nothing was all that bad. He wanted . . .

"I certainly have an appetite now—how about you, Abigail?" The hands moved on the clock face and the deep chime toned eight times while Abigail stared at Willem in disbelief. She finally regained her faculties and blinked at him.

"Eat? How can you think of food at a time like this?" She turned to glare at the dog, who was nuzzling Matthew's face. "And as for this four-legged wrecking crew...I want her out."

Willem saw the boy's head come up. Blue eyes narrowed, and for the first time he saw a streak of defiance in the child.

"I want her." There was a quiet edge of obstinacy in Matthew's childish voice that sent chills up Willem's spine. Something about this boy, this particular boy, struck a chord deep within him. He wanted to see Matthew keep the dog. It was important to him. Willem told himself it was because he prayed his own child had a pet to love somewhere in this big, cold world.

"What? You want to keep her? She's like a clumsy horse and we could never afford to feed an animal that large." Abigail's voice was tight with anger.

Willem was a little fascinated by the depth of her passion. Until now she'd kept a firm rein on herself, and even though he knew she had been flustered earlier she had never lost control of her emotions. It was a revelation to see how deep the waters ran beneath Abigail Cooprel's unflappable exterior. The smoldering embers of his desire were fanned to life—again.

"I would be happy to pay a little extra for the dog's keep." Will heard the words spill from his mouth and yet found it hard to believe.

For the past year, since he had realized he'd never find Moira without help, he had barely allowed himself the necessities of life. He had gone hungry more than once to pay Paxton's team of Pinkertons—and now he was offering to feed a dog without even considering the cost of such a declaration. And all for a freckle-faced boy who tugged on his battered heartstrings. Will had missed out on being able to provide love and tokens of affection for his own child, but he could do something for Matthew.

"I've already arranged with Hans Gustafson at the meat market for weekly deliveries of bones and scraps," Lars interjected. Willem found himself liking the grizzled old miner with the haunted blue eyes.

"She's too big." Abigail sniffed loudly. "She broke my blue vase."

"I'll buy you another," Will said. He felt something warm expand inside his chest and realized with a jolt he'd missed the pleasure of giving. He frowned and puzzled over it. Had he missed providing for Moira that much?

Yes, he had. He missed giving little fripperies to a woman and seeing the pleasure such things brought. He wanted to see that look on Abigail Cooprel's face.

She narrowed her eyes at him and he saw her struggling to erect a barrier around herself. "It was not that dear." She sniffed, and stubbornly avoided his gaze.

He felt the obstinate side of his nature wanting to breach the wall she had built around herself. One part of him wanted to coddle her and give her what she wanted, another part of him longed to dominate her in some hot, primal way he didn't want to examine too closely. He told himself he was doing this for Matthew. He watched the boy's small chin come up a hopeful notch and he knew he should walk away from this melodrama, but he stayed. And he felt another slice of his icy heart melting away.

"She has no home, Mama. She needs me, and I want to keep her." His bottom lip quivered but his voice was steady.

Willem saw Abigail struggle with that bit of information. Twice in one day the apple of her eye had defied her, and now he was doing his best to make her feel guilty about the orphan pup. Willem cocked a brow and watched her face while she thought about it. He made a mental wager with himself that she could not turn the animal away. She was too good and kind.

"Abigail."

She turned to stare at him. He could see she was digging in stubbornly on the subject of the Dane and would not appreciate his interference. He almost changed his mind. It was none of his business, he had other priorities and this should mean nothing to him. Then he looked at Matthew and the thin dog lavishing drool-laden licks on the child's face, and knew he could not abandon their cause, no matter how volatile the situation.

"A boy should have a dog," Willem said quietly.

"Thank you for your opinion, Mr. Tremain," she said. He lifted a brow at her pointed formality.

"Oh, all right, Willem. But I am Matthew's mother—" her hands were on her hips and she was glaring up at him with a determined tilt to her chin "—and I do not appreciate your interference."

Her words stung. He clenched his jaw. Willem saw tiny gold flecks around her irises. She had lovely eyes, which sparkled with strength and intelligence, and a stubbornness he found surprising in a female. This woman would be a handful to any man. He sighed at the bittersweet thought.

Willem nodded at Matthew and the hound. "Look at him, Abigail, and tell me you'd take that dog away from him."

She turned and stared at the skinny Dane and the boy's death grip around its lanky neck.

"He loves her, Abigail. If I agree to help him train her, will you let him keep the dog?" Willem threw caution to the wind.

She frowned and glanced at him before looking back at the animal, who had stretched out across Matthew's lap. The boy rested a protective hand on her neck, and Will knew he would do battle for her if need be.

"I never thought I'd see you turn away a homeless critter," Lars muttered behind her back. Abigail turned and narrowed her eyes at him. Willem sensed there was a deeper meaning to the man's words, because Abigail paled and her lips began to quiver.

"All right. If you will help him house-gentle the animal, I'll do it, but I may as well tell you and Lars right now, I think this is blackmail."

"It'll work out fine, Abigail." Willem fought the overwhelming urge to crush her against him while she tried valiantly to maintain her dignity. He felt his control slip a tiny fraction. "Now can we eat?" he muttered, hoping the normalcy of dinner might quell his odd desire to wipe away the gut-wrenching look in her eyes.

Abigail sniffed. "I doubt there is anything left to eat." The color began to return to her cheeks and her eyes were aglow with banked fire. Willem told himself to stop noticing how her bosom strained against the seams of her plain work dress with each jerky breath she took.

With the exception of Brawley, the newly shaved miners had been watching the latest melodrama from the safe distance of the kitchen, but with the mention of food they sprinted into action. They scurried around mopping up water and righting dishes and chairs.

"I think if you look you'll find that wonderful-smelling meal intact." Willem tried to grin but there was a tightness in his jaw and his chest. The fist-sized knot had grown in size while he bartered with the widow for Matthew's dog. He found her stimulating—both for his mind and his body. It amazed him that he could be feeling so paternal toward Matthew and lustful toward the widow at the same time. He wondered if he was losing all control of his feelings. It seemed as if he was on some sort of skid line, plummeting out of control toward certain destruction since he'd arrived in this town.

"He's right, Missus." Snap's voice wrenched Willem from his meditation. "The chairs were willy-nilly but the table is right as rain."

Abigail sniffed again and wiped her face with the hem of her apron.

Willem looked at Matthew and felt his lips curl into a grin. "Let's get your dog fed."

Lars watched the man with growing curiosity. He sighed and decided he liked Willem Tremain. The man certainly appeared to put the lie to all the stories about him. In fact, compared to the way Abigail was acting, Willem Tremain was docile as a lamb. Lars knew what was ailing Abigail. She was tighter than a clock spring with worry and fear. Her face was pinched into taut lines, and he had never seen her so fidgety. She acted like a cat with its tail caught in a wringer. He knew she had a hundred questions about her baby—and Matthew's mother. He had stayed away so long hoping to avoid those questions. Now he knew he'd have to face her.

"Come on, lad," Willem said. "Let's see if your mama has some extra bread and gravy for your dog. What are you going to name her?" Will's deep voice rippled across the room, and Lars stopped to stare at Will and the boy.

Matthew smiled and rose from the floor. "I don't know. It'll have to be something special 'cause she's a real special dog." Matthew kept one arm around the pup's scrawny neck and urged her along beside him. When he was close enough to Willem he slipped his fingers inside Will's fist.

Lars saw the man freeze into a block of stone. He wondered what the Black Irish was feeling, but the man's face was unreadable.

Will felt his belly drop like a stone. He stared at his hand in mute wonder. When Matthew touched him it felt like four sticks of dynamite exploding inside his chest. He looked down at the boy, smiling up at him as if he were something special, and he knew he'd fallen head over heels in love with the blue-eyed imp. Matthew's small hand inside his own big rough one felt soft and vulnerable. Willem allowed the child to stake a claim to a large, desolate chunk of his soul. The warm, cozy feeling inside him had begun when he saved a lop-eared hound from being tossed into the street. But this feeling was so much more satisfying. He couldn't remember a single impulsive act ever bringing him so much joy.

"Would you sit by me at dinner, Mr. Tremain?" Matthew asked softly.

Willem stared into clear blue eyes that openly adored him. The realization jarred him. He'd never been anybody's hero before, and it was a mighty scary responsibility. It took half a heartbeat for Willem to make a silent vow. He swore to see this child safe and happy. Some inner part of him believed if he nurtured Matthew, then someone, somewhere, would nurture and protect his own child—sort of love by proxy.

An odd thing happened then. The faceless child Will had spent years searching for now had an image—freckle faced and blue eyed. He silently prayed his child was a boy, a son like Matthew Cooprel. A tiny frayed thread from the fabric of his past mended itself in that moment with a small boy's hand inside his. Will took a step toward light at the end of a long, cold tunnel.

"If your mama has no objection, I'd be pleased to sit by you, Matthew." Willem glanced at Abigail. She flicked her eyes from him to Matthew. For just an instant he could've sworn something like hostility burned in them, but she smiled stiffly.

"Sure, honey. Mr. Tremain is welcome to sit on this end of the table if you want him to." She scooted a plate around and nodded her head.

Abigail staggered under the assault of fear. She had told herself it was only her imagination, but now she wasn't so sure. Willem Tremain had wormed his way into Matthew's affections in short order. She told herself it wasn't possible, but she feared Will even more now. Willem Tremain did want something—something from Matthew. The fear she had tried so hard to ignore came into sharp focus. Since Lars had told her the truth she had been waiting for some lost relative to show up.... Could it be that he already had?

Willem managed to smile, but inside he was quaking. The little boy who looked up at him had managed to revive another section of his dead heart. Willem hadn't allowed himself to care for anybody but his faceless child and a missing wife for years. Now he was giving chunks of himself away to a curly-headed boy and a skinny hound. He sat down at the table, numb from the new sensations ripping through him.

Matthew ate with zest while he kept a weather eye on the dog. She polished off two plates of biscuits and gravy, yet her sides were still gaunt.

"Gustafson's daughter will bring some meat and bones tomorrow," Lars promised when Abigail looked at the voracious dog in tight-lipped alarm.

"Shall we start her training tomorrow?" Will asked Matthew.

"I'm ready tonight," Matthew chirped.

Willem chuckled and roughed up the boy's curls. His hair was thick as thatch yet soft as kitten fur. Willem allowed his hand to linger a moment longer than necessary on the boy's head just because it felt so right.

"I'm sure you are, Matthew, but that's probably the first good meal she's had in a while. I think your dog is going to want to sleep." Willem took his hand away and stared at it in awe. A satisfying warmth had snaked up his fingers toward his heart.

"You mean that thing is staying?" Brawley gasped from the doorway. Three livid claw marks blazed a trail down his cheek and one hand was wrapped in a bulky bandage.

"Yes, Brawley, the dog is staying," Lars said, and chuckled.

Willem watched Brawley's gaze sweep over Matthew with a menacing gleam. He felt a wall of protectiveness building inside him. Brawley then looked at the table, his gaze lingering on the only empty chair, the one Willem had previously occupied at the far end of the table. He glared for a moment at Willem, now sitting beside the boy, near the widow, before he lurched toward the chair with a dark scowl.

It was obvious there had never been any affection toward Matthew on Brawley's part. He had been trying to impress Abigail Cooprel with all his talk of discipline and companionship.

"Brawley, I can't imagine what kind of fool notion made you and the other boys go and get your faces shaved naked, but I bet you'll let that beard grow back now that the cat's left his mark on you," Lars quipped with a gleam in his eyes.

Brawley's face turned redder than his hair. He glared at Willem. Will was sure he hadn't heard the last from Brawley Cummins.

Chapter Ten

Willem woke in a cold sweat. Gray and pink fingers of dawn were creeping over the craggy summit of the mountain. He had slept badly. Moira's voice had called to him from a heavy fog but the more he had searched, the more certain he'd been that he would never find her. As if that hadn't been enough, he had dreamed of Abigail and Matthew watching him from a beam of warm sunshine. He wanted to stay where there was laughter and warmth, where he could see the future. He was tired of fog, pain and the hurt of old regrets and mistakes. He wanted to free himself from the past and reach out to life. But the more he wanted a life, the more guilt he found accompanying him. He could never hope to have a normal life, for even if he found Moira and his child, he knew deep in his heart things could never be right. He could and would make any sacrifice for his child but Willem was beginning to face the fact that Abigail Cooprel meant something to him—something precious and unique—and it made a cold knot of fear in his belly.

He threw his legs over the edge of the bed and rose. Willem splashed water into the basin and shaved by the dim light coming through his window. He dressed and poked his head out of his door.

The smell of breakfast wafted up the stairs, and he heard Abigail humming a tune while she cooked. He stopped halfway down and listened. It was a pleasant, simple thing, to stand on the stairs with his back against the wall and listen to the sounds of a woman in her kitchen. Willem smiled a cockeyed grin and thought about how she must look.

Her hair would be pinned up haphazardly, with soft tendrils creeping around the curve of her jawline. She would have flour smudged on her face, the way she had the first time he saw her, and those eyes of hers would be sparkling with life.

Willem opened his eyes and sucked in the smell of corn bread muffins. He sighed and told himself he was headed for heartbreak if he kept weaving fantasies about her in his head. He was married. That made Abigail Cooprel as unattainable as a woman could be for Willem. No, his body would burn to a cinder with hot lust before he made a move toward Abigail.

"Good morning." Will walked into the kitchen. Abigail whirled around and made a small squeak of surprise. She did indeed have a smudge of flour across the bridge of her nose. Willem grinned at himself for knowing she would.

"Willem." She flicked a gaze from the top of his head to his toes and back to his eyes. Willem saw suspicion cloud her face. He turned his back and heard her deep release of breath. It hurt him, the way she pulled herself inside the armor of cool reserve each time he spoke to her. He wondered what he had done to make her so suspicious of him.

"It seems you and I are the only early birds this morning." He took a cup from a peg on the wall and tried to keep the conversation light.

"I always get up early. I have some extra cooking to do for the celebration tomorrow," she explained tightly behind him.

He didn't turn around, but instead poured himself a cup of coffee and moved toward the kitchen window. He wanted to pretend she liked him for just this morning while they were alone in the warm, cozy kitchen. He wanted to make believe that she was not afraid of him. Will wondered what it would feel like to be married—really married—with a wife and a child. Would it be like this? Would he rise and find Abigail, *his wife,* he corrected, in the kitchen?

Willem watched the first brilliant streamers of dawn gild the treetops behind Abigail's boardinghouse and allowed himself to spin yet another fantasy about her. He let his mind construct a story, one where he was husband and father, and Matthew was his child, and Abigail was his wife.

"Ah—yes, the celebration," he mused. He could learn to like that sort of gathering again, if he could see it with Abigail and Matthew.

"I'll have to make half a dozen trips to get everything down to the picnic grounds so I decided to get ahead this morning," Abigail explained.

Willem smiled and let her voice ripple over him. It was nice listening to her plan her days. He could almost believe that he might eventually have this kind of normal life—almost, but not quite.

Abigail watched his broad back, the way it nipped into impossibly lean hips, while she spoke. He made her nervous in some odd, wild way. He was forever sneaking in and surprising her. How could he be so stealthy when every nerve in her body was tuned to him? If he so much as took a deep breath she was aware of it. Abigail frowned and wished she could simply ignore him, but Willem Tremain *affected* her. She could no more pretend he wasn't around than she could sprout wings and fly.

She wished the other men would come down, but it was a good half hour before they would troop in for breakfast.

She grimaced and tried not to notice the way the sun breaking through the window sent a river of blue racing over Will's clean, slick hair, or the way his shoulders bunched with restrained power when he lifted the cup to his lips. Why did he make her feel as if the floor was opening up beneath her feet? Why didn't she trust him? She had spent the better part of the night arguing with herself. It was ridiculous to think Will Tremain had any interest in or claim to Matthew. Years had gone by with her blissfully ignorant of Matthew's true parentage...why should someone show up simply because Lars had finally told her the truth? She had managed to convince herself of the unlikelihood of such a circumstance, yet when she looked at Will Tremain every nerve in her body shrieked in alarm.

"Would you like breakfast?" she croaked out. She had to find some way in which to deal with her feelings.

"No, not yet." He didn't turn around. Instead he closed his eyes and let the aroma of Abigail and her kitchen sluice over him. It was nice, yet it was torture. This simple little pleasure was one he had forgotten. It was such an intimate thing—a man and a woman drinking their first cup of coffee in the early-morning silence.

Guilt and longing warred within his chest. He found himself wishing this moment could go on forever and not be interrupted by the other men who called this place home, but he knew he could not have his wish and he hated himself because he did not deserve it.

"Willem?" Her voice broke through the mist of regret around him. He turned and found her peering into his face as if it was a clear mountain stream. It sent a shiver of heat working its way downward.

"Yes, Abigail?"

She flinched when he spoke her name. It cut him to the quick, the way she shrank from him like a frightened doe.

He watched her bottom lip tremble, then her eyes locked onto his own. Something flashed across the room and drew them inexorably toward each other. Willem had the strangest notion he was being pulled into a bottomless crevasse and once he fell into it there would be no rescue, no reprieve, no salvation.

When sanity returned, he found himself standing two inches away from her. The pulse in her neck fluttered rapidly. She gasped, and fear skittered across her face. He reached up and wiped the flour from her nose, and she lowered her lashes across her luminous eyes. The smell of her—all clean female and spice—drifted to his nostrils.

"Abigail... I..." Willem cupped her chin and tilted her face toward him. She looked at him, and something much like summer lightning seared a path from his hand to his heart.

"Willem... don't..."

He stared at her lips when they parted. He wanted to taste her. Would she taste like cinnamon and tart apples? Or would she be sweeter than summer honey? Or would she be like dark, forbidden wine—intoxicating and addictive?

"I hope those are flapjacks I smell." Snap's rough voice sent her scooting to the opposite side of the kitchen faster than a startled rabbit.

Willem watched while first she went pale and then a bright, hot flush covered her cheeks. She clutched her apron to her chin and blinked. When she focused on his face, accusation and reproach gleamed in her eyes. Then she turned away and avoided his glance while the miners trooped one by one into the room.

Will went to his chair and nursed his cup of coffee between furtive glances. He had no appetite for food, not with the comely widow playing jack-hob with his reeling emotions. Willem would not allow himself to touch Abigail, but that didn't stop him from wanting her with a white hot intensity that burned his soul.

Abigail climbed the stairs and opened the door to number 12. The smell of Willem Tremain hit her like a fist and, combined with the lingering sadness she felt, nearly brought tears to her eyes.

This morning she had finally found her courage and made Lars tell her everything. She would never again be able to admire the blooms on the wild rose behind the church—not when it was the only marker for her daughter's grave. That was where Lars had buried them, the tiny baby and Matthew's nameless mother. Abigail wondered if she should have something more permanent put there to mark their resting place. Then she realized neither one of them had a name. Perhaps the fragrant thorny rose was the most fitting monument to them both.

Abigail crossed the room and flung open the sash. She leaned out and inhaled deeply, trying to fight the heart-pounding response and sense of doom she felt. The past was over and no amount of wishing could change it. Besides, God had seen fit to give her a child. A child for a child. Matthew was her baby in every way that mattered. She had worked hard to give them security. Still, being in Willem Tremain's room reminded her of the dread she felt in his presence.

While she swept under the bed and tidied the room she chided herself for acting like a green girl. Tomorrow was her usual clean linen day but with the celebration in town, she had moved her schedule up by one day. The thought of changing the other eleven rooms made her sigh heavily. After she had left clean towels on the washstand, she stopped and looked at the room.

Only the battered valise proved anyone was staying in the room, yet Willem Tremain could have been standing beside Abigail, she was so aware of him. A dark cloud of approaching disaster seemed to envelop her. She shook her head and told herself it was only the effects of her conversation with Lars.

"Stop acting like a moonstruck calf," she ordered herself aloud. She had never—not in six years of seeing men come and men go—ever reacted like this to a man. She had tonicked herself and even considered going to Sporkin's Pharmacy for a purge. Abigail had no idea what made her react to Willem Tremain the way she did, but he was scaring her to death with his dark power over her. One moment she wanted to fall into the blue depths of his eyes and drown. The next moment she was sure he had some sinister reason for interfering with her son. She had skirted all around her feelings about Matthew and Will, but now she sighed and forced herself to examine them closely.

"Jealous," she accused her own reflection in the mirror over Will's washstand. As much as it galled her to admit it, she was jealous of the newfound worship in Matthew's eyes. He followed Willem Tremain around the way the gangly pup followed Matthew. It hurt her deeply to think her son needed more than she had provided. But that was the way she felt. Matthew was hungry for a man's friendship—for Willem's friendship. At breakfast this morning she had watched her son mimic Willem's gestures while he ate. She was sure the man had no idea of the impact he had on the boy, and that made her even more uneasy.

When winter came, as it surely would in a matter of months, Will Tremain would move on like all the rest of them. Then what would happen to her child's tender heart? She had tried so hard to shield Matthew from the pain of loss. It was far better not to give away your heart at all than to give it away and see it shattered. Abigail was sure that Matthew was a passing fancy to Will Tremain, and when winter came her son would be hurt.

Abigail sighed and moved back to the window to close it. She leaned out and saw Matthew and the spindly dog cavorting on the back lawn. She rested her chin on her crossed forearms and smiled at his happiness.

"Pay something for the dog's keep, indeed." She snorted and repeated Willem's words. He'd told her she had a banker's heart and then implied that he would make a sacrifice so her son could have a pet. She actually liked the dog, but the more Will Tremain pushed, the more he made her want to oppose him. And this was a man she found attractive? She slammed the window shut and resolved to ask the pharmacist to give her something—she must surely be ailing.

Willem stopped by the livery on his way home. He'd spent the better part of the day trying to figure out some way of showing Abigail Cooprel she didn't have to fear him. He told himself he was a fool for worrying about it. He knew he was only adding salt to the raw wound in his heart, but he was going to prove himself to her one way or another.

He stepped into the dimly lit livery. The smell of clean straw, hay dust and leather mixed with the down-to-earth odors of horse sweat and manure. "Hello," he called. Willem leaned against the door to wait for a response. A young man in overalls came from the back of the barn with a bulky gunnysack of feed hefted up on one broad shoulder.

"Can I help you?" The man sloughed the bag at his feet and pulled the white cord, pinching the corners into little cloth ears. The bag opened and sent the scent of robust cracked corn swirling into the air.

"How much do you charge for a day's rental on a buggy?" A voice in Will's head told him to leave before he made a fool of himself.

"Three dollars." The man didn't look up as he scooped up corn with his cupped hands and dumped it into several leather feed bags.

"How much for a wagon and team?"

The man looked up and frowned at Willem. "Dray or light?"

"Light," Willem said with a smile.

"Two-fifty, but I need it back by sundown."

Willem dug into his pocket and pulled out a handful of coins. "How early can I pick one up?"

Willem excused himself from dinner early and went straight to his room. He lay with one arm thrown up over his eyes listening to the sound of voices below. Occasionally he heard the soft soprano of Abigail's voice and felt the zing that accompanied his every conscious thought of her. Matthew's throaty laughter drifted up the stairs, and Willem smiled.

The boy was like a healing balm to him. Each smile or quiet word they exchanged sent a curative shaft sinking deeper into Willem's dark pit of despair. He flopped over on his side and willed himself to sleep. He intended to beat the widow out of bed—a feat he knew would not easily be accomplished—but he would have to be back from the livery before she left the house.

Willem tossed and turned and listened to the bedsprings groan in protest. Finally he resigned himself to the fact he would get no sleep this night. He pulled on his clean clothes, the ones he'd had washed for the occasion, and crept downstairs.

A soft glow from the kitchen caught his eye. He wondered who else was having trouble sleeping. Willem entered the kitchen and found Lars, decked out in overlarge red woolen long johns, sitting at the table alone.

"Up early or out late?" Lars asked while he scanned Willem with cloudy blue eyes.

"Up early, I guess." Willem grinned and helped himself to the coffee on the stove. "How about you?" He pulled out a chair and sat opposite the old man. He saw the gnarled fingers gripping the cup and wondered how the old man survived the cold winters up in the high country.

"The older I get the less I sleep." Lars sighed and rubbed the heels of his hands over his eyes. "Tell me something, young fella. Did you ever do something you knew was not right but you went ahead and did it anyway?"

Willem snorted at the bitter memory of how many impulsive things he'd done. "So many I've lost count."

Lars looked up and smiled. "Well, let me give you a piece of advice—fix what you can and forget the others. As you get older the things you might've or should've done different get mighty heavy on an old man's shoulders."

Willem puzzled over the man's words. Lars continued to rub his palms over his eyes. It almost seemed to Willem the old prospector was trying to erase the picture of some long-ago transgression.

"Surely it can't be that bad." Willem sipped his own coffee and wondered if he was looking at an image of himself in a few years to come—alone and full of regret.

Lars looked up. His milky blue eyes were troubled. "I wish you were right. Lord knows I'd like to end my days believing it will all come to rights, hoping I haven't broken a fine woman's heart."

Willem stared across the table at the old miner in silence. They sipped their coffee and followed separate paths of memory and recollection. Finally the soft padding of dog paws and nails clicking against the wood floor interrupted their mute reflections.

"That was a nice thing you did for Matthew," Lars said when the Dane walked in and looked up at Willem with limpid brown eycs. He reached out and scratched behind one floppy ear.

"Not much. He's a fine lad." Willem smiled when the dog laid her head in his lap and closed her eyes.

"You're good with him. Got any of your own?" Lars asked.

Willem looked up and sighed. "One . . . I think."

"Sowed a few wild oats, did you?" Lars's bushy silver brows rose.

"Yes and no. I had a wife and we were expecting a child...but...things went wrong." Willem slid his palm over the velvet softness of the animal's wide head. She regarded him with solemn dignity and grateful affection. "I've never seen my child."

Lars frowned and looked at Willem a long moment. "How old would your young'un be?"

"Close to Matthew's age," Willem said wistfully. Then he smiled and shook his head for all the lost years. "I don't even know if I have a son or a daughter."

Lars squinted his eyes and watched Willem with a new intensity.

Chapter Eleven

Willem sat in the wagon outside Abigail's boardinghouse feeling anticipation running in his veins. He had walked to the livery and found the young man as good as his word. The wagon was hitched and the horse gleamed with good grooming. Willem couldn't wait to see the look on Abigail's and Matthew's faces.

He jumped down from the wagon seat and strode up to the door. After a quick scuff of his shoes to clean his feet on the rug, he ambled inside. The sound of Abigail moving around in her room drifted downstairs and sent his heart thrumming in his chest. He tiptoed into the kitchen and gathered up two large baskets and the stack of folded linen she'd left on the plank last night. He hurried out to the wagon and loaded them into the back.

He felt the hair on his arms prickle, and when he turned around Abigail was standing there staring at him with wide-eyed surprise.

"What are you doing?" She flicked a glance at him and the wagon. She held a blueberry pie in front of her like a barrier against him while she scanned Will's face.

Willem grimaced. Now that she was standing here with dread and suspicion hanging between them he had serious doubts about what he had done—about what he was going to do. She looked all freshly scrubbed and perky. The bonnet on her head subdued the fine wayward hair, but the robin's egg blue brought out tones of azure in her eyes, which were rapidly filling with angry sparks. The gray dawn made her look dewy and untouched. Willem shuffled his feet at the thought and swallowed a fist-sized lump.

"I rented a wagon so you wouldn't have to walk to the picnic grounds."

She gasped. It was a tiny little sound but it sent a shiver of pure desire surging through him. He wondered if that would be the sound she made before she drifted off to sleep each night.

"You can't," she challenged.

"I already did," he countered.

"Really, Mr. Tremain, you presume too much." She still held the huge blueberry pie in her hands. Willem moved forward to pluck it from her grasp. "What would people say if I rode with you?"

"They will say the widow Cooprel has besotted another wayward miner with her cooking and her charms," he said softly, then turned to deposit the pie in the wagon bed beside the other food.

"Have I?" Her voice was tight and whispery. It froze him like the wind through a snow-covered canyon.

"Have you what, Mrs. Cooprel?" He dared not turn around and look at her for fear of betraying his runaway feelings.

"Have I besotted you, Mr. Tremain?"

He took in a breath and turned. She regarded him with serious eyes, this strange strong woman with a heart soft as eiderdown. He wanted for all the world to scoop her into his arms and taste her lips—just once, only once.

"If I say yes, what will you do?" he asked warily.

"Then I would ask you to find other lodging, Mr. Tremain, and request you never come to my house again."

He laid a hand on the wagon side board for support. Willem narrowed his eyes and watched her. She meant it, meant every word. She would see him gone before she found herself undone by a moment of unguarded passion or loose-tongued gossip. In this tense beat of time he felt his respect for her multiply a hundred times. She had no way of knowing her words would make him want her more. This was a woman of substance, a woman of honor, a woman he could admire from afar, but no more. It would have to be enough, he told himself.

"Then, *Abigail—*" he emphasized her name "—I will say you have captured my admiration and respect and I will endeavor to remember my place from this point on."

Matthew skipped out the front door. "Look, Mama, Willem rented a wagon so you wouldn't have to walk."

"So I see," she said stiffly. The fact that her son was now addressing him as Willem and not Mr. Tremain did not escape her notice.

Willem saw her flick a glance at Matthew's smiling face. If not for the boy he was sure she would turn around and go inside and refuse his offer entirely. A morning breeze swept over them and he smelled her usual scent of spices and soap mingled with a faint trace of rosewater. Passion slammed through his body. He gripped his hand more tightly on the side board and reined in the feeling. She had made herself clear a moment ago, so no matter what Will felt, or fancied he felt, nothing was ever going to come of it. Besides, he had only to look at Abigail to see the anger and distrust in every stiff move she made. He had not succeeded in making her less apprehensive of his motives; in fact, quite the opposite, for now she was on guard and suspicious of his every thought and deed.

Abigail allowed Willem to help her into the wagon bed. She tried to ignore the fluttering in her belly and the way her heart missed a beat when he touched her. How could she have such feelings when she didn't even like him? She had to admit this gesture of renting a wagon seemed kind on the surface, but she was sure there was some other reason, a hidden motive behind it. She had let him know that she would not encourage his flirtation. If he persisted beyond common civility she had every intention of asking him to find lodging elsewhere. So why did her mouth go dry and her legs wobble whenever he came near her? Why did she detest him with every breath, yet feel his masculine heat like sunshine on her face?

Why?

She settled herself on the soft pallet of blankets he had arranged and watched him swing Matthew up beyond the barrier of the side boards. The barking dog nipped playfully at Matthew's feet and Willem gave a deep, throaty laugh. The mingled sounds sent chill bumps along her arms. Abigail felt the nagging resentment creep into her heart when she saw Matthew's face, alight with joy and good-natured roughhousing. Why did Willem Tremain bring out the worst in her? When the man wasn't trying to insinuate himself into her son's affections he was undoing her morality with those haunting blue eyes and seducer's body. What did he really want? She sighed and snapped her eyes shut, away from man and boy and the pain seeing them together brought.

"Mama?" Matthew's voice called.

"Yes, darling?" She looked up to see him standing in the wagon with his palm resting on Willem's shoulder. It sent a ripple of bitter envy rolling through her. For one fleeting moment she wished she could be as carefree and reckless as her innocent young son, for a dark part of her longed to know what Will's body would feel like beneath her own touch. But such thoughts weren't proper—and they certainly weren't ladylike. Abigail felt heat rising to her cheeks at her wicked thoughts.

She saw Will's eyes drift over her neck and face and feared he could see the guilt written there. Instead of seeing smug satisfaction in his eyes because of her weakness, however, she saw a tender longing and sorrow flicker there for a brief instant. Abigail was not prepared for that. She was certain that at best he was a ne'er-do-well, interested in a fine summer of romping with Matthew, and then he'd be gone. But the look in his eyes spoke of a deep loneliness. Abigail shuddered and focused on Matthew while she tried to block Willem Tremain from her notice.

"What is it, darling?"

"Willem is going to be my partner at the games today... if you don't mind."

Abigail's stomach dropped to her feet. When Lars had refused the boy, saying he was too old and slow, she had thought he would ask her to be his partner. This latest development wounded her deeply. She warred with her own desire to see him happy and the hurt she felt at being passed over for another—*for Willem Tremain.* Abigail bit her lip and watched her son. His face shone with hope. She couldn't disappoint him, but she vowed not to feel charitable toward Willem Tremain again—no matter how lonely he seemed.

"Of course, Matthew. I'm sure Mr. Tremain will be a much more suitable partner for the three-legged race." She saw the relief in her child's eyes. It wiped away a tiny portion of the pain.

Matthew settled himself and turned to Willem. "What about my dog?"

"She's going to have the best seat of all." Willem winked before he gathered the gangly animal in his arms. "Have you thought of a name yet?" he asked while he planted the Dane in the wagon seat and climbed in beside her.

"Well, she's real smart. Bright, Lars says. I think I'll call her Brighty. What do you think?" Matthew asked Willem, not Abigail. Again the sting of competing with this relative stranger for her child's attention smarted through her.

"That's a good name." Willem kicked the brake loose and popped the reins. "It suits her real well." The horse cantered off toward town before the other men were even out of bed. Will took a measure of satisfaction, having Abigail and Matthew all to himself.

Abigail sat stiffly, waiting for Matthew to ask her opinion about the dog's name, but he never did. A deep ache settled in her breast. Abigail stared at Will's wide back while he deftly handled the reins. Muscles bunched in his shoulders when he turned the wagon and headed it down the hill. She was stunned to brooding silence by what was happening. The man had upset every aspect of her life since he'd walked into her boardinghouse less than a week ago. What was she going to do about him?

The Dane's head flicked back and forth and her ears perked up at every sound and movement along the pink-shadowed roadside. When the trees thinned out and Guston proper began to engulf them, Abigail tried to push her concerns to the back of her mind. This was a celebration—a day of fun and frolic. She vowed to enjoy herself and not allow Willem Tremain's disturbing presence to cast a pall over her fun.

Matthew grinned and reached up to scratch the dog behind the ear. The hound turned to him and swiped her wide pink tongue up the side of his head. It left a wet cowlick in his curls, and Abigail cringed inwardly. She sighed and told herself it was all part of being a boy—part of growing up—but it took every ounce of control to keep from pulling her hankie from her reticule to clean up his face.

The ache in her heart doubled in size when she realized Matthew *was* growing up. He was reaching an age where he was asserting his independence and letting go of his mama. The days when she would need to fuss and fret over him were flashing by too quickly.

Willem heard Abigail's deep sigh. He could almost feel her conflict, as if she were fighting some kind of battle within herself. He wondered how she would take the rest of the surprise he and Matthew had arranged—and if he would be looking for a place to sleep by nightfall.

Chapter Twelve

A large striped awning flapped in the breeze above fragrant homemade pies lined up on two planks stretched between wooden sawhorses. Willem helped Matthew tie a rope around Brighty's neck in case she decided to enter the pie-eating contest without an invitation.

"How many do you think I'll have to eat to win, Willem?" Matthew looked up, and Will couldn't help but grin at the serious expression on his young face. It brought a measure of poignancy to his naive question. Things like this were so momentous to a boy, and knowing that made it important to Will.

"At least three, I'd guess—maybe more," Willem answered. The boy nodded and frowned. He swept the rows of golden-crusted pastry with wide eyes. Willem laughed aloud at the determination he saw on Matthew's face.

"What's so amusing?" Abigail's voice skimmed over his hide. He felt a shiver start at his toes and slither a warm trail up toward his scalp. The air seemed to heat and crackle around them. Will fancied he could almost touch her anger and his smoldering passion.

"Matthew. He's worried about the contest." Willem nodded toward the pies. He was becoming resolved to his willful body's reaction to Abigail. A gusting breeze brought her scent to his nostrils and he nearly rocked back on his heels with physical awareness of her.

"Oh." Abigail rested her hand on Matthew's cheek and tipped his face up. "Don't eat so many that you get sick, because we still have our own lunch to eat later, by ourselves."

Willem heard the chill in her last words and knew she meant them for him.

"I won't, Mama." Willem saw Matthew cast a sidelong glance at him. The boy shuffled his feet and scratched the Dane's ears. Willem winked conspiratorially at him over the top of Abigail's head. He only wished he was as confident as he pretended to be. His little deception could blow up in his face like a stick of old dynamite. If Abigail didn't like his interference this time, he could be out on the street in short order. Truth to tell, Willem was as nervous about Abigail's reaction as Matthew was about the pie eating contest. He took a deep breath and tried to relax.

A paunchy man with muttonchop whiskers announced the contest was about to begin.

"Wish me luck," Matthew said, then turned and headed for the table. Willem tightened his hold on Brighty's rope and nodded. He heard Abigail's soft sigh and tried to quell the warmth that burst inside his chest. *Damnation,* it was like being chained up inside a brothel surrounded by naked women—one particular woman. His body reacted to her in the most astonishing way with the least amount of provocation. She took a step away from Willem and he felt the air bristling with her suspicion and uneasiness. He hoped he had not made a drastic mistake with his little *surprise.*

Matthew sat down and gripped the edges of a pie plate as if his young life depended upon it. When the starting gun was fired, he plunged his face, nose first, into the crust. He came up for air and Willem saw a bright purple stain of blueberry on his chin and cheeks. The boy concentrated on the task at hand and finished eating his first pie quickly. He grabbed another and attacked it with all the enthusiasm of a six-year-old competing for the first time in his life.

"He'll be sick," Abigail groaned.

"Naw. He's having the time of his life," Willem whispered near her ear. "Let him be a boy."

She stiffened and drew her mouth into a tight line. He saw her turn to look at him with a mixture of doubt and fear in her face. The vulnerability in that look jolted him.

"Abigail?" He stepped closer. Her body went rigid as stone.

"Yes?" She licked her lips and wiped her palm over her throat. Willem saw a drop of sweat on her palm when she lifted her hand from her neck.

"Are you afraid of me?" he asked.

Her eyes widened and she drew in a breath. "Why on earth would I fear you?"

"That's what I've been asking myself."

"Of course I'm not afraid of you, that would be silly. It's just that Matthew has never taken to anyone like he has you."

Willem frowned and studied her face. "He's a fine boy, and spending time with him has meant a lot to me," Willem said honestly.

Abigail snapped her head around and stared at him. "Why?"

Willem shrugged. He wanted to explain to her about Moira, but that thought brought a shroud of guilt drifting over him. "Matthew's friendship means a lot to me, that's all."

She studied him with narrowed eyes. Distrust hung between them. Willem leaned closer and inhaled her wholesome, spicy odor. He had to find some way of bridging the chasm between them.

Willem wanted to tell Abigail what he had done, wanted to tell her now and prepare her for it. "Abigail, there is something I want to—"

"The winner!" A loud cheer went up and pulled Will back from the precipice he'd been standing on. He looked up to find Matthew grinning from one strawberry-covered ear to the other, which sported one fat blueberry. The boy was holding a scrap of bright blue ribbon in his hand.

"Oh, I missed it!" Abigail lamented.

Will grimaced. Because of him she had not witnessed Matthew's triumph. He took a step away from her and tried to harness the jumble of emotions he was experiencing.

"Now we're going to have a little surprise," the man shouted from the upturned wooden keg that served as his podium.

Willem and Matthew exchanged nervous glances behind Abigail's back. Will regretted what he'd done. He wished he had been able to warn her. If he backed out now he would leave Abigail to be humiliated publicly. He could not sacrifice her feelings for his own lack of courage. He squared his shoulders and prepared to face the consequences of his poorly thought out enthusiasm.

"We have managed to persuade all the eligible women in Guston to participate in a little auction," the Mayor announced, his muttonchops puffing up when he grinned. It gave him the appearance of a marmot with his cheeks full of spring clover.

A loud murmur rippled over the group made up mostly of solitary miners and businessmen. Willem glanced around and saw no more than a dozen females among the stags. Abigail was one of a handful of unmarried women and by far the prettiest. He wished he hadn't been so aware of that fact.

"We have some fine box lunches up here," the plump-faced speaker said, and gestured to a row of baskets decorated with ribbons, lace and fresh wildflowers. "These baskets were all donated by the lovely single ladies of Guston. They have very kindly agreed to share their box lunches with the man who bids the highest for theirs. All proceeds will be going to the miners' pension fund—a worthy cause and a needy one."

"Are any of them wimmin under eighty?" a gruff voice yelled from the back of the crowd.

"Shut up, Horace," came a throaty rejoinder from the opposite side of the throng. Loud guffaws erupted at the candid exchange. Abigail giggled behind her hand and Willem found it hard not to smile at the look on her face.

She was a beauty, with the bright sunlight gilding her upturned nose and moist mouth. Funny how she seemed less plain than he had originally thought she was. Perhaps it was the light on her face.

"Let's get to it, then." Willem was jarred from his reverie by a loud voice. The jowly mayor held up a basket with delicate white ribbons tied symmetrically around the handle.

"Seventy-five cents," a baritone voice bellowed.

"I hear seventy-five cents," the mayor repeated.

Soon the bidding was in full swing, with raises of two bits sounding from every corner of the crowd. The final price for the pretty basket was two dollars. Matthew shifted his weight from one foot to the other and looked a little worried.

"Darling, are you feeling well?" Abigail clasped her palm to his forehead.

"I'm fine, Mama." Matthew squirmed to free himself from his mother's hand.

With mixed dread and enthusiasm coursing through his heated blood, Willem watched the auction proceed. One by one the baskets were auctioned off. Blushing maidens and happy miners met by the upturned keg and sauntered off toward a lush meadow that had been roped off for a picnic ground. Abigail smiled at each departing couple. Will fancied he saw a wistful look in her eyes while each couple drifted away in flushed silence toward the clover and grass. Maybe she wouldn't be too upset after all.

"Look, there's the last basket." There was a little catch in her voice when she spoke. It sent an arrow shooting through Will's heart.

He looked up at the basket with the uneven bow tied crookedly around the wicker handle and grimaced. A single sprig of wilted columbine hung loose and lopsided on one side. Compared to the other baskets this one was not very pretty, but the sight of it made the blood rush through Will's ears like a mountain waterfall.

"Well, now, isn't this a fine basket?" the announcer said doubtfully. "Who will begin?"

Silence hung in the air while the group looked on in embarrassed curiosity at the homely little basket. It was plain beyond description and a pitiful example compared to all the others before it.

"Five dollars." Willem's voice was too loud in the stillness. He heard Abigail's surprised gasp mingle with a curious murmur rippling over the remaining crowd. Matthew looked up and graced Willem with a beatific smile that succeeded in giving him hope and more than enough courage to tough out whatever might follow.

"Now then, that's the spirit!" the Mayor choked out. "Who will raise?" He scanned the crowd of shocked miners.

"Five twenty-five," Brawley Cummins drawled from the back of the crowd.

Willem turned and saw Brawley leaning against a slim aspen. He cocked an eyebrow and nodded in greeting. The healing marks on his cheek were bright red today. Willem doubted Brawley knew who the basket belonged to. More likely he was just being ornery to run up the bid against Will.... Still, he might have caught on to Matt and Will's scheme and wished to have Abigail's company for himself.

"Ten dollars." Willem turned toward the rotund auctioneer.

A gasp of shock rippled through the crowd. Abigail frowned and looked up at Willem. "That basket looks familiar to me. Matthew, do you know anything about this?" Abigail laid her hand on the child's shoulder. Will saw disbelief and recognition slowly dawning in her expression. Matt looked at Willem with guilty desperation in his young eyes. All hell was going to break loose soon.

"Ten dollars and fifty cents," Will said.

"Mister, you just raised your own bid," the announcer replied with exasperation in his voice.

"I know." Will felt a knot in his chest. He didn't know who had made the last raise. All he knew was that he had to have that basket—and what went with it. "I'm bidding ten dollars and fifty cents."

"Fine, then. Going once, twice, sold to the gentleman in the blue shirt. This basket was generously donated by Mrs. Abigail Cooprel. If you'll step forward, sir, and claim your prize."

Abigail glared at Willem. There were arcs of anger in her azure eyes. Her mouth pinched into a tight white line. She turned to her son while a deep crimson blush started to steal up her face.

"Matthew, I expect an explanation when we get home."

"Yes, Mama."

Willem moved to the head of the crowd and paid for the basket. He slung it over his arm and returned to where Abigail and Matthew stood.

"I suspect this was your doing," she snapped.

"Yes." Will nodded solemnly.

"Let's go home, Matthew." Abigail spun on her heel and started to leave.

"If you leave now, what will people think? These baskets were all donated, Abigail." Willem hated to use such a ploy to capture her in his snare, but he saw by the set of her mouth and the fire in her eyes that she was not going to be trapped easily. "Do you want folks to think you're less charitable than the other women?"

Abigail's eyes widened.

"You can't just walk away, Abigail," Will said softly.

"It's bad enough you paid such a high price for a box lunch," she whispered. "Couldn't you have made it look a little . . . nicer?"

"Matt decorated that basket."

Abigail sucked in a sharp breath and her hand flew to her throat. "He did?"

"Yes."

"Then let's not stand here while everybody gawks at us."

Willem felt a tiny explosion in his heart when he realized he had triumphed.

"You still paid too much," Abigail said, and smoothed one wild curl on Matthew's forehead.

"I didn't want to take a chance of somebody else outbidding me," Willem admitted honestly. He glowered at

Brawley, who still lingered at the aspen watching them intently.

She paused and looked up at Will. He took a deep breath and tried to stop his heart from slamming within his rib cage when she smiled coolly and raised one delicate brow.

"I certainly hope whatever you two put in there is worth the price." She shook her head in disbelief. "And the effort."

"If the basket was empty it would be worth it to me, Abigail Cooprel."

Matthew romped with Brighty at the edge of the meadow. A pale yellow butterfly flitted just out of the excited dog's reach and brought on a raucous round of barking.

"Please don't be angry with Matthew... it was all my idea."

Abigail's attention was captured by Will's deep voice. He opened the basket and took out the gingham cloth, then bent and spread it on the ground by Abigail's feet. She turned and studied him.

"Willem, just what are your intentions toward Matthew?" She plucked at the beading on her reticule with her fingers.

Willem stopped and gazed at her nervous fingers. He allowed his eyes to trail up her stiff body. Her mouth was compressed into a humorless pout. He knew his answer was important to her and could very well determine their immediate future—and his association with Matthew. He smiled and tried to make light of the question.

"You make me sound like a prospective suitor, Abigail."

"I don't want to see him hurt. When cold weather comes you'll pack up and leave." Abigail knew that was only part of the reason she was afraid of Will. No matter how many times she told herself she was being foolish about Willem

Tremain, she couldn't shake the fear about him and Matthew. "I don't want to see my son's heart broken."

A wash of protectiveness for Abigail and Matthew swept through Will. He had a flash of insight about their past lives. Men would spend the spring and summer under Abigail's roof, allowing her to cook and care for them, then they would vanish like will-o'-the-wisps. The knowledge brought a new understanding about Abigail's touch-me-not attitude and Matthew's aloofness. Any friendships they made would have been tenuous and short-lived. She had seen a cycle of loss and now she kept her heart cloaked against the hurt.

"Are you trying to get rid of me, Abigail?" Will tried to keep his voice light. "You aren't jealous, are you?"

Her eyes widened. He saw a mixture of emotions ripping through her. He had the feeling she might be eagerly looking forward to his departure.

"Jealous?" she whispered.

"Hey, I was joking." Will tried to laugh but he had the notion Abigail was hiding something. "Are you hungry?" Willem lifted out the ham he had bought from Gustafson's daughter. He brought out potato salad and a jar of lemonade and a blueberry tart. "I doubt Matthew will want any of this after all the pie he ate. But I'll cut him a slice, just in case."

Abigail's eyes followed the boy and the dog through the tall meadow grass. She sighed heavily, and Willem felt a tug on his soul. He stepped over the checkered cloth and grasped her shoulders. The searing heat he experienced at the light contact no longer shocked him.

"Abigail, I am not trying to come between you and Matthew. He's a fine boy—I only want to be his friend and yours." His voice dropped to a husky growl when he added the last part.

"I don't need a friend, Mr. Tremain." She trembled beneath his fingers. It made her rail against the power he held over her and the weakness she felt under his touch. "And Matthew—well, Matthew has all the love he needs."

"Then let me be a companion to the boy." Willem's palms burned where he touched her. "That's all I'm asking. Nothing more, nothing sinister, Abigail, just to be his friend." He watched her mouth open and he wanted to claim her trembling bottom lip. She was so soft and fragile beneath his hands that he wanted to hold her and protect her, to prove he would not disappear from her life.

But he knew he could not.

Willem knew a temporary friendship was the only thing that could ever be between him and Abigail Cooprel. An icy shiver cooled his ardor.

A crashing sound announced Matthew's arrival. Will released Abigail and watched her struggle to keep her balance. She blinked rapidly, as if she were waking from a dream. It gave him a new rush of craving to see how his touch shook her iron-willed control.

"Are we ready to eat?" Matthew planted his feet and pulled back on the dog, who was sniffing her way straight toward the roasted ham.

Willem grinned and grabbed the dog's scruff playfully. "I guess we better or there won't be anything left."

"What do you want, darling? I'll fix it for you." Abigail dropped to her knees and ducked her head. Her hands shook while she spooned potato salad and sliced meat onto a small china plate. It made a hollow ache in Will's belly. He hungered to have her hands on him.

"After we eat, can we take a walk?" Matthew tipped his head up toward Will. He saw Abigail stiffen.

"Only if your mother will agree to go with us," Willem said softly. He found himself wishing he was not bound to the past—to a missing wife—then he cursed himself for his thoughts and forced himself to eat in sullen silence.

The dog loped ahead of them through the meadow grass like a racehorse on a carefree gallop. Willem had taken the rope off her neck as soon as they were away from the other picnickers and she reveled in her freedom. Matthew giggled and tried his best to keep up with the leggy animal. Abigail held her skirts up and picked a leisurely pace through clover and wildflowers dotting the rock-strewn meadow.

"Thank you for being Matthew's partner today," she said softly. She wound the blue ribbons of her bonnet through her fingers. "It—it ended up being a wonderful day. . . for him, I mean. It's the first time he's ever won."

Her halting words drew Willem's attention. Several soft strands of long hair had worked their way loose and were dangling by her cheeks. She had undone the top button of her bodice as the day warmed. Her face was softly flushed from their climb. A little sheen of sweat at her throat was exposed to Willem's hungry eyes.

"Thank you for letting me share it with Matthew—and you. I'm glad you aren't mad at me about our little trick with the basket." He wanted to grab hold of her and crush her to him. He wanted her to understand, but how could he expect her to condone what he himself could not? He wanted her with an intensity that rocked him, yet he would never do anything to hurt her reputation or compromise his own honor—not for a short interlude that would leave them both worse off than they were now.

"Matthew is very fond of you, Willem." Abigail stopped and rubbed her hand up her wayward hair. Several pins fell like raindrops around her feet and the mass tumbled down. Willem chewed the inside of his jaw and clamped his fists against his thighs. He wanted to reach out and grab the shiny tresses, to hold them to his nose and smell the essence of Abigail. He wanted to possess her with his body—and he wanted her to give up a corner of her heart.

"Mama!" Matthew's voiced ripped through the red-hot haze of Willem's lust. He snapped his head around and saw the lad standing above them on an outcrop of rough gray stone.

"What have you found?" Abigail turned to look up at Matthew, oblivious to Willem's physical torment.

"A cave. Brighty has gone inside."

Matthew's words swept Will's desire aside like a spring avalanche. He charged past Abigail and up the incline toward the curious child. He saw Matthew standing at the mouth of an abandoned mine shaft. Broken and splintered timbers leaned precariously across the opening, testimony of an earlier cave-in. The space was just large enough for a dog—or a boy—to squeeze through.

"I'm going in after her," Matthew said, and took a step toward the yawning pit.

"No!" Willem moved with a speed born of stark terror. He grabbed Matthew by the shoulders and pulled him away from the crumbling aperture. "Don't ever do that!" Willem cringed at the sound of his hard, flinty voice. He had not raised his voice in six long, lonely years. It shook him to hear the emotion in each severe word after so long a time of harnessing his feelings.

"Mr. Tremain?" Abigail approached and pried Will's stiff fingers from the boy's shoulders. "Are you all right?" Her eyes were wide with concern.

Her expression hit Will's gut like an eighteen-pound sledge. He gulped down the hard lump in his throat and nodded dumbly. Clammy, cold sweat beaded on his brow and upper lip. The churning of his stomach made it difficult to breathe and impossible to speak. He closed his eyes and leaned against the rough stone of the mountainside, sucking in great drafts of air until his lungs felt near to bursting. He told himself to get control of his terror before he frightened the boy—and completely alienated Abigail.

"Mama? What's wrong with Willem?" Matthew's childish whisper cut through the morass surrounding Willem. He opened his eyes and saw concern etched on Matthew's little face.

"I'm fine, Matthew," Willem lied. He placed his palms against the rock and forced himself to stand away from the mountain. He saw the confusion written in the child's eyes and knew he had to explain.

"I had something very bad happen to me in a mine once, one very much like this one." Will's voice was filled with pain and regret. "You must never go in—they're deadly. Promise me that you will never go inside a mine."

The Dane picked that particular moment to emerge from the bowels of the earth. Willem grabbed her neck and hung on to the loose scruff. The smell of damp earth and wet dog wafted upward. "And you, young lady, are going back on the rope."

Willem picked up the dog and strode down the hill toward the picnic grounds. Abigail watched every step he took. She could not dispel the memory of his ashen face. She puzzled over the complex man walking toward the setting sun while she remembered the conversation with the miners.

"The Black Irish," she muttered. Abigail was beginning to see how he'd acquired the name. His actions and expressions were darker than the very pits of hell. She shivered while she followed him toward the wagon.

Chapter Thirteen

Willem lifted the heavy sadiron from the back of the hot stove. He clamped his tongue between his teeth and dragged the iron over his only good white shirt. He'd risen while the moon was still fat and round in the sky, in order to be up before Abigail. He needed his clothes pressed, and for some odd reason found himself wanting to do it without her knowledge. Not that this type of thing normally bothered Will—he believed a man should be able to take care of himself whether that meant skinning a buck or darning his socks. Still, he found himself casting anxious glances toward the doorway and trying to hurry the job along.

Finally the cotton released its tight grip on the wrinkles and began to straighten out. He was going to church for the first time in years and he intended to be dressed properly—for Matthew's sake and no other reason, he told himself.

Abigail lingered in the dark shadows by the registration desk. She watched the single kerosene lamp cast flickering fingers of light across Willem's tousled dark hair. Each time he turned and placed the cooling sadiron on the stove to reheat, Abigail felt her breath catch in her throat.

He was beautiful beyond belief. The soft, silken hair on his defined chest caught deep shadows, which emphasized his physique. She watched while tiny fingers of muscle beneath the gold medallion stretched and corded with each movement. He tapped his foot impatiently, and she found herself smiling. He was wearing thick woolen socks and no shoes. The top button of his trousers was carelessly open. A dark shaft of hair, slender as an arrow, grew downward until it vanished into a V at the loose waistband.

Abigail took a breath and closed her eyes. She had to stop this. She had no intention of finding herself alone and vulnerable because of her silly preoccupation with Will's manly form. But the image of his dark wavy hair, still ruffled from sleep, and the soft, drowsy glow in his eyes, would not be banished so easily. She picked up her skirts and tiptoed up the stairs to her room before the urge to stroke that enticing body overcame her better judgment.

Willem finished his shirt and shrugged into it. He buttoned it while sneaking up the stairs to his room. Once inside his room he dug through his valise and found his old black string tie. He polished his shoes and took particular care shaving and slicking back his hair.

When he looked in the mirror he was marginally satisfied with his appearance. He'd never be accused of being handsome, but he was clean and presentable. He walked out onto the landing just as Matthew and Brighty bounded through the hallway toward him.

"Morning." Willem smiled and ruffled the boy's wild curls.

"Mama just combed my hair, and she's not gonna be happy you did that," Matthew said with a frown.

"Sorry. Step in here and I'll fix it." Willem turned back to his room. He drew Matthew to the washstand while Brighty leapt up on Will's unmade bed. She flopped down with her black muzzle between her front paws and made herself comfortable.

"Getting mighty familiar, isn't she?" Willem quipped while he wet Matthew's hair and recombed it.

"She likes you," Matthew said simply. "I do, too."

Willem stopped what he was doing. "Well, I like you, too." He grinned at the serious look in Matt's crystalline blue eyes. A bolt of lightning ripped through his heart.

"I'm glad you're coming to church with us. Will you sit by me?"

Abigail was walking by Will's room at that exact moment. The sound of Matthew's voice stopped her in midstep. She held her breath and listened to the rest of the conversation on the other side of the half-open door.

"I'd like that, Matthew." Willem's deep voice drifted over Abigail like a hot destructive wind, disturbing every living thing in its path. "Thanks for asking me."

"Mama and Lars and me always sit right up front. You can sit between me and Mama."

"We'll have to ask your mama and see how she feels about that." Will's deep baritone floated over her skin.

Abigail felt the warm tide rise in her cheeks when his words registered. Having Willem Tremain sitting next to her on the narrow pew would do little to inspire any pure thoughts. He brought out the most unholy desires in her while he made her squirm inside. She feared him even while she was attracted to him. It was the most confounding sensation she had ever experienced. She knew with every female instinct she possessed that he was *after* something. She just couldn't for the life of her figure what the elusive something might be. She frowned and slipped by the door before they came out. Abigail sighed and decided this was going to be a long, unsettling Sabbath day.

Lars fumbled with the buttons on his shirt collar until Abigail finally slapped his hand away in mock aggravation.

They were alone in the kitchen now that breakfast was finished.

"Muddled old fingers won't do for me anymore, Abbie. I think I'm about ready for the boneyard." He sighed dramatically. "The cold weather and my age are taking their toll."

Abigail looked at his craggy, sweet face and felt a pang of sadness. Lars had not been a young man when she'd met him and now she found herself wondering just how old he actually was.

"I suspect you have a good many more years left, Lars."

The old man again sighed heavily and frowned. "Perhaps."

His eyes misted over and he seemed lost in thought. Abigail had seen that look more frequently since his return from the mountain several weeks ago. She knew it had much to do with his confession about Matthew's mother.

"Lars, is anything...special...bothering you?" She poured him a cup of coffee and motioned to the table. He ducked his head and avoided her eyes.

"Why do you ask, Abbie girl?" He grasped the cup with twisted fingers and sipped the hot brew.

"You act troubled. I hope you know I'd do anything for you. Matthew and I wouldn't be here if it weren't for you. The rest, well, the rest just isn't important." She saw the color drain from his cheeks above his snowy white beard. His bottom lip quivered and his gnarled hands shook. "Lars? What is it?" Abigail saw misery written in his face and her heart went out to him.

"Nothing, Abbie. It's just an old man's frailty—that's all." He stood up suddenly and pulled on his Sunday hat. "I'll meet you at the church. There's something I have to do before services begin."

Matthew scampered ahead of Abigail and Willem like a young colt out for his first run. Sunshine glinted off his wild, thick curls. The sound of the church bell pealed across the mountainside and echoed in the canyon hollows. A moment later the church whistle screamed.

"Those silly Cornish miners," Abigail mused. "They insisted on having a whistle along with the bell. I don't think I'll ever get used to it."

"I should've rented a buggy," Willem grumbled. "This walk is too far for you and Matthew to make." He wondered when, if ever, Abigail rested.

"I've been making this walk for six years." She felt the same tightening of her insides each time Willem made some comment about doing something for Matthew—and her. She simply could not shake the feeling that he was a threat. Abigail frowned and tried to isolate the anxious feelings she had about Willem Tremain, but nothing would solidify. For one fraction of a minute she thought he might be a long-lost relative—the embodiment of her fears—but then she discounted the idea. After all, if he had come to claim Matthew, he most likely would have done it right away. No, if and when someone came for Matthew, they wouldn't pretend to be a miner, they would simply announce who they were and be done with it. The more she puzzled over it, the more confused she became.

Will Tremain was a mystery.

"I've never seen a gold camp that had a church." Willem's voice ripped her attention back. She looked up at him and saw him staring at the ground.

Will was watching the narrow, pointed toe of Abigail's shoe appear and disappear beneath the swishing, frilly green skirt with each step up the pebbly path. He wondered what color her petticoat was beneath it.

"Guston has the only church that I know of. This church is very special to me—for a lot of reasons." Abigail stopped and picked a wildflower from a trumpet vine. She longed for something to hold, something to keep her from thinking about the grave behind the church. This was the first service Abigail had attended since she had pried the truth out of Lars. Now Will Tremain was questioning her about the church. It was all too much. She felt stripped bare each time he asked her a question. What in God's name *was* he after?

"How's that?" Willem watched her put the bloom near her nostrils. She dropped her lashes for a moment before she inhaled its fragrance. His heart thudded inside his chest.

"Matthew was... born in that church." They turned up the path leading to the gate at the churchyard. Abigail hoped she would find some peace for her troubled soul within the hallowed walls. She avoided looking toward the side of the church where the wild rose grew in a tangled vine.

"In this church?" Willem bent and opened the iron latch. He smelled the faint odor of rosewater and soap when Abigail stepped through the narrow gate.

"Hmm. Lars delivered Matthew on the very church pew we sit on each Sunday. I've always thought of it as God's special blessing to me." Abigail fought to keep her voice steady as she remembered the day Lars had placed the baby in her arms. "I named him Matthew because—because—it means gift of God." Abigail ducked inside and tried to ignore the pounding of her heart when she brushed against Willem. If he noticed her distress he didn't say so. She saw him frown and cast a curious glance toward the mountain behind the small chapel, and for a moment her heart stopped beating.

Willem saw a movement at the side of the church. It was Lars. The old man had his hat in his hand and was kneeling by a huge, wild red rosebush. The tangle of thorny branches reached over six feet up the craggy hillside behind the little whitewashed church. Will wondered what the old fellow was up to.

"Come on!" Matthew's voice snapped Willem from his reverie. He looked down to find the boy watching him with a beaming smile.

"I'm coming." Willem stepped inside the church and let Matthew lead him to the front pew. He saw Abigail glance nervously at him.

"Do you mind, Abigail? If you do, I can find another seat." He felt his heart beat a little faster. Her eyes flicked over his face, and tiny brackets of strain appeared at the corners of her mouth.

"Of course not." Abigail scooted over until the end of the pew halted her retreat.

Willem Tremain's broad shoulders and his tremendous body overwhelmed her even before Matthew and Lars slid in after him. She felt trapped and too aware of him being so near. He smelled like harsh soap, clean, freshly pressed cloth and *him*—that earthy, indolent odor that made her break out in a cold sweat. She dared not look at Willem for fear he would see her unease. When the Reverend Mr. Davis stepped up, Bible in hand, to the narrow podium, she fastened her eyes on his face. She told herself to listen to the sermon, to block out Willem Tremain and all the other thoughts in her head, but it was useless.

Abigail felt every breath, awaited every sigh before Willem Tremain even made them. If he tensed his thigh to find a more comfortable position, she held her breath in anticipation of his unintentional touch. If he frowned, she was aware of it. The entire sermon blurred by and she caught only one or two words. Her heated blood rushed through her ears like a mountain waterfall. Her mouth was dry but her palms were covered with sweat. Abigail felt as if she were being braised over an open fire. She fidgeted in the pew and fumbled with the too-tight collar of her dress.

"Is something wrong?" The deep, husky whisper fluttered the hair beside her earlobe. She felt a million tiny shivers dance along her neck and down her arm.

"N-no," she whispered. She felt him leaning near her to catch her reply and told herself not to look at him, but she did anyway.

One wavy strand of hair was curled over his forehead and brushing the upper edge of his dark eyebrow. His blue eyes intensely scanned her face. Tiny lines framed the corners of his mouth, and his bottom lip twitched slightly. He looked as if he might ask her another question. Then abruptly he swallowed, and she watched his Adam's apple move above his tie.

He was all male and utterly appealing. He lowered his eyes and laid his hand over her own, then gave it a little squeeze. It was an intimate gesture. She glanced at him in wonder, and he bowed his head.

"We're praying, Abigail." His gravelly whisper broke through the fog of her lassitude.

"Oh," she murmured, and ducked her own head while she felt the hot tide in her cheeks. His hand remained firmly atop hers but for some strange reason she didn't try to move it. She allowed Will Tremain to hold her hand, and she found herself oddly comforted by it. When he said, "Amen" and rose, she did, too. They filed outside and she thanked the Reverend Mr. Davis for a lovely sermon, although she couldn't even remember hearing it. He smiled and nodded at her when she and Matthew moved along beside Will Tremain.

"I'm hungry, Mama," Matthew announced in between skips beside the path. Abigail looked at him and saw his hair was rumpled and he had grass stains on one knee of his trousers.

"We'll eat as soon as we get home." She felt as if she was coming out of a fog. Abigail had survived going to the little church and had avoided looking at her daughter's grave, partly because of Will Tremain and the distraction he presented. He walked beside her, careful not to touch her. She sensed his restraint and it made the small space between them all the more noticeable. Lars lagged behind them a few steps. He had been strangely silent since the service, and she was sure he had gone to visit Matthew's mother's grave. Abigail worried he might be making himself sick over the whole thing.

"Are you feeling well?" She turned to Lars, forcing her mind to focus on something other than Willem Tremain.

Lars managed a sort of melancholy grin and nodded. "What I've got there ain't a cure for, Abbie girl." He touched her arm, patted Matthew's head and walked away. She watched him for a few moments, wondering if he would ever forgive himself.

"Is something wrong with Lars?" Willem matched his step with Abigail's shorter stride and once again he was only a hairbreadth from her body. She felt the great magnetic pull of his nearness.

"I don't know. He's had some things on his mind since he returned from the mountain this year." She glanced at Willem and saw him looking at Matthew thoughtfully.

"Do you suppose it's Matthew's friendship with me?"

Abigail frowned and worried her lip. "Perhaps." Lord knew she was uncomfortable with it and maybe Lars felt the same way about the interloper in their midst. Maybe he was as worried as she was about somebody coming to claim her child.

"I can see how it might be upsetting to him for a stranger to show up and have the boy take a liking to him." Willem turned and captured Abigail's eyes. She knew perfectly well he wasn't just speaking about Lars anymore. That Will Tremain could be both sensitive and perceptive took her by surprise.

"Since you brought it up... I am a bit concerned. What happens when winter comes and you move down to warmer country?" She blurted out the question so quickly it surprised even her.

Willem pulled a piece of bear grass from the edge of the path and began to shred it.

"Are you so sure I'm not going to winter here?" Up until this moment he had made no definite plans one way or the other, but hearing Abigail ask the question made his decision fast and easy. He wasn't going to move on when the snow fell.

"What?" She stared at him in disbelief. This was not the news she wanted to hear. Each day it became harder to ignore Willem Tremain, and she had been hanging on to the knowledge that he was but a temporary distraction in her life—and in Matthew's.

"Maybe I'll stay." He grinned, and a flash of white teeth caught her eyes. "You don't already have my room rented out, do you?"

"No. Of course not. It's just that none of my tenants has ever stayed through the winter. Not even Lars. It's always been only Matthew and me—for six years."

Willem watched her face and felt himself coming closer to making a decision, a decision that both thrilled and petrified him.

Chapter Fourteen

Abigail pushed the loose hair back from her forehead. Monday baking loomed before her every bit as large and dark as a mountain thunderhead. She tossed aside the eider quilt and swung her bare feet over the edge of the bed to the cool wood floor. Dawn hung gray and ominous this morning. She could smell rain on the mountaintop.

She pulled on her old calico day dress and tiptoed downstairs with her shoes and stockings in her hand. Matthew had been happily exhausted by the time Willem Tremain had carried him up to his bedroom last evening, with the aging crumpled blue ribbons of their victory still clutched in his small hand. She hoped he and Lars would both sleep in today. She was worried about the old man and the boy.

Abigail paused by the registration desk and took a tentative breath. The smell of freshly ground coffee beans flooded her nostrils. Her brows knit together while she told her heart to stop pounding. Without having to see him she knew exactly who was in her kitchen. The hair on the back of her neck prickled and her mouth went dry. Only Will Tremain had that effect on her.

He looked up and met her eyes when she walked in. He was leaning against the plank near the already hot stove. His hair was tousled and his eyes still bore the slightly drowsy look of slumber, which softened his features and made him appear vulnerable—or at least less threatening. A knot began to form in the pit of her stomach.

His shirt hung open and she had to keep willing her eyes away from his hard, lean midriff and the seductive twinkle of the gold medallion against the curls of chest hair.

"Sorry if I woke you with my banging around down here," he apologized. She could see he was impatiently waiting for the coffee to come to a boil.

"N-n-no." Abigail hated the way she developed a stutter around Willem.

"Tiptoeing this morning?" He raised both eyebrows and nodded toward her hand. She glanced over, mortified to find her stockings and shoes dangling from her fingertips. Her eyes shot back to Will and she found his gaze riveted to the floor. Heat rose from her collar to her hairline when she realized it was her bare toes he was watching with rapt fascination.

"I—I didn't want to wake Matthew." She slid into a chair and pulled one stocking on. "He was so tired yesterday..." Abigail jerked the stocking up past her ankle before she realized Willem Tremain was transfixed by her bare calf, a calf she had blatantly exposed to him. The knowledge made the knot in her belly expand and twist. Would he think she'd done it intentionally?

She glanced up and locked gazes with him. There was a glow within his eyes, like banked embers waiting for a breeze to fan them to life. She swallowed hard while she felt her control weaken by swift degrees.

"Willem, I—" The sound of soft padding broke the spell between them. She looked up in gratitude as the dog walked into the room.

"Ready for breakfast, girl?" Willem squatted down and rubbed Brighty's neck. He looked over at Abigail, and she could have sworn a hot flame licked across the empty space between them. She felt a ribbon of heat snake up her toes and meander toward the soft flesh of her inner thighs. Will's glance scorched her right to the very core of her womanhood.

The dog nuzzled his thigh affectionately. Abigail sighed. He had captured not only Matthew's heart but the dog's, as well.

"I better get started," she blurted out. She shoved her foot into the shoe and wasted no time in covering the other foot with stocking and leather. She felt as if the fires of hell were licking at her back when she grabbed the heavy sack of flour from the cupboard. Suddenly the weighty bulk became light as a feather, when Willem unexpectedly took the burden from her hands.

"That's too heavy for you, Abigail." His voice rubbed over her already prickling nerve endings. She backed up a step to put some space between herself and this man who played hob with her emotions.

"Thank you, that's very kind of you." She glanced at the coffeepot in time to see a bubbling stream of brown liquid come oozing from the spout. "The coffee is done." Of course he could see it was done, she chided herself. It was boiling over on the hot stove and filling the entire kitchen with its smell.

"Will you have a cup with me?" He placed the flour sack on the table and turned toward her. His pupils were so large, only a tiny rim of blue remained around them. It was as if the deepest, blackest pit that ever existed shone in his eyes. Abigail knew if she shared a cup of coffee with this man—alone this morning—she would fall into that pit and gladly remain there until the frosty snows took him away from her. Abigail knew it was an unshakable fact, even if she allowed herself to wish it otherwise.

"No. Thank you." She turned on her heel and fled upstairs. Abigail waited in her room like a coward until she heard the other men shuffling down the stairs. Only then did she feel able to face Willem Tremain again.

Abigail was only a fourth of the way through her baking when she ran out of cinnamon.

"The man is making a muddle of my head." She punched down the lump of dough she had set aside for loaves. A part of her wished it was Will Tremain she was hitting. "Why can't he just go away, or at least be like the others?" she asked aloud.

The kitchen was empty and quiet except for Abigail's voice and the sound of her fist sinking into the soft mound of dough. She cleaned her hands on the front of her apron and sat down with an exasperated sigh. Matthew had badgered Lars until the old man had taken his cane pole, Matthew and the dog fishing over an hour ago.

"If I'm going to get the rolls finished I'd better get myself to town." The last thing Abbie felt like doing was walking down the hill to the mercantile.

She tugged off her apron and took down the small tin from the back of the cupboard. She left the large roll of bills untouched while she extracted a few coins, then covered the rising dough and stepped out of her house.

Sunshine momentarily blinded her and she stood on the steps of her house blinking in awe. The day was fine and sunny, all traces of the gray rain clouds had disappeared. If only her dark mood could vanish so easily. She began to walk toward town, and within a few minutes she was swinging her reticule and humming to herself. For the first time, Abigail noticed the colorful flowers dotting the roadside and the foundation of a new house going up near her own home. She had been so preoccupied with Willem Tremain that she was in danger of letting summer march past her without her even noticing. Fall was only weeks away, and then the first snows of winter would come. Weeks had evaporated since Willem arrived.

Abigail would soon be alone with Matthew...or would she? She willed herself to stop thinking of Willem, but she could not. He had shaken the foundations of her beliefs over and over, and his suggestion that he might not leave with the end of summer had left her both confused and fearful.

Returning with her supplies, Abigail opened the front door of the boardinghouse and found herself face-to-face with a man who could only be described as pugnacious in appearance.

He was big—all over. His neck strained at the celluloid collar of his stiff white shirt and his shoulders pulled at the seams of his fashionable suit coat. A sporty bowler was perched atop his short-cropped blond head. He was a brawny bulldog of a man, and he was blocking Abigail's entrance into her own home.

"Who are you?" she blurted out. Her hand was still fastened on the doorknob. She saw the man frown and take a step toward her. Abigail was forced to either step back or find herself literally nose-to-nose with the brute.

She stepped back.

The man reached inside his vest pocket and drew out a pair of wire-rimmed spectacles. He placed them on his nose and smiled. The change it wrought in his appearance was nothing short of amazing.

"Sorry. I can't see much close up without these." He extended his hand and Abigail stifled a nervous squeak when her eyes fastened on the beefy palm. "I'm Paxton Kane. I'm a Pinkerton agent."

Abigail stared at his hand for a full minute while his words penetrated the fog around her.

"Pinkerton? The detectives?" She weakly grasped his fingers and managed a trembling handshake.

"Yes. I'm looking for Willem Tremain. Is he here?"

Abigail searched the man's face while her mind flew over his question. She had known there was something odd and secretive about Willem from the first—but a criminal? A man being sought by the Pinkertons? She couldn't believe it. He was dark and brooding but surely not a fugitive. He frightened and fascinated her, but...

"Ma'am? Are you ill?"

Abigail felt his hand clamp onto her arms. She had suddenly gone cold and her fingers were numb. The brown-paper-wrapped cake of baker's yeast and cinnamon sticks tumbled from her hand.

"I'm fine," she whispered.

"Well, you don't look fine. Let me help you."

She watched while the man's irascible features melted in front of her eyes. He became a gentle bear who helped her into the kitchen and settled her into a chair with delicate care. She was mute while he drew a glass of water from the pump and brought it to her.

"Here, drink this."

Abigail gulped down the water obediently. She just could not believe that Willem could be wanted by the Pinkertons. Images of Matthew's hero swam before her eyes.

"Mr. Kane?" Her voice quavered.

"Yes, ma'am?"

"What do you want with Willem Tremain? What has he done?" Abigail whispered the question even though she did not want to hear the answer.

"Done?" Paxton Kane frowned and looked befuddled. "Oh, ma'am, I'm afraid I've given you the wrong impression." He grinned and doffed his hat. "Mr. Tremain hasn't done anything. I'm looking for him because I work for him. I have been in his employ for the last year."

Abigail flipped the pan and dumped the golden cinnamon rolls on a blue-painted platter. She had spent the morning watching them disappear into Paxton Kane's mouth. Now she grinned while he licked his fingers clean and leaned back in his chair. A wide smile of satisfaction wreathed his face.

"Ma'am, you are one mighty fine cook. I can see why Willem is staying here." With a grin he accepted the coffee she poured for him. "I must admit, I thought I'd made a mistake when I saw this place...I mean, it isn't exactly what Willem usually picks."

Abigail pulled out a chair and sat down opposite Paxton. "What kind of place does he usually stay at, Mr. Kane?" Tendrils of dread and fear twined around her heart.

"Cheap, no frills. But after tasting the food I can see why he'd pay more—though it does amaze me."

"Why is that, Mr. Kane?" Abigail wanted to bite off her tongue but her curiosity would not allow her to let it alone. She had an opportunity to find out something about Willem and she was not about to pass it up. Perhaps now she could find the reason for her suspicion and distrust. Perhaps she could find a reason to justify her dislike for him. Perhaps she would finally have the reassurance she so desperately wanted.

Paxton took off his spectacles and rubbed the heels of his hands against his eyes. He paused for a moment before he pulled the eyeglasses back on.

"It's against company policy to discuss a client, Mrs. Cooprel."

"I understand. I apologize." Abigail started to rise from her chair, but Paxton reached out and stopped her.

"Please, sit down. I went to work for the Pinkertons about a year ago. Willem Tremain was my first case—and the only one I haven't solved." Paxton leaned back and stared up at her ceiling.

Abigail settled herself and listened quietly, hoping he would continue, even while she felt a twinge of guilt at her nosiness.

"I suppose my pride is bruised. I mean, this should've been an easy case. Frankly, it rankles me to say I'm no closer to solving it now than I was a year ago when Will came to me with it. I like Will Tremain, I can tell you this much." Paxton looked at Abigail and smiled. "He's been searching for...someone. I've come here to give him a report."

Abigail watched Paxton Kane. Her interest deepened against her will, against her better judgment.

"Sorry I can't say more, ma'am." Paxton smiled apologetically.

Abigail tried to smile back. She had hoped to find out something that would make her feel better, but instead she felt more anxiety about Willem. She kept coming back to the same question: why was he here and what did he want from her? Now she had one more mysterious question to add to the list. *Who* was the Pinkerton looking for?

Chapter Fifteen

"I can't do it, Paxton." Willem leaned toward the Pinkerton Agent, while his words drifted across the small table between them. The clock ticking in the empty parlor was the only sound in the house. Everyone else had gone to sleep hours ago and the air in the boardinghouse was thick with quiet.

"I can't give up the search for my child, my own flesh and blood. I'd sooner die."

Paxton saw anguish, guilt and some new, elusive emotion deep within Willem's dark blue eyes. He had known the man would react like this, but still it made his insides curl up to hear the desperate passion in Tremain's baritone voice.

"Will, I've checked every lead. There hasn't been a foundling home or rumor of an orphan in a gold camp—or the whole state, for that matter—that I haven't followed up. I hate to tell you this, but I think Moira found a way to leave Colorado, perhaps the States altogether. Maybe she went back to Ireland. By the time you came to us, the trail was cold. It would take a miracle to find them."

"I know you've done your best, Paxton, and I know it doesn't set well with you to be leaving the Pinkertons with this one case unsolved." Willem leaned back and dragged his fingers through his hair. "Just leave the case file open. I won't ask a new man to be assigned to it, but if any leads come in, I want to be notified immediately. Tell your home office in Chicago. I'll keep paying whatever is necessary."

"Notified? Where? I've had the devil's own time keeping up with you this last year. Just where is the agency supposed to notify you, Will?" Paxton's disgust with Will's nomadic life-style bled into his words. He cleared his throat and glanced at the clock. Ten times it chimed before Willem spoke.

"I know you've had to follow me from one camp to the next while I earned enough money to pay the agency, but that's going to change now." Willem sighed.

Paxton squirmed in his seat. He hated to remember some of the places he'd seen and scrapes he'd fallen into while following his client from one rough-and-tumble boomtown to the next.

"You can tell the agency to send any information to me in care of Abigail Cooprel's boardinghouse." Willem spoke softly. He had been chewing on the idea for days and now his decision was suddenly made.

Paxton could not contain his snort of surprise. He took off his glasses and cleaned them on his trouser leg. When he put them back on, Willem was staring at him with sincerity written all over his face.

"You're serious, aren't you?" Paxton couldn't believe what he was hearing. "This isn't a joke?"

"No joke. I plan on staying right here." Willem tried to contain the little flutter he felt inside his belly when Abigail's image flashed before his eyes.

"After tasting the widow's cooking, I can't say I blame you." Paxton glanced down at his vest, hanging comfortably open over his full stomach, and grinned. He had enjoyed more than one portion of the widow's fine fried chicken at supper.

Will shrugged, for Abigail's cooking had become the least important reason he was staying. He found her, well, irresistible, but Paxton didn't need to know all the details. "She's a good woman and Matthew is a fine boy." Will leaned back in his chair. His eyes seemed fastened on some faraway point.

Paxton wondered if it was the fatherless boy keeping him here or something else. He had never asked Willem about his peculiar penchant for avoiding women. He knew for a gospel fact the man had not been with a woman once since Moira had left him. Whether from a lingering love or some religious belief, he wasn't sure, but the fact was Willem Tremain had been as celibate as a monk for nearly seven years. The widow Cooprel was fetching but could she be enough to banish Will Tremain's wanderlust? No, it had to be the boy. And that made Paxton wonder if Will was setting himself up for disappointment.

"I'm glad to hear you're thinking about putting down roots." Paxton saw Will's head come up. An odd sort of fire glowed within his eyes—the fire of passion—but Paxton dismissed it as a trick of the lantern light in the parlor. Still, if it had been anybody but Willem Tremain he was watching in the quiet room, he would have sworn the man was consumed with lust. But if Will had maintained his control this long, why would it suddenly falter now?

Lars stood on the stairs in the darkness and listened to the conversation of the men below him in the parlor. A warm ribbon of hope mingled with the remorse he still carried. For weeks now he had been watching Willem Tremain, looking for a sign, for some sort of proof to validate his suspicion. He had seen a striking similarity between Matthew's and Will's unusual blue eyes, but then again it could be the wishing of an old man trying to wipe away the last traces of guilt. Matthew's hair had darkened with each passing year. When he was grown, Lars expected the boy's unruly curls would be the color of midnight—just like Will Tremain's thick ebony hair.

Lars knew there had to be a way of finding out if he was right or just plain addled. He fingered the gold medallion hanging beneath his long johns while he mulled over the matter. If only the woman had told him her name before she died.

If only.

Lars tilted his head up and whispered in the dark, "If you want your spirit to have peace, then you're going to have to help me." He hoped Matthew's mother had heard his plea. Then he turned and tiptoed up to his room in the darkness.

Paxton pulled an extra chair up to the table and waited for a lull in the activity before he risked venturing his hand out to snatch the platter of bacon being passed along.

"A man could get skewered trying to eat," he commented.

Willem only smiled and nodded. He seemed oddly distracted this morning. Paxton had slept on a pallet in Will's room and had heard the miner thrashing in the night. He'd known about Will's nightmares, but had thought perhaps Will had attained a measure of peace here in the widow's home.

Willem was staring at something, and Paxton looked over his shoulder to see what captured his friend's attention. He found Will's eyes following the widow around the room as a moth follows a flame through the darkness.

"Willem?" Paxton slid a short stack of flapjacks onto his plate.

"Hmm?" Willem never glanced his way, never looked away from the woman who kept her back to them while she attended to her chores in the crowded kitchen.

"I have a couple of days before I have to leave for Chicago. How about taking me with you to Otto Mears's camp and showing me how you earned your reputation."

Willem glanced at Paxton. His brows drew together, and for the first time he seemed to be paying attention to what Paxton was saying. "How I earned *what* reputation?"

Paxton grinned. "How you earned your reputation as a wizard with explosives. I've heard about it for a year—how you work magic with dynamite. I'd like to see for myself."

Willem shook his head and took a sip of coffee. For a moment he'd thought Paxton Kane was talking about the ridiculous name, Black Irish. He should've known his friend would not do that. "Sure, you might as well come. This is as good a time as any, since I'll be staying at Otto's camp for several nights."

Abigail turned around. "You will be gone?" Her eyes were wide with expectation.

Willem felt his breath catch in his throat at the sound of her question. Some deep part of him wanted to believe she would miss him, but he knew she was more than happy to see him go. It stung knowing that he disturbed her so much she couldn't wait to see him out of her house—out of her life.

"Yes, for a couple of days. Otto is blasting a tunnel for his road and wants me there in case he runs into anything stubborn on the mountain."

"It seems I will have a firsthand opportunity to see how you garnered your reputation." Paxton grinned.

"Every fool on the mountain knows how he got his reputation," Brawley Cummins growled loudly.

Paxton peered through his glasses down the length of the table to the seat Brawley now occupied regularly. Willem noticed the gleam in his eyes.

"Really?" Paxton inquired with a chilling smile.

Willem raised his eyebrows and leaned back. Matthew wandered into the kitchen, still rubbing the sleep from his eyes, and slid into the empty seat beside him.

"Morning, Matthew." Will smiled at the sleepyhead.

"What's going on?" the boy murmured with a drowsy grin.

"Brawley Cummins is telling Mr. Kane how the Black Irish—I mean, Mr. Tremain—got his reputation." Tom Cuthbert chuckled.

Willem flashed the miner a dark glance at the mention of his hated nickname.

"Oh," Matthew said, and yawned. Willem realized with relief that the boy hadn't given the name any notice at all. A warm spot arose in the pit of his stomach just knowing the child accepted him.

"You seem to know a lot, Mr. Cummins. Please, tell me more." Paxton wiped his mouth with the gingham napkin and laid it beside his plate. He pulled off his suit coat and folded it carefully across the back of his chair. Each movement was slow and deliberate.

Brawley blushed crimson. "Ain't nothin' to tell. Any fool knows the story." Brawley shoved a forkful of pancakes into his mouth. A drop of syrup lingered on his chin.

"Are you calling me a fool, Mr. Cummins?" Paxton inquired mildly.

"All I'm sayin' is that citified sissies ought to keep to what they know and not ask dumb questions about what they don't."

Across the room Abigail stiffened and shot a deadly glance toward Brawley, but if he cared about her disapproval, he didn't show it.

Paxton smiled, but his eyes were cool as slivers of mountain ice. "Really? I suppose you think men like me are kind of soft and sissified, is that what you meant?" He winked at Will from behind his wire-rimmed glasses.

"You said it," Brawley snapped.

"Yes, I did. I'm calling you outside, Mr. Cummins." Paxton carefully took off his spectacles and closed them up. He handed them to Matthew. "Will you watch these for me, young man?"

"Sure." Matthew blinked a couple of times as if he were finally coming fully awake. He handled the glasses as though they were a fragile baby bird, fallen from its nest.

"Paxton, are you sure you want to do this?" Willem raised his eyebrows and glanced at Abigail with a meaningful look.

"He needs to be taught some manners," Paxton replied.

Abigail had stopped filling the lunch tins, and now she locked gazes with Willem. The high color of her cheeks intensified while the electricity of their gaze traveled across the room.

"The cat and the dog did enough damage. I'll not have brawling in my house."

"Yes, ma'am," Paxton chirped agreeably.

Willem watched her cheeks turn to dark crimson. She spun back around, and he knew it was to hide her eyes from him.

"Come on, Paxton, Brawley, this is no way for grown men to act," Will reasoned.

"Shut up, Tremain, I can skin my own bears," Brawley growled.

Will raised his hands in mock surrender. "Fine, Brawley, fine, but don't say I didn't warn you."

The sound of boots and the back door slamming punctuated their rapid departure from Abigail's kitchen. Willem followed Lars outside. He found an empty spot, where he watched the men square off on the back lawn. Paxton positioned himself like a prizefighter, both fists held high and poised. He struck a pose and winked at Willem.

"Who does he think he is, bloody John L. Sullivan, himself?" Snaps guffawed while he stared wide-eyed at Paxton's jaunty form.

"Hardly, sir, but I have taken one or two bare-knuckle prizes in Denver and surrounding parts." Paxton snorted indignantly and raised his fists a half inch higher. He thumbed his nose and gave a wide grin. "Ready when you are."

Willem shook his head.

Brawley approached Paxton with all the grace of a lumbering grizzly awakened too early from hibernation. Willem sighed. This was going to be a sad spectacle to watch.

Blood spurted and cartilage tore when Paxton delivered a series of lightning-fast punches to Brawley's shocked face. Will glanced back toward the boardinghouse to see if Abigail was watching. A stunning blow from behind sent him sprawling into the creek on his belly. He looked around and discovered it was Paxton who had put him there.

"Sorry, Will," Paxton shouted apologetically. "I slipped."

Willem pulled himself up. He sat there in the shallow stream and saw the mischief shining in his friend's eyes. When he was certain he had sufficient control over himself, he shook himself off and rose from the icy water. His clothes were soaked and the weight made getting up awkward. He slipped once and went down again. Cold liquid soaked clear up to the neck of his shirt.

Willem glanced up and saw Paxton watching him, then Brawley took a swing and the fight was on again. Will sloughed to the bank, forgotten by all. He slid his hands over his wet clothes to extract as much water as possible while the fight went on.

Paxton's entire lesson in breakfast etiquette took under five minutes, but Willem knew Brawley's battered lips would take much longer to heal. He wondered if the man's pride would ever mend after the public beating—one the other men would no doubt talk about all winter long.

Brawley crawled up off the ground and spit out a mouthful of blood. With his fists held tight against his thighs he glared at Paxton. Brighty sniffed the earth and wandered close to Brawley's wobbly legs. He tried to kick her but the dog was too fast. Sidestepping and snarling at the man, she came to stand at Willem's side. He looked up to see Abigail standing in the doorway watching them all. Her eyes blazed with anger.

"Mr. Cummins, you will please find other lodging! Your language and behavior are not what I want around my son." Abigail looked at Willem with eyes the color of azure embers. He was pretty sure he was the next one on her list for eviction. He couldn't blame her for booting the lot of them out, but the idea of leaving her and the boy sent a cold fist into his gut.

She narrowed her eyes and he winced at the pain her expression brought him. God, he didn't want to go.

"And as for you, Willem Tremain, you will not take one step into my house—unless you strip off those wet clothes first." She wadded up a dry shirt and trousers and tossed them at him before she disappeared inside.

The screen door slammed shut in his face, but all he could do was stand there and grin. Abigail had taken a tiny step toward accepting him. She was going to let him stay. He looked at the clothes in his hand and felt the smile slip a bit. She had gone to his room to fetch him dry clothes. It was a small thing, an intimate thing, the kind of thing a woman did for *her* man. A warm feeling burst inside his chest. He knew he was grinning like an idiot while he fumbled with the buttons of his sodden shirt.

"Wheee! Abbie girl is mad as a wet hen," Lars said with a rasping chuckle. He turned toward Paxton and grinned. "I want to thank you for what you done, young fella. That was a long time coming and I enjoyed seeing it." Lars slapped Paxton on the back.

Willem finished unbuttoning his shirt and peeled off the sodden fabric. He had begun to undo his trousers when he saw Lars's eyes locked on to his chest. The old man's face had gone pale and his bottom lip quivered, while his eyes seemed to lose focus.

"Wh-wh-where did you get that?" Lars pointed at the gold medallion nestled in the wet hair on Will's chest.

"This?" Will fingered the metal, still cold from his dunking. "It's been in my family for generations. It had a twin once, but that was long ago."

Lars's eyes snapped up and fixed on Will's face. The old man seemed to be searching for something.

"Did you—I mean—who did you give it to . . . the other one like it?" Lars's old voice was barely a whisper.

Willem frowned and glanced at Paxton, who was blinking at the old man like an owl in bright sunlight. Kane took a step closer and peered at Lars curiously. Will knew he could barely see without his glasses. "Why do you ask, Lars?"

"Tell me, Black Irish—Willem—tell me. Who did you give it to?" There was desperation in the old man's voice.

Willem was worried about the old miner. He had lost his color and was trembling like an aspen leaf in a strong wind.

"I gave it to my wife on our wedding day," Willem said softly.

Chapter Sixteen

Lars stood by the flowering rose and let his tears fall on the crimson petals like raindrops. After all these years someone related to the dead woman—to Matthew's *real* mother—had appeared. His worst fear and his most desperate hope had materialized in the embodiment of Will Tremain. Lars sniffed and dragged his sleeve across his nose.

"Forgive me, but I don't know if I can do it," he said to the woman and baby buried beneath the bush. "I don't know if I can tell Abbie the truth. It was hard enough telling her that Matthew was not her child." Lars sat in the morning sun and considered where his impulsive deed had taken them all and what the final outcome would be.

For years he'd longed for the dead woman's kin to find her, but in all those years he'd never considered it would be her husband, never considered the consequences to Abigail, never conceived that Matthew's *father* might come to claim him. Now he sat with his head in his hands and felt a deep pit of fear widening in his chest.

"The Black Irish—Matthew's father is the Black Irish." His voice was a harsh, raspy whisper in the cool mountain air.

When Willem Tremain learned the truth would he pack the boy up and take him away from Abigail? Lars moaned aloud and pulled the gold medallion from beneath his long johns. His gnarled old fingers could not undo the clasp, so he held the metal between his palms and prayed for a way out of the maze. Prayed to find a way for Abigail to be spared heartache for what he had done.

Lars thought back to that day. He had wanted to tell her, but the look of joy on her face had frozen the words in his throat. Finally, after his conscience had eaten at him, he had told her the truth, but he would never forget the look of pain and betrayal in her eyes. He wasn't sure he could do it again. He wasn't sure he could tell Will Tremain he was Matthew's father.

Paxton stood by an outcrop of jagged stone and watched the old man. He had sent Willem on to work at Otto's camp, feigning aches and pains from his fight with Brawley, agreeing to meet him later. He'd had a hunch that had made him follow Lars to this church. The old man's face had been a picture of remorse and recognition when he'd seen Will's pendant. Paxton knew that look—he'd seen it on a hundred fugitives' faces. Lars knew something about the disk. So he had followed the old man here.

Lars's shoulders shook and Paxton felt shame at watching him weep. Funny, the reverent way the old man was bent toward the tangle of wild roses, it put him in mind of someone visiting at a . . . grave side.

A grave.

Paxton listened to the old man babble between wrenching sobs. Slowly bits and pieces of the solitary conversation began to make sense. He took a step, and loose rock crunched beneath his boots. Lars's head snapped around in surprise.

"Is this where you buried her, Lars?" Paxton moved up beside the old man and squatted down. "Here, beneath the rose?"

Lars blinked rapidly a couple of times and nodded. "I made their caskets that night and buried them here side by side." His bottom lip trembled and his blue eyes got milkier. "I didn't want them to be alone."

"Them?" Paxton held his breath. He didn't know if Willem could withstand hearing that both Moira and his beloved child had both died.

"Yes. The red-haired woman and the baby girl." Lars's shoulders trembled.

"She died in childbirth?" Paxton plucked a red bud from the tangled bush. He rolled it between his thumb and index finger.

Lars opened his palms and sunlight glinted off the dragon on the medallion. "Yes."

"She had a baby girl?" Paxton felt a sick feeling in the pit of his stomach. How was Will going to take this?

"What?" Lars looked up. He clenched his fist around the gold disk.

"Moira, the woman who wore that, her baby was a little girl?"

"No. Her baby was a healthy, strapping boy."

"I don't understand. If Moira is buried here with a baby—then whose baby is it?" Paxton tried to make sense of what the old man was saying.

Lars looked up and blinked. "The baby girl buried here is Abigail's child. Not the red-haired woman's child. It's Abigail's poor daughter." Lars's face crumpled in grief.

Paxton stood and crushed the bud in his hand. "Do you mean to tell me that..."

"Yes. I laid the dead woman and Abbie's tiny stillborn daughter side by side that night." Lars's voice was steady but his gnarled old hands shook.

"If Abigail Cooprel's baby is dead, then who is Matthew?" Paxton felt the hair on his nape rise.

Lars looked at him and frowned, suddenly stunned to icy composure by the question. "He's Willem Tremain's son, born just minutes before his mother died. Will Tremain is the father of Abigail's child."

Lars swallowed hard. Just hearing the words spoken, after so many years, took a small portion of the burden from his shoulders. He was glad it was the Pinkerton he was telling, and not Abbie or Will, for it was somehow easier to tell this stranger.

Paxton felt an invisible fist the size of a ham knock all the air from his chest. He slumped back down beside Lars and stared at the rosebush. The reality of what he had just heard settled over him like a funeral shroud.

"We've got to tell him. Dear God, we've got to tell him."

Lars nodded in agreement. "I hope Abigail will be able to forgive me—one more time—for what I've done." Lars stood and squared his shoulders. "You go find Will and tell him, tell him that Matthew is his son. I'll go talk to Abbie."

Paxton paced back and forth in the road beside Otto's camp while the sun dipped lower in the west. Lars had given him the medallion at the church and started for Abigail's boardinghouse hours ago. He drew his watch from his vest pocket and looked at the face. Five-fifteen. Willem should be coming along this path any minute now. A part of Paxton was bristling with excitement. After so many years and dead-end leads, the question of Moira Tremain and Will's missing child had been answered. Paxton shook his head in amazement.

She died in childbirth...that's why the trail went cold, he thought. *That's why Will couldn't find her right away.* Paxton held up the gold medallion and watched it spin in the waning light. It was a wyvern, a mythical winged dragon, etched on the face. In all these years Paxton had never looked closely enough at the one hanging around Will's neck to identify the mythical creature. He shoved the medallion back into the shallow pocket with his watch and looked up. The sound of a harness jingling signaled the arrival of the dray. He waited until the driver pulled up beside him.

A half dozen brawny men covered in dust sat in the back. Willem was among them. He grinned broadly and waved.

"Paxton! Come to meet me now that all the work is done?" Willem jumped down from the wagon. Paxton watched Willem with the other men and saw a changed person. Gone was the quiet, brooding man who had hired him a year ago. The group exchanged some joke, and deep laughter echoed through the canyon.

Paxton studied Willem's face. There were lines of laughter around his eyes where the grit of his labor had not remained. Two more deep grooves of humor bracketed his mouth. In all the time Paxton had worked for Will he had never known him to laugh, but apparently he did now—and from the look of him, often.

"Feeling better?" Willem slapped Paxton on the back and grinned. "You look a little peaked, my friend. Don't tell me ol' Brawley hurt your hand with his face." Will stifled a chuckle.

"Will...I need to talk to you." Paxton fell into step beside his friend while they walked toward a haphazard group of tents. A scruffy cook was dishing some nameless stew onto tin plates. Willem grabbed one plate for himself and handed another to Paxton.

"I'm all ears." He straddled a long bench and sat down at a lopsided table beneath a spindly aspen tree.

Paxton took a deep breath and thought about how he was going to tell Willem. He had spent the better part of the day practicing and rehearsing, but now all of his speeches fled. Not a single word would come to his lips. In frustration he reached inside his vest pocket and pulled out the medallion. He held it aloft so the light would catch it.

Willem stopped with the fork halfway to his lips. His eyes narrowed and the smile drained from his face.

"Where in God's name did you find that?" He reached out and let the medallion slide into his own dirt-covered hand. It lay across his palm like a bright star in the dusky twilight. He reached inside his shirt and drew out his own as if to make sure there were really two of them. Paxton watched emotion rip across Will's face.

"Lars had it."

"Lars?" Willem closed his fist over the chain and drew a deep breath. He appeared to be summoning his strength. "Where is Moira?"

"Buried beneath the rosebush behind the Guston church."

"Dead? She's dead? How long—when?" Willem shook his head in disbelief.

"A long time, Will." Paxton saw unshed tears well up in Willem's eyes.

"And—and my child?" Will's voice was a thready whisper. "Where is my child? Not dead—please, not dead."

"Alive. A fine, healthy boy."

Will's face shattered and a dull moan rumbled deep in his chest. His chin quivered. "A son? I have a son? Have you seen him? Where is he? Is he well? When can I—"

"He's fine, Will." Paxton dreaded what eventually must be said.

"Where? How?" The questions tumbled from Willem's lips like an avalanche. He thought of all the things he would do for the boy... the places he would take him... things he would teach him. "When can I see him?"

"You already have." Paxton gripped the edge of the rough table. He had no idea what Will's reaction would be.

"I—know him?" Bewilderment permeated in his voice.

"Yes. It's Matthew Cooprel. Matthew is Moira's child... and yours, Willem."

Chapter Seventeen

Willem stood and stalked away from the table. He kept the medallion clutched in his fist while he paced like a great catamount. He could not dispel from his mind the picture of Abigail's face. All those times he saw fear, dread and doubt in her eyes—now he knew why. She must have known, he thought bitterly.

She had been deceiving him. Duping him about the most important thing in his life. No wonder she wanted him to leave. She had been masquerading as the mother of—*his child.*

"Abigail kept this from me?" Willem felt the sharp sting of betrayal. He had come to respect and trust Abigail Cooprel. It made him cringe inside to think of all the times he had lusted after her while she was playing him false.

Paxton was stunned. Willem's face was a mask of misery. He had expected many possibilities, but this had not been one of them. After all this time, he expected tears of joy, jubilation, but not this distress, and certainly not about the widow Cooprel and the part she had played in this tragedy. He started to explain, to correct Will's mistake, but Will rapidly fired questions at him.

"How did it happen? How did Moira die?" Willem slumped back onto the wooden bench. After six years of searching he had come to the end of his quest. A cold numbness seeped into his body. He was not a married man anymore—had not been for a while. He wondered how long Moira had been resting in her grave while he searched in vain.

When Will seemed to have finally ran out of words, Paxton seized the opportunity. "Moira died not long after she left you. Lars was working at the church in Guston when Moira showed up. She was in labor, and Matthew was born just before Moira died." Paxton watched Will's face for a reaction.

"Did she suffer much?" Willem intended to see a proper headstone was erected, and he would speak to the minister about a memorial service. It was the least he could do, knowing she had died alone.

"I don't think so. She never even told Lars her name. He took the medallion and hoped that somebody would come looking."

Willem's head came up and he narrowed a gaze on Paxton. "How long has Abigail had my son? How long has she been raising my son as her own?" He felt a cold void inside. Willem had tried so hard to resist temptation, and now he felt twice the fool knowing Abigail had what he had so futilely sought.

"It's too much of a coincidence to be anything but the truth, I guess." Paxton sighed and shook his head in amazement. "Lars claims she showed up right after Moira passed away, also about ready to give birth."

Willem snorted at the fantastic tale. "You believe that?"

"Yeah, I do. The old man has been carrying around a lot of guilt for what he did."

"Guilt? Over what?" Willem just couldn't believe that he'd been under the same roof with Matthew and hadn't known that Abigail was keeping this secret from him. No wonder she quaked in his presence. He tried to tamp down the fuming anger building inside him. He found it hard to accept that those clear blue-green eyes had lied to him—every day since his arrival.

"Lars never told Abigail." Paxton couldn't get the image of Lars's grief-stricken face out of his mind. "Abigail never knew."

"What the hell are you telling me?" Willem shouted in his agitation.

"Abigail's baby was born dead, a little girl. Abigail never saw Moira, never knew another woman was even in the church. Lars switched the infants and never let on."

Willem's face drained of all color. Even by the glow of the camp fire he looked deathly white.

"Paxton, are you telling me that Abigail *believes* Matthew is her own child?" Willem's head was reeling with the impact of what Paxton was implying. A flame of hope flared inside Willem. He realized that beyond anything in his life he wanted Abigail to be innocent of this horrible deception.

"That's exactly what I'm telling you. Until a few months ago she never knew. Lars says he didn't know what else to do, so he gave Matthew to Abigail and let her think it was the child she birthed. He helped her care for the boy. Finally his conscience got the better of him and he told her, but only recently."

"Oh, Lord," Willem groaned. He leaned over, hung his head on one hand and slouched wearily. "This changes everything."

Paxton looked at him for a long moment. "What do you mean?" He felt a frisson of dread meander up his spine. Something about the set of Willem's jaw worried him, made him think his friend was in peril. Paxton saw the visage that had earned the name Black Irish. Willem was a picture of dark, primal passion.

"I can't allow Abigail to suffer for what happened between Moira and me. No matter what happens, Paxton, I want your promise." Willem narrowed his eyes and fixed his gaze on Paxton's face. "I want you to swear you will never tell Abigail the truth about Matthew... never tell her that I am Matthew's father." Willem felt the fires of protection and devotion for Abigail burst inside his chest. "Just let her go on like she has."

"You can't be serious. All these years you've searched. This last year you've lived like a pauper, paying me to find Moira and your child, and now you don't want her to be told?"

"Not yet. I have to think about this." He searched his mind for a solution. There had to be one—he'd just have to work it out.

"What is there to think about, Will?"

"Abigail and Matthew. This would destroy their world." Willem's eyes narrowed. "This would kill Abigail. She adores that boy, and if, as you believe, she had nothing to do with what happened at his birth, then she and Matthew are the only innocent ones in this whole mess."

"I do believe Lars when he says she didn't know until recently, but what about you?" Paxton found himself seeing Willem's point, but it still amazed him.

"I'm not the important one. The boy and Abigail are the only ones who matter."

"So what do you plan on doing?" Paxton crossed his arms at his chest and watched Willem.

"I don't know yet, but I don't want Abigail to be told that I am the boy's father." He turned toward Paxton. "Promise me you won't tell her." Will's voice trembled with emotion and steely determination.

"You've found your son and all you can think of is the cost to Abigail Cooprel?" Paxton studied Will's face and realized the truth. "Do you care that much for her, Will?"

"That much and more. You've got to promise me. She must not be told. I'll not take my happiness by destroying hers. I need time to think about this, to find a way out."

"It's too late. It's out of your hands, Will." Paxton saw the impact the words had upon Willem.

"What?" Dark brows drew together. "What do you mean, it's too late?"

"Lars went to tell her hours ago. The old man couldn't live with the secret. When he saw your medallion he realized who you were. Moira died without ever telling him her name, but he has felt her spirit crying out to him for years—or at least, that's what he thinks. He unburdened part of his conscience when he told Abigail about her daughter, but it was not enough. He wants her and Matthew to know who you really are."

"Oh, Lord. What will this do to Abigail?" Willem held the medallion tighter in his hand.

"By the time you get back she will have already been told," Paxton said softly.

Willem wondered how she would react to the news. He wished with all his heart he could be there with her. Of course she had never trusted him, and she certainly would have more cause for that sentiment now.

Will flung back the thin blanket and left the tent. He felt as if he were suffocating. The canvas walls had closed in on him the moment he shut his eyes. The nightmare had come as usual, but this time it was different, worse. He was locked in the black, bottomless, airless pit, but instead of being alone, Abigail was there with him. The memory of his dream sent a shiver quaking through his body. He shuddered and rubbed the heels of his hands against his eyes. She had been trapped, alone and terrified. No matter how many tons of rock he moved, or how hard he tried to reach her, he could not free her from the trap they shared.

Willem groaned and walked a few paces from the tent full of snoring men. Night sounds enveloped him and he saw a flicker of wild green eyes glowing in the tall pines near him.

He puzzled over the dream. He understood the one that came with heart-pounding regularity, the one in which he was forced to relive the accident that had robbed him of friends, taken his wife and saddled him with that grim hated name, but this one had seemed different. This dream had been vivid to the point of terror. Instead of vaguely painful memory blending and merging, this had been new and crystal clear.

Willem fancied he could still smell the dank, musty odor of a mine shaft clinging to his shirt even now in the clean night air. Even Abigail had been too real to be part of the nightmare he carried within his scarred soul. This dream seemed more a graphic portent of things to come than a reminder of past events.

"Prophetic," he whispered. He tipped his head toward a dark sky and prayed it was not so.

Chapter Eighteen

Abigail couldn't feel her fingertips. She saw them, knotting up her tear-stained kerchief, but she couldn't feel them anymore. She couldn't feel anything except cold devastation in her heart. At last she knew what Willem Tremain wanted from her—and why she had felt such an unconscious threat from him.

"I don't care what you say, Lars, he knew from the start. That's why he came here—he knew and he came to take Matthew from me."

Visions of how Willem had wormed his way into her son's—into Matthew's—heart assaulted her. She had been wise to fear him, but not wise enough to send him away or to steel herself against his dark potency over her. He held in his hands the power to destroy her utterly, now that Lars had told her the truth of who he was, and she didn't doubt for a minute that he would do it—the black-hearted Black Irish.

"Paxton Kane knew," Abigail mused. "He must've found out the woman, Moira, had come here and that Matthew had been in my care. Willem came ahead of him so he could get to know Matthew first. I thought Mr. Kane was so nice..." Her words trailed off.

She stood and walked to the window. Shafts of mauve and silver glistened in the moonlight and sent long shadows across the meadow behind her house. Suddenly she felt trapped, caged. She had to get outside, get away from the boardinghouse, away from the images of Will Tremain. It was too late to take Matthew and run, she knew that, but she had to put some distance between this place and herself.

"Lars, I need to take a walk. Will you be here in case Matthew wakes up?" She thought of her child, *her child,* sleeping peacefully in his room down the hall, unaware of the calamity going on around him. Unaware that the security of his home was being shattered like thin ice over a pond.

"Yes, I'll be right here if he needs anything. Abbie, do you—do you hate me?" His voice trembled in pain.

She looked up at the old man and new tears sprang to her eyes. "No, Lars. I don't hate you." She managed to walk toward him. "You gave me a little boy to raise and love as my own. How could I hate you for that?" Her room seemed like a void, as if she were trapped in a dream without end.

"I didn't know what else to do—for any of you," he said when her fingers touched his thin, sinewy shoulder.

"We'll talk again when I get back. Now try to get some rest, and don't worry."

The old man nodded bleakly. He managed a tremulous smile when she squeezed his gnarled fingers affectionately. Abigail pulled on her heavy woolen shawl and went outside. The crisp evening air was spiced with the sharp, urgent taste of approaching fall. She inhaled and knew the first killing frost was not far away. Her heart already felt as if the edges had been scorched by a cold so deep she might never feel warm again.

"What am I going to do?" she asked herself while she made her way up the gravelly slope. There in the moonlight she found her place—a place of solitude and secrecy. A place she had been coming to often since Lars first told her about Matthew and her baby.

She neared the flat smooth boulder in the small sheltered hollow. The place was hard to find even if someone knew what they were looking for. Abigail sat down and felt the cold of the stone permeate her thin calico skirt. She didn't care. In fact, she didn't care about anything except the shocking truth she had learned.

Abigail sniffed and remembered the joy and relief she had felt when Lars put Matthew in her arms. Matthew was her life, her child.... Surely she could not love him more if he were of her blood. Surely Willem Tremain could see that.

She heard a twig snap nearby and sat a little straighter on the slab of cold stone. Something moved near a tiny dark hole in the middle of the hollow. Some nocturnal creature had built itself a home in the depression since Abigail's last visit. She saw a blur through the fallen leaves when the small animal entered its burrow. She relaxed again and tried to think. She had to find a way to remove the threat of Willem Tremain. When he returned tomorrow he would surely want to pack Matthew up and take him away. She had to prevent that—no matter what the cost.

When Lars had described the events of Matthew's birth several months ago, Abigail had thought nothing could hurt or shock her again. Now she found herself wondering about why the woman was there in that church, alone without her husband, without... Willem.

Maybe all those rumors about him are true, she thought as she pulled the shawl tighter around her shoulders. A pregnant woman would not run from the love and protection of her husband without good reason. Abigail wondered what terrible thing Willem had done to the poor woman that made her run from him. It gave her little comfort, to believe that Willem Tremain was capable of all the sins people laid at his feet, and it made her more determined to do whatever was necessary to prevent him from taking Matthew away from her.

Abigail heard an owl hoot nearby from the deep shadows in the trees. The urge to flee gripped her. She could return home, pack up Matthew and be gone before Willem Tremain returned. The plan took form in her mind.

She had money—plenty of money. Years of cooking for miners had made her financially secure. The tin in her kitchen contained enough to start over. They could catch the train.... She could take Matthew far away from Will...from his father. Abigail wrung her hands together and thought about it.

A part of her—a very small part—did have compassion for the man. She had felt the loss of her own baby deeply, even though the little girl had been dead for years before she learned of her existence. How would it feel to lose a child twice in one lifetime? Slowly the desire to run away was replaced by a feeling of remorse.

She pictured Willem's eyes, haunted and pain filled, and knew she could not disappear with Matthew. No matter how badly she wanted to remain in Matthew's life she could not do it by ripping Will's child from him a second time. That would be a cruelty she could not administer to anyone—not even him, no matter what terrible thing he might have done to cause his wife to run from him.

There has to be a way. And I'll find it, I swear to God. I will find a way to keep Willem Tremain from taking Matthew from me and still let him know his son.

Abigail rose from the chilled stone and turned back toward her home. She raised her chin a notch higher and let the steely resolve wash through her. She was determined to find a way to keep Willem from taking Matthew from her, but she would not run from the man in order to do it.

* * *

Abigail turned and looked out the window. She could see Matthew below, milking the Jersey cow in the weak rays of the morning sun.

It was odd. She hadn't felt any differently after Lars had told her Matthew wasn't her son. Her heart still beat faster when he laughed and her arms longed to hold him close. She frowned and wondered if she should feel otherwise—*could* feel otherwise—now that she knew Willem had sired him.

The knowledge that she had a daughter—one who'd entered this world dead—had made her sad and rent a corner of her heart, but it did not diminish the feeling she had for Matthew. If anything, it only strengthened her resolve to see him loved and nurtured. Now fate had given her another bitter pill to swallow.

"I suppose Mr. Kane and Willem will be here soon." Abigail saw the long shadows of purple and gray receding from her yard.

"Yes, I 'spect so." Lars's voice sounded weak and defeated.

Abigail shook herself and looked at him. He suddenly appeared old and frail. She knelt beside him.

"Lars, listen to me. You did what you thought was best...I don't blame you. Matthew is my son in every way but blood. Nothing has changed just because his father has shown up." Abigail was shocked by the force of her conviction.

"But Willem Tremain...what about him?" Lars's milky blue eyes were wide with regret.

"I don't know yet," Abigail replied, then stood and marched to the window. "But I'll think of something. I have to think of a way to handle him." She patted Lars's cheek. "Don't you fret. It will all work out."

"I've been thinking about it, too, Abbie." Lars stood and walked to the window to watch the boy playing outside.

"Have you?" She smiled at the old white-haired man. She loved him like a father.

"I've thought of a way, Abbie." His voice dropped to a whisper. "A way we can all have Matthew."

Abigail stepped nearer. "Really? A way to keep Willem Tremain from taking Matthew from us?" She felt the zing of excitement and hope. "Tell me, Lars."

"It's reckless and it may not work, but I think it might—if you will consider it."

"What is it?" Abigail felt a tiny frisson of trepidation trail up her spine to her nape.

"Hear me out before you say anything."

"All right." Abigail returned to her chair and sat down. She gripped the warm mug of coffee a little more tightly and told herself not to get her hopes up.

"He's alone now. I mean, Will Tremain is a widower, right?" Lars licked his lips. Abigail saw his eyes flick over her face.

"Yes, his wife is dead so that would make him a widower." She sensed Lars was having a hard time putting his thoughts into words.

"He's a man without roots. From what Mr. Kane said, he has no family anywhere else. He's lived like a gypsy looking for his wife and child."

Abigail shrugged. "Yes, I think that's true. Mr. Kane made it sound like Willem went from town to town like a rolling stone." For some reason Abigail felt a shaft of charity slam through her at the thought of such loneliness. She had seen the way Will settled in her boardinghouse like a man grateful for a warm meal and a clean bed. He had acted hungry for hearth and home, like someone who had not known much *love*. She shook her head and forced herself to listen to Lars.

"You've made a proper home for Matthew, Abbie."

"You've helped do that, Lars."

"I've not done much, but I have to tell you there is an account in Matthew's name in Silverton. It's there for the boy to use if he ever needs it."

Abigail's gasp of surprise brought his old gnarled hands up in protest. "No, I don't want to argue about that now, Abbie—we have the other problem to deal with."

Abigail nodded and sighed. "You're right. Go on—tell me about your plan."

Lars took a deep breath and stared at her with his pale blue eyes. He grimaced and shook his head. "The way I see it, there is only one possible solution to this problem."

"And what is that, Lars?"

"Get Willem Tremain to marry you."

Chapter Nineteen

"I could delay my departure for Chicago if you'd like me to stay for a while." Paxton shifted the valise to his other arm and offered his hand to Willem. People waiting to board the train jostled them out of the way. The platform in front of the Silverton depot was crowded today. Most of the passengers were traveling one way, leaving the high country ahead of the snow.

"No. You have a job waiting. I'll work this out." Willem grasped Kane's wide hand and shook it. "I want to thank you—for everything."

"I can't say I did much. I am glad after all these years you know what happened to Moira." Paxton had seen a great burden lifted from Will's shoulders. He knew that any affection Will had had for his missing wife had died years ago, but the uncertainty of what had happened had always shackled Will. Now perhaps he could put the past aside and have a real life. "What are you going to do about the boy?"

Willem shrugged and looked over the heads of the passengers waiting to board the train. "I don't know. All I know is that I don't want to see Matthew hurt and confused, and I don't want to cause Abigail any more pain than she's already had."

Paxton raised his eyebrows and tried not to laugh. Willem Tremain had just received the most astounding news of his entire life and all he could think of was sparing the widow's feelings.

"Paxton, keep in touch. Let me know how you like the big city and that new job of yours."

"I will—and you do the same. After the past year of searching, I feel like I've got an investment in that boy."

"I know." Willem grinned. "It still seems like a dream that I have a son."

Paxton nodded. He watched while Willem bolted off the step toward the dusty street.

"Where are you going in such a hurry?" Paxton called when Will turned to wave.

"I need to see what can be done for a proper headstone for Moira, then I'm going to see my son. It's a meeting that's long overdue."

"What dates do you want on the stone?" the mason asked, and scratched his head and stuck the end of the pencil against his tongue.

"Dates?" Willem was puzzled by his question.

"You know, the date of birth and death."

Willem had not asked what date Moira died. He realized with another surge of cold reality that it would also be Matthew's birthday. Somehow it didn't seem right to him, to put Matthew's birthday on Moira's tombstone. "Just leave the dates blank."

The mason shrugged. "Let me see if I have the rest right. Moira Tremain. Wife And Mother. Rest In Peace. Is that it?" the man asked with his brows raised. "Any best beloved or anything like that?"

"No." Willem felt a stab of conscience, but he didn't want to be a hypocrite. He had to admit that finally having

Moira's fate settled had released him from a terrible responsibility. "That's it. When will it be ready?"

"I'm sending a load of garden stone up your way in two weeks. Is that soon enough?"

"Yes, that will be fine. I guess after six years there's no rush." Willem turned to step outside and found himself staring into the face of Snap Jackson.

"Black Iri—Tremain." The man doffed his hat in greeting.

"Jackson. What brings you to Silverton?" Willem wondered how long the man had been standing in the doorway.

"I'm on my way to Creede. Heard news of a big strike up there."

Willem frowned and shook his head. How many times had he heard the same story and in how many gold camps? "I thought you'd been working near the Yankee Girl."

Snap Jackson shrugged. "I have, but it's time to move on, anyway. My bones tell me the first snow will be here soon. I don't want to get stuck in Guston for the winter! Mac and Skipper are going with me. Now with Brawley gone, the widow's house will be just about empty."

"Yes, I suppose it will," Will said thoughtfully. Images of Abigail flitted through his mind and left a trail of heat in his middle.

"I, uh, I heard you found your wife." Snap nodded his head toward the stonemason, who was rubbing his palms over a slab of rough gray stone.

Willem frowned. So, Snap had been listening to the conversation. "Yes, I did."

"How about you, Tremain? Are you planning on moving to new fields before winter hits?" Snap raised an eyebrow.

"I have no plans to."

Snap grinned. "Tom Cuthbert asked Gustafson's daughter to marry him, and he's moving into the little clapboard house beside the meat market. Guess you and old Lars will have the widow's, uh, cooking all to yourselves." Snap slapped Willem on the shoulder and turned away.

Willem wondered how long it would take for this bit of news to travel up the steep mountain to Guston. He also wondered where he and Matthew would be living when the first snow fell.

Willem walked up the hill toward Abigail's house and felt a heavy weight settle more firmly on his shoulders with each step. How was he going to approach her? How was he supposed to act?

He sat down on a large boulder beside the street. A buggy passed him and he had a vague impression of someone waving, but he didn't see who it was. His mind was a jumble of questions that he had no answer for. He had waited six years to find his child, and now that he knew where the boy was he couldn't find the strength to go to him.

Willem tried to figure out what was the matter with him. He loved the child—had started loving him the moment the grubby boy walked in and dropped trout at Abigail's feet—so what was preventing him from marching into Abigail's house and declaring that love?

"Abigail," he whispered. He had to face the truth. He cared about Abigail deeply, and he was afraid of what this would do to her. One part of him wanted to go and claim his child, to raise him, to be a part of his life. But another part of him died a little inside for Abigail and what this would no doubt do to her.

Willem wondered when he had allowed himself to fall so completely under her spell. He couldn't remember the exact time, but now he realized with profound shock that he cared for her. He wasn't sure if it was love, since he'd had so little experience with the emotion, but he held her in high regard and he'd sooner cut off a finger than harm her. He longed to hold her and comfort her and reassure her. Then in the next breath he wondered how he could. After all, Matthew was his son. He must make provisions for the boy...provide a home, take responsibility...but in order to do all those things he was going to have to wrench the heart out of Abigail. It filled him with a sadness so deep and wide he nearly wept. If only there was some other way—but there wasn't.

There wasn't any way out of this mess.

He solemnly forced himself to put one foot in front of the other. He inhaled and smelled fresh bread and cinnamon rolls, and Abigail Cooprel. Praying she would not hate him for what he had to do, he trudged up the hillside and felt his pulse increase as he got closer to Abigail's house. A blur of color shot out from beside the hand pump.

"Willem!" The childish voice sent a chill up his back. It was so hard to keep from reaching out and crushing the boy to his chest in happiness and love. He wondered if Abigail or Lars had said anything to Matthew, then realized they would not.

No, they would not be anxious to tell the boy. Will stared at Matthew and marveled that he had not seen the resemblance before.

They were alike in so many ways. Willem's physical stamp was on the lad, no denying it. His shoulders had a breadth and his legs a length that were unusual for a six-year-old. And then there were his eyes... he had the Tremain eyes.

"Matthew, how are you, lad?" He forced himself to keep his emotions in check.

"I missed you. You were gone a long time." The child smiled, which sent an arrow of love ripping through Will's heart.

"Not so long—only a few days. It only seemed a long time." A blur of gold announced Brighty. She bounded playfully around Will's legs, weaving in and out in her excitement.

"Did you bring us anything?" Matthew asked.

"Well, as a matter of fact, I did." He reached inside his shirt and brought out a brown-paper-wrapped object. He gave it to the boy and chuckled when Matthew ripped it open.

"A knife! My very own knife!" Matthew squeezed it in his hand as if the small bit of metal was the most precious thing in the world. Will's chest filled with pride.

Will could feel the hair on the back of his neck rise as the smell of spices and Abigail filled his nostrils. He didn't even have to turn around to know she was standing there watching him.

"Look, Mama!" Matthew held out the small knife to show her. Willem turned and caught the clear glint of disapproval washing across her narrowed eyes.

They met gazes then above Matthew's curly head. Will probed her aqua eyes for some clue as to her feelings, but she had erected the wall. No matter how hard he tried, he could not tell what Abigail was thinking. She glanced from him to Matthew and back again while he stood mute, waiting for some indication of what she expected him to do.

Abigail tried to arm herself against him. Against her will she found herself comparing his and Matthew's eyes. It sent a chill through her. Will's were dark, swirled with age and too much pain. Matthew's were clear and hopeful, as yet untouched by tragedy and loss. She prayed the truth would not taint the boy's outlook in the same way heartache had changed Willem's over the years. She shook herself and wondered how she could possibly know that life and tragedy had changed him, but she did. She looked into Willem's face and saw the toll that fate had taken upon him. She vowed she would not let his past destroy the happiness she and Matthew had found.

"Hello, Abigail." Will's deep voice pulled her from her musing.

Matthew shifted the new knife from one hand to the other proudly. "Can I go show it to Lars, Mama?"

"Yes, darling, that would be nice. You run along. Mr. Tremain and I need to talk."

Willem drew in a breath. So, he was back to being Mr. Tremain. That bit of information didn't bode well. He braced himself for what Abigail had to say.

Chapter Twenty

"Please, Mr. Tremain, come inside." Abigail avoided his eyes. The somber glint inside them sucked the courage from her heart and the breath from her body. She turned away from him but continued to feel the itchy sensation that always accompanied him.

Willem saw the stiff set of Abigail's shoulders. He wasn't sure what he had expected, but it was not her tight-mouthed rigidity. He frowned and wondered if he had misread Abigail. Perhaps she intended to fight him...perhaps he had been right when he'd thought she was somehow involved in keeping Matthew's parentage a secret from the very beginning.

No.

He could not believe it of her. No matter what, Will was certain Abigail Cooprel wouldn't have lied to him and kept Matthew's identity a secret if she had known he was the boy's father. He took a deep breath and tried to ignore the powerful feelings she awakened in him.

He wanted her—God in heaven, he wanted her—and now Moira no longer stood between them. Only Abigail herself prevented Willem from telling her how much he had come to care for her. Abigail and the rock-solid wall she had erected between them.

Abigail turned and watched Willem Tremain walk toward her. His face was bland and expressionless while each muffled tread on the patterned Chinese rug brought him closer.

She wanted to see his eyes—to read the emotion in them, to see what his intentions might be about Matthew—but they were hooded by his dark eyebrows and thick lashes.

His hair was slicked back. Her eyes skimmed over his clean shirt, open halfway down the front, exposing the wide expanse of his chest. The kerosene lamplight flickered over the gold medallion on his chest like a firefly caught in a jar.

She knew Lars had learned who Willem was because of the medallion's twin. For a fleeting moment she cursed it, wished that Lars had buried the wretched thing with the dead woman, then she drew in a ragged breath and told herself it was God's will.

"That which does not kill us serves to make us stronger," she whispered aloud.

"Abigail?" His voice skittered over her raw nerve endings like velvet in the quiet room.

Her own pulse began to thrum so loudly in her ears that she could no longer hear the clock. The vibrations of the last chime traveled through the soles of her high-buttoned shoes.

"I—" Her voice cracked. She wrung her hands and tried again. "Lars told me you are Matthew's father. I never knew, I swear." She wondered why, after all the hours of logic and reasoning, she should feel compelled to apologize to him for something she had no control over.

"I know that." He took another step until only a hand span separated them. "I'm sorry about your daughter."

"Thank you." Abigail blinked back unshed tears before she managed a tremulous smile. The pain of her child's death had become a dull ache in her breast. Now she forced herself to worry about the living child, the one she longed to protect and nurture.

"I made coffee for us. Would you like a cup?" She gestured toward two cups sitting on the table. Abigail sat down on the sofa and looked up at Will. No matter how hard she tried to keep her eyes off his stern face, she could not. Even now, when he had the power to destroy her world with a single word, she could not deny the attraction she felt for him. It maddened her to be so weak and feel so wanton when she was with him. A small part of her still feared him, but that fear brought a rush of untamed sexual excitement along with it. She bit her lip and tried to ignore the lure of his eyes... his body... the clean manly scent of him.

"Fine, that's just fine. I'd like a cup." Willem felt his mouth dry out like a powder keg on a summer's day. He started to sit down, then hesitated halfway. He was unsure of how he should act around her now that so many things had changed.

"Please, sit." Abigail touched the settee next to her.

He nodded and bent his knees until he was, more or less, perched stiffly on the edge next to her.

"We need to talk about—Matthew." For a moment he had almost said "our son."

Willem took the coffee she offered and was grateful for something to wrap his hands around. He squeezed his fingers against the solid mass of the cup and wished that he had the guts to tell Abigail how he felt about her, but when he looked up into her eyes, shielded from him by the icy wall of condemnation, he knew he could not.

Willem could not risk it. She didn't like him, he knew. Matthew's parentage had not changed that—if anything, it had made her feel more animosity toward him. He could feel it in the room along with his own unflagging desire.

"I guess we do have to sort this all out—for Matthew, of course." He groped to find the right words.

"Lars didn't mean any harm..." Abigail began. "Six years ago he did the only thing he could think of. There were few women on the mountain then, and fewer still who would've cared for an—orphan boy." She stammered over the words and he heard the painful catch in her voice.

"I'm just grateful that he was there to help Moira—and you. You've done a fine job with Matthew." Willem saw her look at him in surprise. "It's also a comfort to know that Moira—my wife—wasn't alone at the end."

Abigail looked at him with her great azure eyes, and all the air was suddenly sucked out of the room. "It's a lovely name, Moira Tremain...." Her voice was a husky whisper.

"I'm having a stone made in Silverton to mark her resting place." Willem felt a catch in his throat. "I'd be happy to have one made for your daughter, too."

Abigail's eyes filled with unshed tears and Willem wanted to kick himself for reminding her of the dead baby. He wanted to wrap her in his arms and comfort her, to stroke her soft hair and promise her a future filled with love and laughter, to wipe away the hurt he saw etched in her pretty face. He set the cup on the table and raised his hand to touch her but she stiffened abruptly. He drew his hand back as if he'd touched flame. He chewed the inside of his jaw.

She was lovely in this muted light yet there was a wariness about her, an uncompromising reserve that made him uneasy. He fought to ignore the enticing aroma of Abigail—the faint trace of rosewater and the spicy wholesome smell that followed her everywhere.

"I've been giving this a lot of thought since Lars spoke to me about you being Matthew's father." She pulled a hankie from her skirt pocket and dabbed at her eyes.

Her face was so animated and expressive. The more she talked the more he wanted to kiss her and tell her it would be all right.

"I've come up with a solution." She sniffed and sat up straighter. Willem felt the hair on his arms stand on end.

"You have?"

"Yes. I believe once you give it some consideration you will agree that to tell Matthew the truth right now would only confuse him." She glanced at Willem from under tear-spiked lashes.

Willem crossed his arms at his chest and leaned back. She thought he was such an uncaring brute that he would hurt his son for his own selfish needs. That knowledge cut a raw, jagged hole in his heart. He was stunned to silence.

"You already live here, so there would be no need to change that arrangement—of course, you would no longer pay, Mr. Tremain." She wrung her hands together in the hankie. He raised an eyebrow at her continued formality and felt himself stiffen in response.

"Really? And why is that?" Her tidy banker's heart was showing again. He wished she would quit babbling such nonsense.

"You are now a free man, since your wife is dead. I am, as well—free, I mean. In order to serve all of us, I have the following proposition for you, Mr. Tremain."

"A proposition, Mrs. Cooprel?" He kept telling himself no matter what outrageous thing she suggested, this was still sweet Abigail behind the icy barrier she had put between them.

"Yes. An arrangement. A business arrangement of sorts. You can have all the comforts of a family—home-cooked meals, clean clothes and, most important, the company and companionship of your son. I will continue as Matthew's . . . mother, until such time as we both agree he's old enough to understand what happened. I will see that you are comfortable in every respect, Mr. Tremain. Nobody but you and I will ever know that we are anything less than a real family."

"Abigail, are you asking me to marry you?" A tug-of-war was going on inside him. One part of his heart leapt for joy at the prospect, while his honor and his manly pride withered up at the manner in which this was taking place. This was not how he would've proposed to Abigail. He wanted passion and love, not an arrangement, not a *business proposal.*

"Well, yes—no." She took a deep breath and her delicate brows knit together. "I'm not making this very clear, am I? It would be a marriage of convenience—for the sake of Matthew. I mean, it's not like you and I have any true feelings of affection for each other, but I think under the circumstances we could learn to respect each other. For all outward appearances we would be a happy couple—for Matthew's sake." She fidgeted nervously beside him.

Willem looked up abruptly. It took every particle of control he possessed to keep from bolting off the sofa and dragging her up against him. She was so soft and pretty. Her hair was piled on her head and the calico brought out the color of her eyes. He wanted to show her just how much she meant to him, how much he was dying inside that she didn't want him to be a real husband to her. How angry her words were making him.

"Of course, I would not expect you to endure any hardship, Mr. Tremain. As a husband, I mean," she stammered in a great rush of words, and roses bloomed in her cheeks.

"Indeed? And how have you worked out that small difficulty, Mrs. Cooprel?" Willem tamped down the arousal and anger building inside him.

She twisted her hankie into a tight knot. "I would not ask you to behave any differently than other men. I would be a wife to you in every respect. I wouldn't expect you to settle for anything less."

Willem closed his eyes and breathed deeply. He clenched his fists and forced them to the tops of his tense thighs. The woman had no idea what it cost him to keep from jerking her up from the sofa and shaking some sense into her. He was so besotted with her it was painful, and she was telling him that she would *endure* his physical attentions?

"I can see you've given this matter a great deal of thought," he growled.

"It would be the perfect solution to our, er, problem. A marriage of convenience, for the sake of Matthew."

He stared at her with his mouth agape. Willem was afraid to speak, afraid if he said anything he would not be able to stem the tide of words. He wanted her, but not as a housekeeper and cook. Not just as a substitute mother for the son he'd finally found.

He wanted her in every way a man could want a woman. He wanted her for his wife, his helpmate. He wanted her in his bed—willingly. Not enduring his touch like a thing that could not be avoided.

He drew in a long, slow breath and found to his chagrin it was perfumed with the lovely odor of her enticing body. He forced himself to focus on her pale, worried face. It wrenched him deep inside to think of living with her each day and not being able to hold her and touch her and taste her in the way he wanted to.

The idea that she would submit to him in order to retain Matthew sent his soul curling in despair. This was not what he wanted. Not what he had imagined for the remainder of his life.

"I'll have to think about this, Abigail."

Willem rose stiffly from the sofa and strode out the front door into the dark, cool night. He hoped it would cool his lust and the slow, simmering burn of anger inside him.

Abigail stared at the closed door for long minutes. A part of her wanted to run and open it and call Willem back. He had left so abruptly she was paralyzed.

He hadn't refused, and that was at least something to pin her hopes upon. Yet he had not agreed, either. She stared at the door and wondered if he would rip the child of her heart from her.

"No," she whispered aloud. He was a hard man with a haunted past but he was not cruel. She had seen proof of that time and again. She thought of how he had championed the dog, and she thought back to Willem's words when he had offered to pay for the animal's keep. In light of what Paxton Kane had told her, that was an act of generosity beyond any reasonable expectation, knowing how Will had suffered to pay the Pinkertons to search for Moira.

No, he would not take the child from her. She sighed and felt a small measure of dread winnow from her heart.

Abigail worried her bottom lip and found herself oddly piqued by Willem's silence. She had not admitted it, not even to herself until this very moment, but she had wanted him to refuse her offer. She had wanted him to yell and rail at her, to tell her she was a fool. She had wanted him to react as any man would when a woman suggested such an arrangement. She was sure he would've—if he thought of her as a woman.

Abigail sighed and admitted he did not. Willem Tremain saw her as a possible solution to their difficult problem—a good cook and housekeeper, a dowdy widow well beyond her prime.

A secret part of Abigail's heart longed to see Willem react to her passionately. She realized with a slight warming of her face that she wished to see some of his control slip in her presence. She wanted to be able to penetrate the cool armor of indifference and have him want her.

As a woman.

Well, he doesn't. You are a plain widow who runs a boardinghouse and loves his son as your own. You've put it to him plain enough—he would be a boarder, but not a boarder, a husband, but not a husband.

She told herself she should pray he would agree to do what she asked, what she claimed she wanted. But if that was true, why did she feel so bereft?

Matthew would be spared any heartache. She would have her beloved son and the security of marriage. As long as she never gave her heart away she would be fine. Even if Willem Tremain decided to follow the other miners and find a new fertile gold camp she would still have Matthew, which was all that mattered.

Will Tremain might be willing to make this sacrifice for his son, but Abigail knew he had no feeling whatsoever for her. She really had no right to expect anything more from Willem—if he agreed—than a marriage of convenience to protect Matthew and secure his place in her life. She raised her chin a notch and vowed to keep her silly notions to herself.

She would not allow herself to care, to be vulnerable. Abigail pushed herself up from the settee. She stared at the cold cups of coffee and felt a new wave of hot tears surge forth. Why did she always lose her head around Will Tremain?

She sniffed loudly and picked up the dirty cups. The clock sounded nine chimes. She needed to see Matthew tucked in before she went to her empty, cold bed.

* * *

Willem strode through the streets like a great dark shadow. He encountered a miner he recognized now and then, but after they looked up into his face and stammered a greeting to the Black Irish, they moved along as if they had seen their own destruction mirrored in his eyes.

He grated his teeth until his jaw ached, and still the slow, simmering resentment in his gut would not be quelled.

Who does she think I am? What does she think I am? Willem paused by the glow of a gas street lamp and stared at the few stars twinkling over his head.

He was not a man who could be called eloquent, for words didn't come easily to him. If they had, maybe he could have made Abigail understand how he felt, which was what he had hoped might happen between them. Willem had exorcised his guilt about Moira and he wanted to get on with his life. He had lived alone with his demons for so long that Abigail and Matthew blazed into his dark life like a ray of summer sun.

He wanted them both.

Will raked his fingers through his hair. He was shocked and he was wounded by Abigail's opinion of him. As much as he hated to admit it, the widow had managed to get beneath his thick, protective shell. Her barbs had sunk right into his soft underbelly with her "business offer."

He snorted and resumed his walk. The very idea of her thinking he would agree to such an arrangement appalled him. Marriage was a lasting commitment, a covenant that could not be broken or bartered—not even for Matthew's sake.

Or given by half measure. No, by damn, a marriage is a marriage. All or none. But he knew deep in his heart that Abigail didn't want it all. At least, not with him.

He looked up to find himself standing outside the boardinghouse. Willem had negotiated a great circle through

Guston and come back to Abigail once again. He saw the pale glow of lamplight through a third-floor window and knew it was from her bedroom.

"If you only knew what you do to me, Abigail," Willem whispered in the wind. "You'd know I could sooner cut out my own heart than live with you on the terms you suggest."

He stood there in the dark while the cool blanket of evening engulfed him. By slow degrees he felt his indignation dissipate. Willem shook his head and found himself smiling in bewildered silence.

"She's some woman," he said, chuckling to himself. He leaned on the hand pump and watched her window. The faint silhouette of Abigail pacing back and forth across her room held his attention. He saw her lift her hands, then the curtain of her hair cascaded down her back in shadow. He saw the silhouette of her dress being pulled over her head and felt his heart slam against his ribs.

My God.

Searing hot desire flared within him. His body became like iron and Abigail's image the forge. She blistered him into a painful erection. He stood there and felt the disappointment and lust mingle as one emotion inside his chest.

Willem knew he could not agree to marry Abigail on her terms. He watched the film of her night rail settle over her body and came to a decision.

He would do this her way—for a time. But he promised himself he'd not see spring come without having her in his bed—willingly.

She bent toward the lamp and the shade darkened.

I will marry you, but, by all I hold dear, I swear you will come to love me as much as I love you.

Morning found Willem wide awake and anticipating his conversation with Abigail. All through the night he had plotted delicious methods to insure her downfall. He yawned and pulled on his clothes with restless energy.

He felt primed and ready for the challenge he knew his "bride" would give him. She was a strong woman and whatever lay ahead, he was ready to face it.

Willem grinned and glanced at himself in the mirror. He saw the glint in his own eyes and chuckled. The widow would get what she bargained for and much, much more.

He strolled downstairs, whistling a tune. The morning was fine and sunny. A slender shaft of light touched the settee where he and Abigail had sat last night. A tendril of heat curled from his belly to his groin.

He stopped and cocked his head to listen.

She was humming in the kitchen. A sudden burst of happiness gripped him. Soon she would be his wife. He would wake to her every morning. The idea of her in his kitchen, cooking his meals, and spending the night in his bed made him almost giddy with joy.

He crossed the parlor and entered the kitchen. She whirled around and gazed at him with wide, expectant eyes. He resisted the urge to smile at her.

"Fine, Abigail. We will be married as you say—for love of Matthew. Just tell me when to show up at the church."

Chapter Twenty-One

"Church?" Abigail swallowed hard. "You are expecting to have a church wedding?" She fumbled with the coarse cotton dish towel in her hands.

"Of course. What did you have in mind?" Willem leaned the backs of his thighs against the breakfast table, where only four plates now sat, and crossed his arms at his chest. He smiled inwardly when Abigail licked her full bottom lip and blinked in confusion.

"I—I hadn't really thought about it. I guess I just thought we'd go to the courthouse in Silverton and have the justice perform a simple ceremony or something like that."

Willem shrugged. "I suppose we could, but after all this time of you remaining a widow there's bound to be some gossip. I thought for appearances, for Matthew, you might want to do this thing up a little. Make it a special occasion, so there'll be no doubt about our willingness." He scanned her face to gauge the effect his words were having upon her.

"For Matthew...yes, I see what you mean. People would be inclined to talk less and all, if we had a church wedding."

"I thought so. In fact, I think I should buy you a ring and announce our engagement in the local newspapers," Willem said, barely managing to suppress his smile when her eyes widened in shock. They were the color of peacock copper this morning. He had never noticed before how they changed colors with her moods.

"Engagement? Newspapers?" Abigail sagged against the hand pump. "I never thought... I mean, it all seems so...public."

The morning sun was slanting through the window to tip her lashes in gilt. He wanted to step forward and grasp her stubborn chin. He wanted to tilt her face up and deposit kisses across her lids. He wanted her to know that he would gladly climb to the top of the church steeple to yell his happiness to the world.

Willem wanted to tell that world that he was marrying Abigail, and glad of it, and not for reasons of convenience. He wrenched his thoughts away from what he would like to do, and focused on what he had to do, to win this woman.

"Abigail, I know this is a lot of fuss over—uh, how did you put it? A business arrangement? But I think we owe it to Matthew. Particularly since the other miners have moved out."

"You know about that?" Abigail gasped.

Willem smiled while he sat down and poured himself a cup of coffee. Things were shaping up nicely.

"Yes. I ran into Snap in Silverton. I'm sure he has told the world about Moira." He glanced up. "Do you want to be the one to tell him, or shall I?" He saw Abbie's back stiffen and her head snap up at his question.

"Tell him? Tell who about what?" She blinked and worried her bottom lip with perfect white teeth.

Passion slammed through him. Willem wished he were a poet so he might tell her what was in his heart. He longed to have her know what the sight of her hair hanging in silken wisps about her face did to him. He inhaled and savored the flavor of spices, coffee beans and Abigail. With iron-fisted effort he armed himself against the growing fire inside him and set the cup down on the table.

"Matthew should be the first to know about the wedding." He felt the rush of love and amazement that accompanied every thought of his newly found son.

"Of course," Abigail said, and wondered how she could have overlooked such a thing. After all, this entire plan was being done for Matthew—wasn't it? "I'll speak with him after breakfast. Unless, of course, you feel you should do it."

Willem speared a stack of flapjacks. "No, that will be fine. I don't expect things to change overnight, Abigail." Each time he looked up he caught Abigail watching him with a look of bemused curiosity and wonder on her pretty face. It made him all the more eager to make her his bride. He hurried through breakfast and made his way to Otto's camp on feet that barely touched the ground.

Abigail stared at Matthew's beaming smile and felt the tension flow from her body.

"Are you sure, darling?" She couldn't believe it had been so easy—after spending hours fretting, while she did the laundry—to tell him. "You really are happy about me marrying Willem?"

"Sure. I like him." Matthew scratched behind the dog's ear and giggled when her hind leg started moving like the arm on a locomotive. "Should I call him Pa or Willem?" Matthew asked.

A lump formed in Abigail's throat. She blinked rapidly but a wash of hot tears blurred her vision. Images of Willem's face swam before her eyes. It tore at her heart to know he had been searching for this child—her child—and now she had blackmailed him to silence with a sham marriage.

"I think you should ask Willem what he wishes," she finally whispered.

"I will. I hope he lets me call him Pa." Matthew scampered up from the grass and grabbed the Dane around the scruff. They tumbled to the ground in a heap of rambunctious boy and slathering, pink-tongued dog.

"Matthew?" Abigail watched his blue eyes fasten on her face and she felt a shiver. They were the same exotic shape as Willem's. Why hadn't she seen the striking resemblance before now?

"Yes, Mama?" He peeked over the dog's shoulder and Abigail realized for the first time that the dog had put on some weight since she'd arrived.

"Would you be my ring bearer?" She held her breath while his face scrunched up and his brows knit together. Again, the arresting similarity to his sire bowled her over. It had been right in front of her all the time, and she was so blinded by her own love she had never seen it. Or perhaps she had been afraid to admit it, even to herself.

"What do I have to do?" Matthew glanced at her suspiciously.

"Just carry the ring and give it to Willem when he's ready to slip it on my finger." Abigail felt a rush of heat flood her face. She denied the possibility it could be anticipation of her coming matrimony.

"I'll do it."

"Good. We'll get you a new suit of clothes." Abigail stood and brushed away dry grass and a few golden aspen leaves that were beginning to fall. The line full of clean sheets and laundry flapped in the breeze and sent the smell of strong lye soap wafting toward her.

"New clothes?" Matthew bounded up. "You never said anything about wearing new clothes!"

Abigail laughed at the stricken look on his face before he and the dog bounded off. She picked up the empty wicker basket and tucked it under her arm.

Maybe getting married to Willem Tremain wouldn't be so bad. Since he'd agreed to all her terms it might be rather pleasant having someone to talk to in the evenings after Matthew was asleep. She felt heat flood her cheeks at the thought of intimacy between them. She told herself she could maintain the charade of a happy family life as long as she didn't give herself to him body and soul. As long as she kept her heart from him it would be all right. She could do it, she promised herself. She could live with him and take care of his needs, but she must never give him her love.

To give your heart is to risk it being broken, she thought to herself. *Yes, I think this will work out fine.*

Willem ducked his head. Loose rock and shale covered his arm and dusted his face with fine grit. He looked up and saw Otto climbing the crest of jagged rock toward him from the opposite direction.

"Morning, Otto." Willem extended his hand. He chuckled at the thunderous look on his employer's face.

"Vhat you vant? I had to leef a pile of vork to come." Otto placed his hands on his hips and glared up at Willem from under his jaunty cap.

"I need to take a few days off," Willem said, then grinned at the agonized expression washing over Otto's face.

"Vhat? You can't mean it. The road is behind schedule. I need you. Vhat you vant time off for, anyvay?"

"I'm getting married."

A smile twitched at the corners of Otto's mouth. It climbed his face until his blue eyes glittered with mirth. He swept off his cap and shuffled his feet. "Vell, now. Dat is fine. You take a veek—more if you need it. But vhen you come back I vant you vork twice as hard. The snow vill come soon. I vant you to agree to come finish dis damned road vit me in the spring."

"I'll do that, Otto." Willem grinned and shook the man's sinewy palm.

"Married... By Sheminie, dat is just fine," Otto muttered when he turned and ambled back down the mountain. "Who vould have thought any voman vould marry the damned Black Irish, anyvay?"

The words made Willem laugh. The deep sound echoed over the rocks and down the craggy ravines into the mauve-colored gorge below.

He was happy—happier than he'd ever been in his life. Now all he had to do was figure out a way to seduce Abigail and make her learn to love him.

"I'm going to Silverton to get some things for the wedding." Their voices mingled together and blended when they spoke simultaneously. Willem grinned and Abigail blushed at their unintentional concert.

"You go first," she mumbled while she plucked at the seam of her bodice. Abigail focused on Willem's face and tried to stop the tide of heat rising to her face. It was uncanny they had said the exact same thing at the same time.

"No, Abigail, you go ahead. You wanted to tell me about going to Silverton," He leaned back on the settee and sipped the coffee she had poured for him. It was nice, sitting with her like this in the quiet parlor of an evening. Visions of the long winter ahead danced enticingly in his mind.

"No, you go first." She fumbled with the handle of her cup and fidgeted nervously. How could he ever have thought her plain? Her face was a canvas, which blazed in infinite color and beauty with every thought she considered.

"I wondered if you and Matthew might like to come with me to Silverton. I need some new clothes. And I want to buy you a proper wedding ring."

She ducked her head and he saw the pinking of her cheeks. It sent a frisson of longing shooting through him.

"You don't have to..." Her voice trailed off.

"I want to. Besides, we can put the announcement in the papers. There's a nice hotel, and I'd like to show Matthew some of the sights."

Her head snapped up, and he saw something like disappointment written in her eyes. It gave him both a stab of guilt and a thrill of exhilaration. Maybe she wasn't as eager to be married just for Matthew's sake as she would like to have him believe.

"That would be nice... for Matthew. I need to get him a suit for the wedding." She smiled and her whole face lit up. "He's agreed to be the ring bearer."

Willem felt all the air leave his body. His son, Matthew, carrying the rings for his wedding to Abigail. He shook his head in wonder at the way things had come about.

Without warning the frightening nightmare returned to him. He felt a cold fist of dread close around his heart. Now that he was so happy and had so much within his tenuous grasp, he worried that something would snatch it from him. He vowed he would not let anything come between him and Abigail—not now, not ever.

Willem set the cup on the table at the same moment Abigail put hers down. Their knuckles brushed together. He felt a ribbon of fire at the small contact. They looked up into each other's eyes and froze in place.

"Abigail..." Willem reached up and cupped her cheeks. They were smooth as polished marble and cool beneath his fingers. He inhaled, and her essence lingered on the tip of his tongue.

He had to taste her. He could deny himself no longer. He bent his head toward her and captured her mouth gently, tentatively.

She felt a shudder run through his fingertips cupped around her cheeks. His kiss was gentle, reverent and tinged with awe. She felt special in his grasp. Abigail leaned into him and returned the light pressure. She lost herself in the earthy scent of fresh air, wool and man. It made her part her lips in wonder.

Willem felt her mouth open, and he fought to control the hot fire inside him. Without conscious thought he slid his tongue inside her mouth. She gasped, and a trembling rippled through her. He wanted her so badly his body throbbed with a dull ache.

Abigail's thoughts swirled and shimmered. Willem was holding her lightly within his wide rough palms. She felt a flutter in her belly the like of which she hadn't known before, and misgiving shot through her. She jerked away in fear.

"Willem—I—we—" she stammered, and touched her lips. They were soft and glistened with his kisses. He looked into her eyes and saw them wide and unfocused with latent passion. It was all he needed to see.

"I forgot myself." Willem pushed himself up and stood rigid beside the couch. A war was being fought inside him. The wild, lusty man who had lived celibate for so long wanted to toss up her skirts and bury himself inside her. The man inside him who cared for her wanted to tease and taunt and bring her to his bed, begging for completeness.

That man easily won out over the lust.

"I'll see you at sunrise," he said softly, then bent over and deposited a chaste kiss on her forehead. He heard a moan escape her throat. "Sleep well, Abigail."

The look on her face and the confusion in her eyes when he raised his head made him want to shout for joy. He had hope now, real hope of winning her. He turned and walked up the stairs.

"Good night." Her voice drifted to him when he reached the second-floor landing. He could swear it was huskier than usual.

He paused on the stairs. "Do you think you might start calling me Will?"

"Perhaps someday, Willem." The sound of his given name on her lips filled him with happiness and a bright flame of hope.

Chapter Twenty-Two

Matthew looked as if he was abandoning his best friend. The boy's solemn expression tugged at Willem's heart.

"Lars will take good care of Brighty while you're gone." He gently rested his palm on the boy's shoulder and felt a catch in his chest when Matthew turned misty blue eyes up at him.

"I know. I just hope she isn't too lonesome without me." Matthew dragged his sleeve under his nose and attempted a smile that ripped Will's heart apart. God, how he loved this child.

"Of course she will miss you, just like you're going to miss her, but Lars will take good care of her. And we're not going to be gone very long, I promise." Willem nearly crushed the boy to his chest when a faint smile trembled at the corners of Matthew's young mouth.

"Where is your mama?" Willem asked.

"She's in the kitchen putting some food up for Lars." Matthew rolled his eyes expressively.

"I see." Willem grinned. "Why don't you spend a few minutes with your dog, and I'll go fetch her."

Willem turned and stepped inside the house. The sound of feminine humming and the smell of freshly ground coffee beans engulfed him. This house had more warmth and love in it than he had ever known existed. He felt his chest tighten when he thought about Abigail being his wife.

His wife. Not the widow Cooprel, not the lady who ran the boardinghouse, not Matthew's mother. His wife.

Abigail would be his soon. The impact of that made him grab the registration desk to support his liquefied knees. When he recovered his strength he stepped inside the warm kitchen.

The breath caught in his throat when he saw Abigail. She had her hair pinned up beneath a wide-brimmed hat. Only one wisp had managed to escape from under the soft brown velvet ribbons. A short, curved, blue feather swayed above the brim.

Abigail stopped humming and turned. Her eyes locked onto Willem's face. He felt the temperature in the room rise ten degrees and saw her shoulders tense. It had the usual conflicting impact on him. She made him want to sweep her up in his arms and cover her face with kisses until she no longer stared at him like a wary, trapped creature, and it cut him to the quick to know she feared him still.

"I—Matthew said you were in here," he stammered.

She was beautiful. He knew right then and there he should pay a visit to the fellow in Silverton who made spectacles. Obviously he needed a pair more than Paxton Kane. Any fool who ever thought this woman plain had to be half blind or addlebrained.

"Are you ready, Abigail?"

"Yes. I was just making sure Lars would have plenty to eat before we go." Abigail's hand trembled slightly when she picked up a fringed reticule and slipped the cord over her wrist. She was wearing a bright blue, black and yellow plaid frock with a white shirtfront. Her full skirt was brown velvet, the same color as the inside of her hat. Willem was certain she had never looked prettier, or more reluctant.

"Matthew is saying goodbye to his dog." Willem couldn't peel his eyes off her. A self-conscious smile tugged at the corners of her mouth and he knew he was staring but was powerless to stop. "Abigail, I've never seen you look—you're pretty."

He felt the fool for stammering like a schoolboy, but a bright wash of color crept up her cheeks in response to his compliment. He forgot his own embarrassment when he realized she was pleased.

"Thank you. I'm going to run up and say goodbye to Lars." She slipped by Willem and he followed her into the parlor. He groaned inwardly at his body's immediate reaction to the sight of her ankle when she raised her skirt to take the first step. He watched the attractive sway of her hips while she climbed the staircase. When she disappeared from his sight he felt the life and the warmth leave the room. Willem shook his head and marveled at how much he coveted Abigail Cooprel.

Everywhere Abigail looked from the narrow window of the stagecoach she found crimson and gold blanketing the mountains. The crisp autumn air filled her lungs and tugged at her heart. In years past, this time of year signaled the departure of the men from her home. This year it heralded the beginning of a new way of life and the continuing distraction of Will Tremain. She trembled inwardly thinking about it.

"Are you cold?" Willem leaned across the stage and peered into her face. His warm breath smelled of mint leaves and *him*. Abigail cringed inwardly at her inability to ignore him.

"No, why do you ask?" She raised the defensive shield of ice around her heart and prayed it would be enough to keep Willem out.

"You looked like you were shivering a moment ago," Willem said as he raised one eyebrow and looked at her speculatively. She wondered if he knew how much turmoil was going on inside her.

The sensible part of her nature warned her to keep her guard up. The woman inside her cried out for something more. She wasn't even sure what that elusive thing was any-more—it had been such a long time since she'd allowed herself to really care about anyone except Matthew. Hot and cold currents of emotion had left her confused and irrita-ble. She dreaded the coach arriving in Silverton and sizzled with anticipation all at once. Abigail could never remem-ber behaving in this manner before.

She was scared to death.

Being with Will reminded her of standing on the pond in winter. Sometimes she went out too early, before the water had frozen all the way through. The ice groaned and cracked under her feet. On those occasions she knew she couldn't stand still, that she had to return to shore, but with each cracking step she feared she would plunge into the frigid water. She felt like that now; she knew this situation could not remain stagnant but she was fearful of what lay ahead of her.

"Where will we stay in Silverton?" Matthew's voice ripped into the shroud of doubt and bewilderment sur-rounding her.

"I've heard the Grand Hotel is the best," Willem said with a grin.

"The Grand?" Abigail gulped down her surprise.

"Was there somewhere else you'd like better?" Willem leaned back in the swaying coach and fastened his blue eyes on her face. She felt the heat of his scrutiny begin to melt her pitiful facade of indifference. It was frightening the way he could control her with a single, candid look.

"N-no." Abigail forced her heart to stop fluttering. "No. I just never . . . that is, I didn't . . ." She let her words awkwardly trail off.

"We'll have separate rooms. It will all be very proper." Willem flicked a glance over Matthew's face. "How would you like a room all to yourself, Matt?"

"My own room?" Matthew chirped with a beaming smile.

Abigail felt the color drain from her face and her eyes widened. "That would be too dear. I'm sure he can share a room with me."

"Listen, Abigail, I've supported the Pinkertons for the last year. What I earn will gladly be spent on Matthew—and you. I'll not have you or the boy think I'm miserly." Willem's face had gone stern and his eyes flared with blue fire.

It startled Abigail the way he could change like a chameleon, one moment smiling and jovial, the next firm and unyielding. His dark brows knit together over his blazing eyes. She thought he looked for all the world like a thundercloud building over the mountain.

It was sobering. She reminded herself of his reputation and nickname. When he was like this she found herself believing he was indeed the Black Irish in every respect, and that every evil deed whispered about him was true.

"Whatever arrangements you make will be fine." She compressed her lips together and leaned back in the coach. Learning to submit to Willem's husbandly control was going to be a trial, she decided with a heavy sigh.

Willem watched Abigail withdraw from him by slow degrees. Her eyes fastened on some faraway point outside the coach and her lips pulled into a tight line.

She was angry again. He leaned back against the leather seat and folded his arms across his chest. Getting to know what set her off was going to be a full-time job, he mused.

He had thought the idea of staying in the finest hotel and allowing Matthew the privilege of having his own room would appeal to her. Evidently, he was wrong. He sighed and found himself oddly saddened by her reaction. He had hoped she would relax and enjoy the trip, but if Abigail was going to balk at his every attempt at kindness, this was going to be an ordeal for them all.

Willem closed his eyes and pretended to sleep while he mulled the situation over. He heard her soft release of breath and felt his skin prickle all over. He shifted in the seat and stretched out his legs a bit. It was pure torture, sitting in the cramped space of the coach so near Abigail. Each time they hit a bump in the steep hairpin road, she shifted in the seat and sent a hot ribbon of desire snaking toward him across the narrow coach.

He lifted his lids a fraction and looked at her. The bonnet brim obscured part of her face but he could clearly see her soft mouth and one dark-fringed eye.

Willem held his position and watched her. Abigail's lashes flicked upward and he saw a tiny smile tug at the corners of her mouth. It was thrilling in an odd sort of way—to be watching her while she was unaware. A strand of hair was fluttering against her cheek and she swiped at it impatiently. He longed to reach out and take the bonnet off her head and kiss her.

The coach lurched and hit a bump. Matthew giggled, and Abigail was tossed toward Willem's outstretched legs.

"Oh, my!" She squeaked, and fought to regain her balance.

He locked his hands on her shoulders and they held there, the two of them, suspended in time by a rope of desire and caution.

He found himself not more than an inch from her face. He could smell the mixture of rosewater and clean starched cotton. It sent a river of desire through his body. If he crushed her lips beneath his would she struggle or would she respond? He longed to find out. "Are you all right?"

"I think so." Her eyes were wide and luminous. The tiny, dust-laden shaft of light gilded her lashes and the tip of her nose.

He wanted her. God, how he wanted her.

"Good." He felt his lips curve into a tiny smile. Her eyes flicked from his hair to his chin, then to his mouth, where they paused for a moment. He felt—knew—she was wondering what his kiss would feel like.

"Willem, I..."

He leaned closer and grazed her mouth with his own. It was tender and wild, and a hundred tiny sticks of dynamite exploded inside his chest. They touched for no more than one pulse beat of time, but Willem felt an iron bond forge around his heart.

He not only wanted her, he was falling in love with her. The knowledge tugged at him like a current in a rain-swollen river.

"Silverton—next stop." The stage driver's voice intruded before Willem could do any more than blink at his discovery.

He pushed her gently back into the seat and forced his hands to the tops of his thighs. He made himself a promise to continue this journey of discovery with Abigail—soon.

Willem carried the bags up the stairs to the third floor of the Grand Hotel. Matthew scampered a few feet ahead of Abigail, chattering excitedly with each new treasure he found. Willem found it difficult to listen because his attention was focused on Abigail's alluring form. Each step she took sent a shaft of lust pulsing through him.

"Here it is," Abigail said. She stopped abruptly and Willem blinked in surprise. He hadn't even realized she'd turned down a branching corridor and located her room. He cleared his throat and tried to reclaim his wandering senses.

She fumbled with the key on the door and it finally opened with a jerk that sent her lurching inside the room. Her bonnet went cockeyed on her head and the one stubborn strand of hair tumbled down her shoulder.

Willem smiled inwardly. She was so cool and proper on the outside, but more and more he glimpsed a fiery inner person. He had a burning curiosity to know Abigail's most private thoughts, and he found himself chafing at having to wait several more weeks for the privilege.

"You can set the bags down now." Her voice brought his fantasy up short. He realized with no small amount of consternation that he'd been standing in the doorway staring at her like a dolt, with a bag in each hand.

Matthew had settled himself on the window ledge and was peering through the glass at the busy street below.

"Right." Will's voice was gruff with lust.

"Matthew, let's see your room, shall we?" Abigail walked to a closed door and threw the bolt back. Matthew darted toward it and squealed in delight when Abigail swung it open. The sound of the boy's happiness sent a warm feeling flooding through Willem. He watched them, Abigail and Matthew beyond her in the adjoining room, and felt a completeness he had not known could exist within himself.

He felt good. Not quite content, but after all this time of living in numbed agony he felt that true happiness might be within his grasp. He no longer had the lonely sensation that he was watching Matthew and Abigail through a pane of glass. Now when Will looked at Abigail and Matthew, he felt they were within his reach—and coming closer to him all the time.

"I've made arrangements for dinner in the hotel dining room," he said softly.

Abigail's head came around and he saw her look of surprise. She narrowed her eyes, and he knew the wall was coming up. He decided not to allow her to erect the barrier, not this time.

Willem stepped over the bags on the floor and strode forward. He closed the distance between them in three long strides. When he reached out and took her by the shoulders she responded with a short gasp. It fueled his passion, that soft sound.

"Abigail..." He bent his head and kissed her. Not like the first time. This kiss was hard and full of need. He felt her lips part and he took the opportunity to plunge his tongue deep inside her soft mouth. She quaked within his grasp, but she didn't stiffen. He felt her body go warm and she became pliant in his hands. A burst of pure delight shot through him. She didn't return the kiss, as he'd imagined in his mind, but she accepted what he offered. Her response was tentative and cautious, but there was an underlying curiosity in her touch that sent hope rippling over him in a great hot cascade.

When he raised his head she still had her eyes closed. He grinned at the light flush on her cheeks. Her lids fluttered open and she blinked like a woman waking from sleep. Her mouth was soft and dewy from his kiss.

"I'll pick you and Matthew up at six." He deposited a quick peck to her forehead, forced his fingers to release her and turned on his heel.

A thousand pinpoints of electricity seared his flesh when she sighed softly behind him. He closed the door to her room and stood in the hallway grinning. *This will be no marriage in name only, Abigail—not if I have anything to say about it.*

Willem turned and walked down the hall to his own room with the scent of Abigail still lingering in his nostrils and the taste of her on his lips. He longed to hold her and hear her call him Will. He wanted to win her love and ignite her passions. It was all he could do to keep himself in tight control while he anticipated the evening ahead.

Chapter Twenty-Three

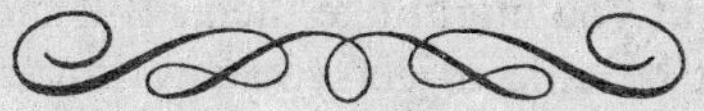

Abigail allowed her eyes to drift over the dining room. The many patrons were aglow in lantern light from the huge candelabra hanging overhead on a heavy chain attached to the pressed tin ceiling. She admired the heavy carving in the wooden bar and the enormous mirror behind it.

Several rough miners entered the basement with a burst of rowdy noise. A large portion of Silverton was squeezed into the stone building this evening. The hotel occupied the third floor, food and drink was served in the basement and the county leased seven rooms on the second floor for offices and the court. The Grand Hotel appeared to be the mecca of life in the bustling mining town.

"Did you miss us?" Matthew's voice asked behind Abigail. She turned and looked at him. He was grinning from ear to ear.

"Of course I missed you. Where did you two go?" Abigail allowed herself a quick glance at Willem. His hair was wet and slicked back and he wore a smile almost as wide as Matthew's.

"We had to get something," Matthew said, then nudged Will in the thigh with his elbow. "Didn't we?"

"Sure did." Willem brought his arm from behind his back and laid a large bouquet of flowers on the table in front of Abigail.

"For me?" She shifted awkwardly in her chair, aware that people were watching them. Some of the women wore envious smiles and Abigail found her cheeks flushing with heat.

"Will thought you might like them. It'll snow soon and then we won't be able to get you any flowers until next spring," Matthew explained solemnly. "'Sides, these are nicer than the ones I picked."

"Oh, darling, they were beautiful." Abigail lifted the paper-wrapped stems and held the blooms to her nose. The delicate fragrance engulfed her. She glanced up at Willem. "And so are these. Thank you—both."

Willem's gaze locked on her face, and a feeling of hot anticipation slammed through her. His eyes—those magnetic orbs—held her transfixed. She saw something within them, something tender and yearning she had not seen before, and it shook her. She tried to rip her glance away but found her resolve weakening with each thud of her heart. He was not a man she could trust, for he had come into her life and upset everything. He was a threat to all she held dear. She told herself this while the room seemed to shrink around them until there was only the two of them locked in each other's gaze.

"Would you like menus, sir?" A smooth male voice ripped her from the web Will had spun around them.

He looked up at the waiter and one side of his mouth twitched convulsively. "Yes, that would be fine."

Abigail felt like a sleepwalker. She watched half-dazed while Matthew scampered around the table and Will scooted the boy's chair in. She felt heat rise in her cheeks. She could not take her eyes off the dark-haired man who sat down opposite her. This kind, considerate, quiet man with undisguised need shining in his eyes.

"Are you hungry, Abigail?"

"Yes, I am," she managed to say without her voice breaking. It was growing hot in the previously cool basement dining room. She wished she had not worn the long-sleeved blue serge. She tugged at the neck and squirmed.

"You look lovely tonight." Will reached out and lightly touched the back of her hand where it still rested on the bouquet. A trail of fire ignited under his fingertips. She felt surprised when she saw that her hand was not on fire where Will's long, work-roughened fingers caressed her.

"Thank you. You look fine, too." She stumbled over the words. Abigail glanced at Matthew and found him smiling in genuine happiness. It sent a ribbon of bittersweet emotion sailing into her heart. He truly was happy about her upcoming marriage to Willem. She was glad, but a tiny part of her still cringed at the thought of sharing him—even with his real father.

"Are you ready to order?" The waiter reappeared and Abigail realized she had no idea how long she had been staring at Matthew. Time had taken on a languid quality, which made it difficult for her to discern the measure of its passing.

"Are we?" Willem captured her attention with an inquiring look.

"You order for me. Whatever you decide will be fine."

Willem grinned and seemed inordinately pleased by her suggestion. It occurred to Abigail that he might have misinterpreted her words and she regretted saying them, but it was too late. He was already telling the waiter to bring three plates of roast beef.

She frowned. It would not be good to let him think he could make all her decisions. She resolved not to be so agreeable.

"Willem and I have a surprise for you tomorrow, Mama," Matthew said, eager as a pup.

She smiled and smoothed down one stubborn curl above his eye. "Really? What?"

"Oh, I can't tell. It's real nice, though." Matthew nodded at Willem, and Abigail felt a tendril of alarm snake up her back. The last time they had conspired together she had been trapped into a picnic. She pondered Matthew's words and tried to avoid Will's probing gaze. He seemed to be searching her face for something. A knot was growing in the pit of her stomach with each beseeching glance he gave her.

"I saw a prospector I knew while Matthew and I were getting the flowers," Willem said conversationally.

"Really?" Abigail refused to look up.

"Yes. He said the first storm hit in the high country last night."

Abigail's head came up with a snap. "How soon do you think it will be here?" If they got caught on this side of the pass when the snow fell, getting home could be a risky affair. Chains and anchors had to be used to keep the wagons and coaches from sliding off into the canyons. Men died every year trying to navigate the snow-covered mountain passes with supplies.

"Another couple of days." Willem was still studying her face intently. She had the strangest notion that he wanted to tell her something but was hesitating.

"Does this mean we'll need to cut our trip short?" Abigail didn't know if she was happy or sad about the prospect. Being in Silverton with Will was disconcerting, but when she returned home he would be there—in her house. The thought sent a shiver coursing through her.

"Cold?" He seemed instantly aware of her every action. It was a sobering thought.

"No, I was just thinking," she confessed. The waiter appeared with a large flat tray, which he set on a nearby table. He placed oval platters heaped with savory beef, fat rolls and garden vegetables in front of Abigail before he moved to Matthew and Will.

"This smells good." Matthew leaned over and inhaled deeply.

"I'm sure it's not as good as your mama's cooking." Willem winked at Abigail. She felt pleasure at his compliment. Abigail told herself it was foolish vanity on her part, but she liked knowing that Willem appreciated her talents.

"Thank you," she said softly.

He picked up his fork and smiled at her. The lump in the pit of her stomach got larger while she watched him. He was a handsome devil, and if she wasn't careful he was going to charm his way into her heart. She ducked her head and vowed not to let him do that. She would marry him when they returned to Guston but she promised to take care with her heart. Willem was more man than she had ever known—a thought that brought anticipation thudding through her breast.

Abigail felt the distinct crisp flavor of fall when she raised the window and looked down at the street below. She had dressed early this morning, wanting to get Matthew to the haberdashery on the main floor and find him a proper suit.

A knock on the door drew her attention and she frowned, wondering who would be calling this early. Abigail opened the door and found herself staring at Matthew and Willem. They were both dressed to the teeth and grinning like a couple of foxes in a henhouse.

"Morning," she said tightly.

"Get ready, Mama," Matthew chirped happily.

"Ready? For what, dear?" She felt foolish, standing in the doorway having a conversation with her own son.

"Willem and I have a surprise. Remember?" Matthew slipped by her and ran to the window.

Abigail looked up at Willem and frowned. It irritated her that he had gotten Matthew up without her knowledge.

"What is going on?" She fixed her gaze on his face. True alarm sizzled through her.

"Matthew and I did one or two other things yesterday evening before we got the flowers," Willem said smoothly.

"Oh? And what exactly have you two done this time?" Abigail glanced at the bouquet in the glass vase and found herself remembering the picnic in Guston.

Willem grinned tightly and raised his eyebrows. "I have spoken to the judge.... The arrangements have all been made."

"Arrangements?" Abigail saw a flicker of something in Will's eyes that sent her pulse racing.

"Yes. They are waiting for us now." Willem took a step toward her.

"Who is waiting for us?" Abigail was becoming exasperated with all this mysterious sidestepping.

"The judge, Mama." Matthew scampered up behind her and grabbed her hand. He jerked her toward the door, toward Willem.

"Matthew, what on earth are you doing?" Abigail tried not to grin at his mischievous expression.

"Taking you to the judge." Matthew laughed.

"Abigail, I've made arrangements for us to be married here—in Silverton." Willem stood squarely in the doorway.

"What?" She looked up at him in alarm while Matthew tugged her even nearer to Willem. "When?"

"Abigail, I want us to be married here in Silverton, not in Guston."

"I couldn't—I mean—there are things to do," she stammered, and finally halted Matthew's progress.

"Matthew and I have done everything." Willem fixed a hard stare on her face. "You haven't changed your mind...about our *arrangement?*" Willem's flinty voice sent a chill through Abigail. She swallowed a hard lump in her throat. He flicked a glance from her to Matthew and back again. If she had forgotten how high the stakes were in this game, Will's cold glance certainly reminded her. This had been her idea, her suggestion, and now she would have to go through with it—or lose Matthew.

"No, of course not," she snapped.

"Then there is no reason to wait, is there?" Willem's voice was low and stony.

"I—I suppose not." The cool wash of reality engulfed her. If she was going to secure Matthew's presence in her life, then she would have to go through with the illusion of marriage. "I thought you wanted a church wedding for appearances." She tried to pluck up her courage.

"Why wait? The weather may prevent us from getting back like we planned. Wouldn't it be better to be married quietly here and avoid any rumor about our traveling together?"

"I suppose. All right, Willem. I'm ready. Let's go get married."

"I do." Abigail felt her knees turn to water. Willem's fingers tightened on her left hand while he slid the gold band over her knuckle. She turned instinctively toward him. He was leaning toward her with an odd expression in his eyes.

"That does it, young fella. You're now man and wife." The portly judge winked. "You can kiss your bride."

She told herself she would not respond to his touch. This was a business arrangement, a plan she and Lars had concocted to secure her right to Matthew, and nothing more. She told herself a kiss—the kiss of her new *husband*—would mean nothing to her.

She told herself the lie, but she knew it for the falsehood it was the minute his hand touched her face. Willem tilted her chin up and bent forward. His mouth was warm and tender. The sensation was poignant and powerful and totally unexpected. It left Abigail feeling vulnerable and eager and confused. He tightened one arm around the middle of her back and pressed her against the entire length of his hard body. Liquid fire burned along her breasts and thighs. It was wondrous, and it was frightening.

Will released her and stood back, staring down at her as if she were something precious to him, as if she really mattered and the vows they had taken were real and not a hollow sham. Willem looked awkward and unsure of himself for the first time since this morning began.

Abigail was not prepared for that, it caught her unaware and melted away another chunk of her frigid resolve.

"Mrs. Tremain, shall we go celebrate?" Willem's voice skimmed over her skin like velvet.

Matthew jumped up and down with glee. He clapped his hands together and hung on to Willem's leg. "Yes! We're married now. Let's have a party."

"Celebrate?" Abigail's head seemed full of cotton batting. So much had happened in such a short time, her mind was still spinning. She toyed with the slender gold band with the delicate braided design on her ring finger. It felt foreign. She felt foreign to herself now that she was Abigail Tremain and not Abigail Cooprel. The lingering taste of

Will's mouth also made her skin feel as if it was shrinking around her bones.

"Mmm. I've arranged a wedding breakfast in the dining room."

Abigail found herself smiling at this unexpected act of kindness. Maybe it wouldn't be so bad being married to Will Tremain. She could adjust. The boy laughed and launched himself at Willem. He swooped Matthew up and tickled him thoroughly.

Abigail frowned. If Will's moods could be gauged by the time they had spent together in Silverton, he would not be a difficult spouse. Perhaps it would all work out in the end.

"Yes. Let's all three go and have our celebration." Abigail tried to join in the ebullient mood. Matthew slipped his hand inside her fingers and she felt Willem gently wrap his arm around the small of her back. She breathed deeply and tried to quell the rapid beating of her heart. She assured herself it was only the excitement of the moment and not some crazy attraction for Will Tremain that made her feel light-headed and breathless.

The trio spent the day strolling arm in arm around Silverton. Will took great pleasure in showing Matthew the section of toll road he had helped Otto build. The boy was so exhausted he was happy for dinner and an early bedtime. Abigail had objected to leaving him upstairs, so Willem had hired the third-floor maid. The girl had agreed to come and get them if Matthew should stir or need anything.

Abigail laughed and bit into the sweet Willem held in front of her lips. The tiny voice in her head told her she was acting like a giddy schoolgirl, allowing her new husband to feed her in a manner that lovers shared, but she ignored it. Willem leaned across the table and popped another bite into her mouth. His deep, throaty chuckle sent her nerves prickling. He had been feeding her rum-soaked cake for the past half hour.

"How do you judge your first day as my wife?" Willem's words were light but his eyes burned with an intensity that let Abigail know he was more than marginally interested in her answer. Abigail stared at him while she puzzled over why he should care—after all, this was a marriage of convenience.

The wayward lock of ebony hair fell over one thick brow and made him look boyish. She momentarily forgot herself and allowed her hand to graze across his forehead while she pushed the strand back in place. It was a gesture that sent a shaft of surprise and unanticipated delight rushing through her.

"Well?" He caught her fingers in his wide, rough hand and held them close to his mouth. His warm breath fanned out over her palm. It sent a thousand goose bumps up her shoulder and down her chest toward her tingling breasts.

"I must confess...today has been wonderful. More than I expected." Once the words were said she almost felt relief at speaking the truth. She expected him to glower at her honesty, but he did not. His shy pleased smile tugged on her heartstrings.

He cared what she thought, or so it seemed. She heard the tiny voice of reason tell her to be cautious. Abigail kept telling herself this was not a true marriage. She would do well not to change her opinion of Willem Tremain. He had become her husband in name, but that did not erase the threat he posed to her happiness. She held on to the thought until Willem popped another piece of rum cake into her mouth. Then she forgot everything except the smell of him and the warm sensation skipping through her middle.

Abigail perceived the heady bouquet of liquor coursing through her mouth and downward. Her limbs began to relax while the alcohol mingled with her heated blood. A part of her heart—the cool, reserved part she kept concealed from Will Tremain—began to thaw. His face and manner seemed to soften with each passing moment and along with it her resolve weakened. Willem beckoned to her with his charm and his man's body.

He pulled his chair around to the other side of the table to be closer to Abigail. She was enchanting tonight. There was a timid curiosity about her that sent his libido rising. He couldn't get enough of her. He watched her every move, listened to her every word. Her hair was gossamer in the soft glow of candlelight, her form inviting, and he was drowning in a sea of sensuality.

The hotel staff had outdone themselves with the delicacies for dinner, and the dessert he now fed her had been designed to intoxicate and liberate—a delightful combination for newlyweds. Willem splashed some more claret into Abigail's glass and tipped it toward her lips. He wondered if she had any inkling what possessive feelings had shot through him when he'd slipped the newly purchased wedding ring on her finger.

She turned to him, wide-eyed and dewy looking, and he felt passion slam through his belly. She was a seductress, an enchantress, his *wife.*

The thought made him tingle from scalp to toe. He was married to Abigail Cooprel—

No. Abigail Tremain. He could no longer think of her as Abigail Cooprel. It gave him a burst of satisfaction so strong it rivaled the feeling of finding his son.

He had it all. Child, wife and a future after so many bleak years of having nothing. Happiness was so close. All he had to do was find a way to make Abigail fall in love with him.

"I want to propose a toast, Abigail." Willem raised his glass and watched her face light with a feminine smile. It was temptation itself to sit so near he could inhale her scent with each breath. It sent his pulse racing and his thoughts skipping along with desire. For six years Willem had been celibate. Now the prospect of lying with his wife sent him into delicious flights of fancy.

"I propose we try to make each other as happy as we are now, tonight, until the day after forever," Willem said without smiling.

Abigail felt a hot lump form in her throat. She would never have imagined Willem had a poet's soul underneath that brawny body. She blinked to keep the hot burn of tears from cascading down her cheek. It was a lovely toast—even if it was a game of pretend. She wanted to pretend right along with him. What would it hurt to act as if this had all been real? What could it matter if just this one evening they acted as if it had all been for love and not just for one small boy?

He tilted his glass toward hers and they met in a sharp crystal clink. She nodded her agreement. If Willem wanted to pretend this was a real marriage, just for tonight, then she would let him.

"Yes, Willem. Until the day after forever." A part of her wished for a fleeting foolish instant that this was not pretend and that she was truly Willem's bride in every respect.

She brought the wineglass to her lips. The liquid was robust and warm and it sent a frisson of slow, drowsy heat meandering through her mouth and middle toward her languorous limbs. She breathed deeply and found her tongue tingling with the strong, lingering taste of Will's earlier kiss. Her belly coiled with a strange tension each time she looked at him and remembered her husband's ardent kiss.

Her husband.

Tonight she would lie with him. Her first time in over six years. The prospect filled her with anticipation, self-doubt and sadness. Sadness that his toast and their marriage was only a sham. She found herself wanting to believe this magical night could last forever.

As ridiculous as it was, she allowed him to open a locked door to her heart and step inside. A part of her still feared that he would take Matthew from her, but the woman prayed he might not. She held the glass to her lips and drained the liquid in one shaky gulp.

Willem unlocked his room and opened the door. The matching kerosene lamps on the marble-topped chest cast a romantic glow over the rose-hued velvet folded at the foot of the turned-down bed.

"Where are we?" Abigail was tipsy and giggly and utterly delightful.

"In my room—our room." Will shut the door while keeping a protective arm looped around her waist.

"Oh." Her lips formed a little circle. She leaned against him and giggled. He found the weight to be a pleasurable burden, one that fanned the smoldering fires of latent passion inside him. He wanted to kiss her but she swooned and he wasn't able to catch his balance and capture her lips at the same time.

"Let's get you out of these clothes and into bed, Abigail." Erotic images sizzled through his stimulated mind. She giggled when he swept her up in his arms. She felt feather light and softly padded.

He crossed the room in two long strides. Abigail blinked at him and sighed heavily when he laid her on the big bed. She was all doe-eyed, sweet temptation. It took every ounce of control he possessed to slowly undo the long row of tiny buttons down her bodice. He wanted to bury his face in her hair and rip the dress from her inviting body.

"Are you…undressing me, Willem?" She blinked at him and he paused to watch her face pucker in pretty confusion.

"Yes, I am." He heard the deep husky sound of his escalating desire. It made him realize again how much he cared, that he was truly falling in love with Abigail.

"Oh." Again her dewy mouth made a small O. "I just wondered."

Will undid the last button, and the bodice of her dress opened. He closed his eyes momentarily when she rose to lift her arms. He slipped the fabric down over her shoulders to her waist. It bunched up above the seductive flare of her hips.

Abigail looked up at him and he felt a thousand charges explode inside his belly. Her hair had tumbled free and it lay like a cloud on her creamy shoulders. The tight-laced corset pinched her breasts into delectable mounds that he longed to kiss and lave with his tongue.

"Willem?"

"Yes, Abigail?" He stood there contemplating her perfection, trying not to lose control. He didn't want to frighten his beautiful new bride with his ardor. He forced himself to slowly, deliberately remove his own clothes while he fought for control.

"I hope you won't be disappointed in me." Her voice cracked a little and she ducked her head shyly.

It was his undoing.

He came to her then, all hot fire in his blood and longing need in his soul. He collapsed with a harsh moan on the bed beside her and busied himself freeing her body from the corset for his starving eyes to feast upon.

Willem ran his hands over her smooth skin and caught his breath. She was even more lovely than he had contemplated. Her limbs were long and slender. She had supple muscles that shivered and moved beneath his questing palms.

In his rush he had not extinguished the lamps. They allowed him to devour her with his eyes while he experienced the feel and smell and taste of her.

"God, Abigail, you are lovely."

"And you, Willem, your body is pleasing." She sighed.

He tilted his head and realized she had no shyness about looking at him—all of him. It gave him a heady thrill to see her glance rake over his chest, belly and lower. Her eyes paused at his groin and he felt his erect shaft jerk spasmodically in response to her approving stare.

Being with her and having Abigail find him satisfactory was like ascending to heaven. He gently pushed her shoulders back on the bed and claimed her mouth with his own. He straddled her slender waist with his naked thighs and cupped her jaws in his hands. She was warm and sensual and he reveled in her openness. He lowered his head and kissed her. It was nearly as explosive as a stick of dynamite being ignited.

Abigail returned his kiss and wrapped her arms around his neck. She felt her body respond to him by lightning-fast degrees. It was shocking after so many years, but the combination of wine and rum cake and her own primitive attraction to Willem made it easy for her to forget any inhibitions. She stroked and caressed his smooth, hard muscles with her hands. She allowed her body to open to him, to enjoy the sensations swirling through her. Abigail gave of her body freely, but the deepest part of her heart remained untouched.

Willem laved his tongue over her breast and she moaned. He kneaded her mound with strong, sure fingers and she sighed—but at no time did Abigail open the final closed door to her heart and allow him inside.

Will yearned to give her pleasure, hungered to show her how much he cared for her.

"Tell me what makes you feel good," Will whispered while Abigail groaned and dug her nails into the flesh on his shoulders. He pulled her atop him, then drove himself deep inside her. She fit over him like a hand in a glove. Abigail started to moan and buck, and Will knew she was reaching the shattering point of her pleasure. A feeling bloomed, grew, and exploded in his heart. He loved her so much.

Long silken strands of her hair hit him in the face when she tossed her head from side to side. Then she stiffened and collapsed toward him. He captured her mouth an instant before every muscle and sinew in his body tightened and then sprang free in a great spinning arc of pure pleasure. The blood rushed from his head, and then he was floating above his body.

"Abigail, dear sweet Abigail," he whispered.

It was an experience that was more intense and all the sweeter for having been denied him for so many long, lonely years. Willem looked at Abigail and could not remember ever loving another woman before her. It was a revelation that pierced his heart.

"Lordy, Abigail, that was something."

She whimpered and squeezed her thighs against his hips. He felt another spasm tighten her hot flesh around his staff. He realized with a large dose of male pride that he had pleasured his new wife. It gave him a rush of satisfaction. He knew if he held a mirror up to his face right now, he would find a silly smile looking back at him.

Abigail regained her senses slowly. What she had experienced with Willem took her breath away and filled her with a confused emotion that was bittersweet. She had not planned to let herself get so swept up by emotion. Of course, she had expected their coupling to be *nice,* but she had not anticipated such a shattering experience. She would like to have believed it was the wine and rum cake, but she knew it wasn't. Ever since Will had marched into the boardinghouse she had secretly been wishing for this, and now it had come to pass.

Even while the rippling delight coursed through her body a tiny voice in her head told her she should not be altogether pleased about it. The man was too seductive, too experienced. She knew she would fear him even more now that she had seen how he could level her defenses. He was her husband, but she dared not let herself care for him—not like this. If she gave all of herself to him, and he did take Matthew from her, she would be devastated doubly—losing her son and her heart.

She pulled the sheet up to her chin. She must guard against it and not allow him to vanquish her feelings, or else the brooding Black Irish would consume her utterly. She must not succumb to this physical temptation again or he would possess her very soul.

Loud laughter drew her attention to the group of men drinking at the bar. They were dressed in the usual manner of Colorado miners with beards, heavy shirts and dust-covered trousers.

The dining room was an odd assortment of fashion. Ladies in silks and satins shared space with the roughest of the boomtown's men. Abigail shifted in her seat and wondered what was keeping Will and Matthew. Upon arriving in the cool basement-dining room she realized she'd forgotten her wrap. They both insisted on retrieving it for her. She sighed at the thought of how they had looked together—two gallant knights on an errand of chivalry.

"I tell you it *was* the Black Irish." A harsh, gruff voice drew Abigail's attention to a group of men drinking at the bar.

"Curly heard it from Snap," another heavily accented voice delcared. "The murderous devil was buying a tombstone. Snap saw it with his own eyes."

Abigail sat a little straighter and ran a finger over the gilt rim of her crystal water glass while she strained to catch every word. Her conscience cringed at eavesdropping, but hearing Willem's nickname was a bait she could not resist.

"So, little Moira killed herself, huh?"

Abigail stiffened and a cool blanket of dread settled over her shoulders. She turned the braided gold band around and around on her finger.

"Who knows? She's dead as stone now, and however she died, we all know who was the cause," the first man said before he sloshed back a swig of pale amber beer from a long-necked bottle.

"I was there, you know—in Leadville—when it happened," the miner with the accent added. Several men murmured and nodded.

"Are the stories true?" a grizzled, wiry, gnomelike creature asked. Abigail found herself glancing at the stairwell, hoping Will would not choose this precise moment to return. She wanted to hear what the men had to say about him.

The small man shrugged. "As far as I know. Only one man knows what really happened down there—Sennen Mulgrew—and he's vanished like woodsmoke."

"No. I'm not talking about the cave-in. I mean the story about how he treated his wife. You know, what he *did* to her after they brought him out," the man clarified.

"What do you think? Why would any woman leave her man, especially when she has a belly full of his brat, unless he'd done something mighty bad? You heard how he was when they brought him and Sennen up from that hole."

All the shaggy heads nodded in agreement. Abigail felt her blood congeal in her veins. Up until now she had only wondered in passing about Moira's actions. Now, with the reminder of the Black Irish and all the rumors surrounding that name, Abigail began to wonder why Willem's first wife had risked her child's safety.

She frowned. What *had* Willem done to cause his wife to end up dying in a deserted church all alone?

"Mama." Matthew's voice ripped into her reverie. She turned and saw him and Willem standing side by side, and a cold shaft of fear stabbed her heart. Willem was glaring at the group of men with a look so dire it sent a shiver through her. It was obvious he had overheard at least some of the conversation.

"Good...you brought my wrap." She took the shawl and wrapped it around her shoulders, but the cold remained. "Thank you."

Willem moved like a man in a dream. She saw his eyes narrow more each time he glanced toward the group of men drinking at the bar. One man grinned and nodded in recognition when he caught Willem's dark gaze. When Abigail looked back she found Willem studying her with a pensive expression. He sat down opposite her and never took his eyes from her face. His eyebrows were drawn together in a somber slash above his blazing scrutiny.

"We've been here long enough. We'll head for home tomorrow morning." His voice held a tone that sent a finger of fear tracing a cold trail down Abigail's back.

She watched him turn to glare at the men once more. She wondered if she had made the biggest mistake of her life by marrying Willem Tremain.

Willem had seen the fear and accusation in Abigail's face when he had returned to the dining room. He knew instinctively something was wrong. Her face was white as death and her eyes held the wary look of an animal on the run.

Then he had seen them—and heard part of what they had been saying.

He'd known who they were instantly. Two of the men had been in the crowd when they'd dug him and Sennen out of that accursed hole. He held himself rigid against the murky terror lurking on the edges of his mind.

The nightmares had been coming less frequently, and he had foolishly thought the past was behind him. Now he looked over at the men and heard them whispering about the Black Irish and all the terrible things that he had done in Leadville. How long would it be before Abigail heard all the stories or what he had done to Moira? How long would it be before she looked at him with loathing and contempt?

He could not lose her and Matthew. He would get them back to Guston, where nobody really knew him. He would make sure he got them out of Silverton before she learned the truth and turned away from him in fear.

Willem stalked the length of the room and back again. He felt trapped, suffocated. He opened and closed his hands at his bare thighs and looked at Abigail. She was asleep, her hands curled into tiny fists beside her cheek.

What a fool he had been.

He had hoped—even believed—that their marriage was a new beginning. Now, in the unrelenting blackness of night, he faced the truth. They suited each other well enough in bed, but in the harsh light of day she looked at him with fear and suspicion. He had felt it grow between them through dinner like a cancer. Each time he glanced up she had been staring at him with a glint of indictment and knowledge in her blue-green eyes.

He had watched her cast surreptitious glances at the group of miners. The men had drunk more and talked more and several times they had spoken openly about the Black Irish.

Willem shoved the heels of his palms into his eyes and wished he had never brought Abigail and Matthew to Silverton. He looked up and saw a soft snowflake drift by the window. Willem sighed and leaned his forehead against the cold glass. He didn't even care what the weather was like tomorrow—he had to get them back to Guston before Abigail heard about his haunted past.

Willem strode to the bed and looked down on the woman who had consented to be his wife. She was lovely, and he wanted to believe that somewhere deep inside her a kernel of affection and trust had been sown.

She made a soft sleeping sound and he felt passion rip through him. She was his wife in name only, for love of the child they now shared.

The coach driver was busy loading anchors and chains in case the trip over the pass proved to be treacherous. Abigail flinched when Willem suddenly appeared at her elbow to help her inside the coach. He had been sullen and more fierce looking while they made preparations to leave Silverton, and he frowned at her now with an intensity that made her stomach tie itself into knots.

Matthew hopped into the coach, his face a flushed canvas of excited pleasure. Abigail was grateful he seemed to be unaware of the frightening change she saw in Willem.

"Isn't it pretty, Mama?" Matthew's eyes glittered ice blue from the pale reflection of fallen snow.

"Mmm. It is. You scoot over here by me and stay under this lap robe." Abigail tucked the heavy tapestry around Matthew's thighs while he squirmed and wiggled. She wanted him on her side of the coach, away from Willem. She felt trepidation at having the Black Irish too near the boy. Abigail frowned and realized that since last night she had begun to think of Willem as the Black Irish more and more, not Willem—certainly not Will. Still, he was the boy's father and no amount of wishing could change that.

"Oh, Mama. I'll bet Willem won't cover up," Matthew protested, then looked up, grinning. Willem's dark head and wide shoulders obscured the open door of the stagecoach.

He was glowering at her again. Abigail locked gazes with him and a shiver skittered up her arms. She squirmed worse than Matthew under Willem's harsh scrutiny.

"Well, Matthew, I want you to stay warm." She swallowed hard and forced herself to remain calm while Will's brows furrowed deeper.

"Matthew, do as your mother asks." Willem's words were uncharacteristically sharp. Matthew looked confused.

Abigail found her temper rising. Willem Tremain could do as he liked with her, but she would not allow him to mistreat Matthew. She challenged Will's steady gaze and hoped he saw her censure. He must have, for he narrowed his eyes before he spun away with great agitation in his movements. She heard his deep baritone voice raised in anger. A moment later one of the miners she had listened to in the dining room swung into the small coach.

"Ma'am," the man said, and laid his index finger up against the bridge of his nose. "Looks like we're in for a rough ride, don't it?" He settled himself across the coach from Abigail and allowed his gaze to linger on Willem. She did not miss his double meaning.

Abigail noticed with some consternation that the miner's knees nearly touched her own. She shifted positions and tried to increase the distance between their legs but it didn't work. When Willem swung inside he raked one hot glance over Abigail and the nearness of the miner before he turned his face to the window in brooding silence.

Abigail sighed and wondered if she was going to witness the wrath of the Black Irish firsthand. The more she looked at his scowling face and rigid body, the more she found herself believing that all the rumors *might* be true.

Willem stared out at the falling snow in silent misery. He had seen the cold look in Abigail's face when he'd snapped at Matthew. It sent an icy fist squeezing his heart. Then Grady Dawson had shown up before he could apologize for being short-tempered. The snake had the gall to speak to Abigail as if he knew her, and Will noticed how close he sat, nearly touching her with his legs. Now Willem wondered just how much gossip Abigail *had* heard in Silverton. Knowing Grady Dawson's reputation as a tongue-wagging skirt chaser, it was reasonable to assume he would make a point of telling Abbie every black story he could recall—if he hadn't already. Willem glanced at Abigail and felt the chill of fear surge over him.

He didn't want to lose her. He had fallen head over heels in love with the woman. He sighed and wished he could put his feelings into words. The closest he had ever come to speaking what was in his heart had been that clumsy toast. He had never been much good with words. He tried to show Abigail how he felt about her with his body, his touch. He looked at her pale face, her lips drawn into a tight line, and he knew he had failed in the attempt.

"It's been a long time, Irish." Grady broke the thick silence inside the swaying coach.

Willem snapped his head around to glance at Matthew. He was relieved to see him asleep with his head nestled in the crook of Abigail's protective arm. He looked up at her but she lowered her lashes to avoid his gaze. It made his gut twist painfully.

"About six years by my count. Is that about right, Irish?" Grady raised his bushy eyebrows.

"About that," Willem snapped. He could tell Abigail was listening with every fiber of her being.

"I understand congratulations are in order." Grady inclined his head toward Abigail.

She glanced at Will from under her lowered lashes. It sent a ribbon of anxiety threading through him.

"How did you hear?" Willem saw her glance up at Grady, and he wondered if Abigail herself had told the skunk about their relationship.

"All the hotel staff could talk about was the happy couple," Grady said, smiling coolly. "I heard about Moira, too, Irish."

Willem felt the cold fist around his heart squeeze tighter. Abigail raised her lashes and stared at him. She had a curious hurt look in her eyes. Willem wanted to hold her close and tell her everything would work out, but the trouble was he was having a hard time believing it himself at this particular moment.

"I expect you're glad to have that part of your life dead and buried, so to speak, aren't you, Irish?" Grady smirked.

Willem wanted to hit him. He balled up his fists and tensed his arm, then he looked at Abigail. Knowledge flickered across her face and he knew she was damning him silently. If he laid into Grady, he would be doubly damned, because then she would have no doubt about the rumors.

He met her eyes and prayed she could see what lay in his heart—what he wanted to say and could not. Willem held her gaze until she looked away. It tore a bit of his soul apart. He felt an invisible door slam shut in his face. He turned back to the cold white world outside.

Abigail felt the knot in her belly grow. Willem was brooding and sullen but when he spoke to the miner she saw pure hatred blaze in his cerulean eyes.

Matthew stirred. She pulled the lap rug up higher to keep him warm and safe. So far the trip had been cold but clear. The driver had managed to negotiate the narrow, snow-covered passes without difficulty.

She glanced at the shortening shadows outside and realized if they continued at the same steady pace they would reach Guston in another hour or so. She felt relief and dread mingle in her knotted stomach. Once she was back in Guston she would feel more secure—being in her own home.

She hoped that Willem would decide to follow the other miners and strike out for Creede. On the heels of that hope she remembered their wedding night. Pure, raw longing coursed through her. She remembered the fantasy she had spun around Willem's romantic toast, but when she glanced at him across the small stagecoach she could not believe it was the same man. The person she saw curling and uncurling his fists was worthy of the name Black Irish.

Willem felt the deep chasm of loneliness opening up in his soul again. He looked at Abigail and felt sharp desolation. She withdrew from him more each minute. He had felt her accepting him, at least for a few hours, in Silverton. Now with each passing mile he felt her rejection. It was the cold, harsh reality of his past settling firmly between them.

It ate at him. He wanted to grab her by the shoulders. He wanted to look into her eyes and tell her he was the same man she had given her body to. He wanted to beg her to love him. But when he glanced at her and saw how her arms were folded over her bosom like a tight little shield, and she kept her eyes averted when he looked at her, it sent a flash of wounded anger coursing through him.

He hurt deep inside. The hurt made him want to yell, to tell her she was wrong, but he couldn't. So he sat in miserable silence and hated the part of himself that had frightened her. He loved Abigail, but no matter how much he wanted her to love him in return, he couldn't force her to feel about him the way he felt about her.

They reached Guston by late afternoon. The clean smell of the first snow hung in the mountain air. Abigail took a great breath of it, hoping it might clear her head and calm her nerves, but to no avail. Each time she looked at Willem her heart slammed painfully in her chest and her mouth went dry. His face was stern and forbidding.

Grady Dawson lingered around the stagecoach until Willem jerked him aside by the front of his shirt. He yanked the man close to his face and snarled like a wild animal. Abigail told herself it was not right for her to listen, but she couldn't resist. She pretended to be fussing with her shoe buttons while she strained to catch every word that Willem hissed out.

"Stay away from my wife, Dawson." His words were colder than the frost clinging to the board sidewalk.

"Why? Are you afraid I might tell the little woman th truth?"

"And what truth would that be?"

Abigail glanced up and saw Willem's face. It sent an ar row of alarm through her. His brows were knit together i a great dark slash and his eyes snapped like the crack of doomsday, but his words were low and controlled. She was glad Matthew was inside the depot beyond earshot. She didn't want him to see the violence in Willem.

"The truth about how you killed those men, and how your wife ran from you before you could do the same to her."

For a moment Abigail thought one of the beams supporting the roof of the stage depot had snapped under the weight of the snow—but it was too light to cause such damage. Grady hit the thin crust of ice faceup and slid backward past the luggage. Abigail was horrified to see his nose twisted crookedly to one side of his face. A maroon trail of blood was meandering over his beard-stubbled chin.

"I mean it, Grady. Stay away from my wife. Or I swear I'll..."

"You'll what? Kill me? Like you did the others?"

Grady staggered to his feet and wiped his arm under his nose. Abigail held her breath while she waited to see if the man would challenge Will further, but Grady spat out a mouthful of blood and made his way up Blaine Street without another word or a backward glance. Abigail stood mute, stunned by the depth of violence within Willem. Her hand was trembling when she grabbed the wooden railing for support.

Willem picked up the bags. When he reached Abigail he stared at her with a mixture of pain and confusion in his eyes.

"I'll tell Matthew it's time to go home now," he said softly before he turned and strode up the hill. His boots crunched in the snow while Abigail bit her lip and tried to hold back the tears. The miner's words had left her shocked and numb. Willem had not denied the accusation. Now after witnessing the rage inside him she feared she had indeed married a murderer.

With each step Willem felt his heart breaking. He had seen true fear in Abigail's eyes and knew she had heard every word Grady had said. The fact that she knew about his past and believed it tore at him. He saw a tendril of smoke coming from the boardinghouse. Instead of feeling the excitement of coming home he felt a gray desolation opening up inside him. It hadn't been so bad before he arrived in Guston. For six years he had thought of nothing but finding Moira and his child. He'd never thought about happiness, until Abigail and Matthew changed his life.

Now he knew what happiness and love tasted like. The loss of that emotion sent a torrent of despair flooding through him. He'd savored a brief sweet encounter of family life, only to have it yanked away from him. It was the cruelest punishment of all. He grimaced and shook his head. All these years he had thought the nightmares were his purgatory but now he knew better. The real retribution was having found real love only to lose it again.

Chapter Twenty-Four

"How was Silverton?" Lars met Abigail and Matthew at the parlor door. Matthew launched himself at Brighty. The dog responded by collapsing in a tangle of legs and paws with the boy on the closest Chinese rug. They writhed happily in front of Abigail's snow-dampened skirt hem.

"I see you got the furnace going." Abigail didn't want to talk about Silverton—not now. Not with Willem watching her and listening to her every word. She wanted to confide in Lars when Will wasn't listening, and get his advice about how she could get out of this mess. "It's nice and warm in here."

She took off her cape and tried to control her trembling fingers while she hung it above the metal floor grate to dry.

"We got married," Matthew said between licks from the ecstatic dog. "By a judge."

Lars's white eyebrows shot up. "Married?"

"Yes. Willem decided—" Abigail saw him rake her with a glance. "That is, we *both* thought it would be foolish to make a big to-do and wait longer. We had a small ceremony in Silverton."

The muscles in Willem's jaw jumped spasmodically and Abigail felt the pit of her stomach drop. It was like walking on tacks barefoot. He seemed to be watching her—judging her every word—and it put her more ill at ease with each passing minute.

Lars frowned and Abigail knew he could sense the tension arcing back and forth between her and her *husband.* He flicked a quick look down at Matthew, who was still frolicking with the Dane.

"We need to celebrate the occasion." He walked to Willem and extended his hand. "Congratulations, Will."

Willem stared at the gnarled fingers and swallowed hard. It was the civil thing to do, but he felt as if he'd just been hit with a sixteen-pound sledge.

"Thanks," he managed to grate out.

The old man smiled, and Willem saw compassion and perhaps sadness flickering in the depths of his blue eyes. It made him cringe inside knowing the old fellow would regard him with open contempt if he knew what Abigail knew.

"I 'spect Otto will be glad to have you back early." Lars studied Abigail while he spoke to Willem. She was biting her bottom lip and was nervous as a cat.

"Why is that?" Will tried not to notice the hurt and fear written in her face, but it wasn't easy; it wasn't even possible. He loved her so much it was painful to see her suffering and know he was the cause of her misery.

"He has been hiring double crews trying to get track laid through the pass before the heavy winter snow hits," Lars explained.

"Is he having any luck finding men to work?" Willem wondered how many men Otto could find with news of the silver strike in Creede on every tongue from here to Leadville.

"He's found a few. They've been coming in by mule train and stage since you two left for Silverton. For what he's paying, I 'spect he'll find plenty."

Willem narrowed his eyes and thought of Dawson. That would explain what the son-of-a-buck was doing here with winter coming. He wondered how many more specters from his past would show up to haunt him and Abigail.

He glanced up and found Abigail watching him with round, wary eyes. The look in her eyes made him want to flee her condemnation, but at the same time he wanted to remind her of the intimacy they had shared.

Willem tore his gaze from her face and told himself to forget it. She had offered marriage because of Matthew, no matter how much he might wish it was otherwise. He had seen the look in her eyes and knew he should come to grips with the loss.

"I'm going to go pack up my things." The words were out of his mouth before he knew it.

"You're leaving?" He didn't miss the hopeful note in Abigail's surprised voice. It sent a lancet of pain through his heart.

"Yes, I am." He picked up the valise at his feet. For half a heartbeat he considered giving her what she wanted. For the tiniest fraction in time he thought about making it easy on Abigail, but then he looked at her face and felt a love so strong it hurt. She seemed almost like the woman he had married in Silverton. There was a bright expectancy in her eyes and lips that made his pulse race. He wanted to kiss her.

"I'm moving into your room, Abigail. Since we are married it would seem peculiar for me to stay in number twelve. Don't you think?"

He saw the disappointment in her eyes. He hurt deeply inside, knowing that he could only make her happy by going away and knowing he would die before he left her.

Willem turned and climbed the stairs. He could feel her eyes on his back with each step.

"What is going on, Abbie?" Lars asked as soon as Willem was out of earshot.

"Oh, Lars, I think I've made a terrible mistake," Abigail whispered. She glanced at Matthew, but the boy was still playing with the dog, unaware of the tempest brewing around him. "Matthew, why don't you take your dog for a walk?"

"Yeah. I'll bet she likes the snow." He looked up and smiled. "I'll get my sleigh."

"I don't think there's enough for sledding yet." Lars chuckled.

"Maybe—but I'll give it a try and find out." Matthew was already running out the back door with the leggy Dane in tow.

"Now, Abbie, come into the kitchen and let me pour you a cup of coffee." Lars put his arm around her shoulders. "Tell me what this is all about."

"Do you believe Willem Tremain is a murderer, Abbie?" Lars laid his rough hand over her own. The kitchen was flooded with bright winter light but she felt chilled to the bone.

"He didn't deny it. The man accused him of murder and—" She tried to forget the words. "He said Moira left Willem because she was afraid he would hurt her like he did the others. And I saw a side of him . . . It was frightening." Abigail shivered.

"I must admit I've always wondered why a woman would be out in this country all alone when her time was so near," Lars said, and shifted in his chair. He had thought the dead woman would finally be laid to rest, but now he began to have doubts.

"Oh, Lars. What am I going to do?"

"I don't know, but I'll be here in case you need me, Abbie girl."

"It's so terrible. But before that man, Grady, showed up, well, I had almost started to... to trust him and..." Abigail let her words trail off. She had started to tell Lars that she had begun to have feelings for Willem. Feelings that had nothing to do with her heart fluttering like a hummingbird each time he looked at her, but warm feelings of confidence and admiration.

"Tell me, Abbie." Lars focused on her face.

"He was a different person, Lars. He was kind and considerate. Being with him was nice. I had started to think it would not be so bad." She swallowed the hot, dry lump in her throat. "Until he saw those men. Then it was... well, I see why they call him Black Irish."

"I'll ask around and see if I can find out anything."

"Please do. I have Matthew's happiness and safety to think of."

The sound of Will's boots on the stairs brought Abigail up short. She felt the hair on the nape of her neck bristle when he stepped into the kitchen. It was all she could do to keep from cringing in fear from the forbidding scowl he wore.

Willem felt Abigail's alarm with dread. He watched the tense set of her shoulders and saw her straight back stiffen even more while he watched her. A strand of silky hair lay across her nape. He wanted to kiss her neck, to hold her and hear her moan in ecstasy. He wanted to show her with his body all the things he could not put into words. He wanted her to realize he cherished her and could never do anything to cause her harm, no matter what she thought he was capable of.

"Abigail..." He saw her start when he spoke her name. "I want to talk to you."

She turned, and he took a quick breath. The sight of her trembling lips and tear-spiked lashes sent a spear of compassion and guilt blasting through him. God, how he loved this woman.

"I have to go down in the basement and tend the furnace." Lars excused himself tactfully. He stood and took his coffee cup to the dishpan, then he opened a narrow door and disappeared down the steps.

Willem forced himself to ignore the yawning darkness of the cellar, and took a step toward Abigail. He saw her eyes widen. If she could just forget his past he was sure they could find some happiness.

"Abigail," he began, knowing he had to try to put his feelings into words. He swallowed hard and prayed he could make her understand.

Just then the kitchen door flew open and Matthew darted inside. "Mama, come help me! My dog just got sprayed by a skunk!"

Willem paced the floor and tried to quell the burning inside his heart. He had tried in vain all day to get Abigail alone so he could confront her about what Grady had said. Each time he tried, she found a way to escape him. After dinner she had pleaded a headache and vanished upstairs. Now he paced the parlor and wondered what he should do.

He looked up at the darkness at the top of the stairs and knew what he wanted to do. He wanted to go to Abigail. He wanted to hold her and kiss her and make sweet love to her until the haunting past was driven away from them both. But if he went to her now, like a rutting boar, would she misunderstand? Would she judge him a beast, a man only interested in his physical pleasure and unconcerned about the wide, empty chasm between them?

He raked his hand through his hair and wondered what he could do. He wondered why he couldn't just go up the stairs and take whatever she offered. Her body responded to him—he could have her passion—but the idea left a sour taste in his mouth. He wanted more than that.... He wanted her *love.* He longed to have her mind, her body, her trust. He yearned to hear his name on her lips.

Willem stared out the window at the snow beginning to fall and wondered if there would ever be a time when Abigail would trust him. He wondered if there could ever, on God's earth, come a time when she might care for him.

Chapter Twenty-Five

"Lars, would you keep an eye on Matthew when he wakes up? I'm going for a walk." Abigail pulled on her heaviest shawl and tried to forget the past three days and nights. She had feigned a headache, or some other malady, and managed to avoid Willem—so far. She had done a poor job of ignoring his probing gaze across the table or denying the attraction she felt for him. It was getting harder all the time.

This morning at breakfast he had mentioned the rumors of the silver strike in Creede. She found her heart beating a little faster. He would be leaving soon, she was sure of it. All she had to do was stay away from him and keep her own rebellious desires under control until he left. Something that was far easier said than done.

"It's cold out there, Abbie girl. Are you sure you want to leave this warm house?" Lars knew he had caused this most recent heartache by interfering—again. When would he learn? If not for his suggestion that Abigail marry Will, she would not be so troubled now. He had watched her try to avoid the man, while it was obvious she really wanted to be with him. It was a constant source of sorrow for Lars that Matthew's real father caused such a conflict in Abigail.

"I have to get out for a while to think. Where is Willem?" she asked softly.

"Spent the night in his old room again." Lars listened each night to Willem pace the floor in the parlor until the wee hours of the morning. The sun was a gray finger on the horizon before he climbed the stairs to his old room each morning for a few hours of rest.

"I see." Abigail hated to admit it, but she missed Willem. She missed his body in her bed. She missed his hands on her. For long hours after she went upstairs each evening, she lay there torn between hope and desire. She wished for Will to come and ignite the fires within her body, all the while hoping he would just leave her and Matthew in peace. What kind of woman was she to lust after a man who terrified her so, a man who was rumored to be a killer?

"I'll watch the boy." Lars patted her shoulder with his gnarled fingers. He hoped that Abigail could work this out—for Matthew's sake as well as her own. Brighty padded into the room and scratched at the back door. She turned her liquid brown eyes up to Abigail.

"Looks like someone wants to go along."

Abigail smiled. She had come to like the dog and her faithful company. "Yes, it does." She rubbed the animal's wide head with her open palm. "We'll be back long before noon. I'll fix you something special for dinner."

She opened the back door and stepped out into the sparkling white landscape of newly fallen snow.

Abigail tossed a stick and chuckled while the dog plowed through a shallow drift. Snow sprayed up in all directions as Brighty dug down through the crust to find the hidden stick. Abigail laughed and allowed her thoughts to wander.

She found herself thinking about the time she had spent with Willem in Silverton. His kindness and generosity had surprised and delighted her. She thought back to the bouquet of flowers and the look in his eye when he presented them.

Abigail leaned against a bare stripling of an aspen and closed her eyes. She could almost taste the intoxicating rum cake on her tongue. A shiver ran through her. Willem's kisses had been equally potent. She sighed and realized that she was starving to know his touch again.

"If only," she said aloud.

The dog's head came up with a snap at Abigail's words. Her voice was loud in the wintry silence. The sun gilded the snowy crust with sparkles of silver and diamond like ice. A tiny cracking sound accompanied a sploosh of snow when a slender, dry branch broke nearby. The dog perked up her ears and barked low in her chest.

"It was nothing, silly," Abigail said to the dog, and walked on toward her place of solitude. The path was nearly obscured by the snow, but she navigated on instinct and habit alone. A scatter of large boulders suddenly appeared in the middle of the old path. Abigail stopped and frowned.

"Did I take the wrong direction?" she asked aloud. She looked up at the craggy mountain and realized she was in the right spot. "There must've been a landslide since I was here last time." She shook her head and climbed over the large boulders. There was the hollow and the flat smooth stone, now pillowed in fluffy snow. She wiped the flat surface clean, then dried her damp, cold palm on her shawl.

It was quiet. She hoped in this pristine silence she would find the solution to her problem—an answer she could live with about Willem's guilt. Abigail looked up and saw the dog digging at the mouth of a burrow.

"Stop that, Brighty, you'll wake somebody who will not be happy to see you." She stood and walked toward the depression in the ground. The dog glanced up for a minute but went back to digging with great enthusiasm.

Abigail moved forward. She laid her fingers on the animal's loose scruff to lure her away.

Then she heard the sound.

The groan sounded almost human. The ground under her feet began to sift away like white flour through a sieve. She jerked back and tried to find purchase but the damp earth was slick beneath her shoes. She slipped toward the deepening center of the hollow.

"Oh, my God!" She grabbed a slender sapling growing near the depression. Her fingers closed around one slender branch, but it broke off in her hand like dry kindling.

Horrified, Abigail saw more dirt fall away from under her feet. The end of an exposed beam jutted upward near her leg. With a sickening thud of her heart she realized that the dog had uncovered an abandoned mine shaft.

"Brighty—get back!" Abigail managed to croak before the earth beneath her opened up and she was engulfed by darkness. The dank smell of soggy earth and rotting wood surrounded her before she lost consciousness.

"What time did you say Abigail left?" Willem walked to the window and looked at the dark formation of mauve and black clouds scudding toward the mountain's highest snow-covered peak.

"Early this morning. She took the dog and went for a walk." Lars hated to admit it, but he was beginning to worry about Abbie, too. He glanced at Matthew and nodded toward the window. Willem acknowledged his gesture and stepped closer to the old man.

"I don't want to upset the boy—" Lars's voice was a harsh whisper while he watched Matthew sipping a glass of milk "—but I'm starting to get worried."

Willem poured himself a cup of coffee. He had slept little and his mind was sluggish. He had not been able to rest more than a few hours a night since they'd returned from Silverton, and he'd felt a dark foreboding when he woke today and found Abigail gone. He told himself it was only his imagination, but the hair on his arms was standing on end. A restless anxiety that would not go away had seeped into his soul with each passing hour.

"What time did she say she was coming back, Lars?"

"Before noon."

Willem looked outside and frowned. The late-afternoon shadows were stretching toward the east. "Did you say Abigail took Matthew's dog?" He saw a blur of fawn-colored fur moving in the tree line. Willem felt the hair prickle along his nape while he scanned the horizon.

"Yes. Why?" Lars leaned closer to the window. His breath fanned out and fogged the cold pane of glass, completely obscuring his view.

"That's Brighty." Willem rushed to the back door and flung it open.

"Is my mama back?" Matthew stood beside him watching the dog lope across the open meadow toward the house.

"I'm not sure, Matthew." Willem squatted down and grabbed the dog as soon as she reached him.

"Look at her...she's been digging." Lars's voice cracked.

"Yes." Willem touched the mud-encrusted fur with trembling fingers. "She's covered with it."

"Look at this." Lars reached out and plucked a sliver of wood from the fur near Brighty's ear. He turned it over in his fingers before he handed it to Willem.

"It's a piece of rotted mine timber." Will's heart slammed in his chest like a jackhammer.

"Where's my mama?" Matthew tipped his face up to Willem, and it ripped into his guilt-ridden soul. He knew right then he should never have agreed to Abigail's crazy suggestion.

It was a foolish idea, but he had wanted it all. He should have gone away and left her and Matthew in peace. All he'd wanted to do was raise his son and love the woman who had been the only mother the boy had ever known, but now because of his selfishness he had driven her to disaster.

"I don't know, Matthew, but I promise I'll find her for you." Willem yanked on his coat and put his belt around Brighty's neck. "Lars, can you watch over Matthew?"

"What are you going to do?"

"There's a storm coming. I'm going to see if I can find Abigail's tracks before they are covered. Maybe Brighty and I can find her before the storm hits." Willem looked down at the boy's pinched face and forced himself to smile. He prayed the child couldn't see his own fear.

"Good idea." Lars slipped his hand over Matthew's shoulder. "Let's me and you take a look at that furnace, Matthew. I think it needs more coal. I'll bet by the time we get finished, your mama will be making spiced cider for us." Lars winked and the boy nodded. Willem felt his heart swell with love and pride for Matthew.

"Come on, Brighty—find Abigail!"

Willem had not even left the shelter of the steps before the first snowflake fell on his heavy wool coat. He sloughed on through the rapidly deepening snow while the temperature plummeted. Frost and tiny spikes of ice formed on his brows and eyelashes. He swiped at them to clear his vision and knelt to warm Brighty's nose. The smooth-coated animal was ill equipped to live in the mountains of Colorado, but as soon as the ice was clear she whined and tugged on the belt clutched in his cold fingers. She seemed anxious to move on, and that sent a shiver of fear through Will.

The sun was obscured behind thick gray clouds and falling snow. He looked up at the faint round glow and prayed he could find Abigail before nightfall. The thought of her out here alone and maybe hurt made his heart constrict. He loved her, and because of his rash actions she was in jeopardy. Guilt weighed heavily on his shoulders.

"Please, God, don't let anything happen to her. I'll go away—I'll leave them in peace, only please..." His words trailed off in the wake of a mournful howl. Brighty's high-pitched wail echoed off the canyon walls and bounced back to him.

"What is it?" He encouraged the shivering dog forward.

She danced in a tight little circle, then lunged toward a mound of boulders. Willem scrambled to keep up with her and hang on to the belt at the same time. He scaled the slick, wet rocks and slid down the other side, cracking his leg on a large piece of shale when he landed in a scrub oak.

The dog was barking furiously now and straining to move forward. Willem regained his feet, ignoring the pain in his shin. He followed the excited animal into a depression. The snow was deeper here, reaching nearly to his knees. Slender aspens surrounded the hollow, their snow-laden branches dipping toward the growing drifts.

"What is it, girl?" He watched the dog flounder through the snow toward the center of the hollow. She started to dig. At first only white flakes flew in a rooster tail behind her, then slowly it turned muddy and dark. Loamy earth and finally shards of rotted timber began to pile up beside her wet body.

"Is Abigail in there?" A hard knot formed in Will's throat. He dropped to his knees and dug side by side with the dog. His fingers ached from the snow but he continued to grab handfuls of frosty earth and pitch them away. Finally, with one last mournful whine, the dog broke through the thin barrier of dirt and slush.

Willem sucked in the wet air and sat back on his haunches. His head was spinning and he tasted bile rising in his throat. He stared into the black pit and knew he was looking into the face of his own private hell. A hell he must enter to save his wife.

Abigail opened her eyes but the world around her remained dark and quiet. She tried to get up but something heavy held her fast. With her hands she felt around and discovered she was lying on stone with a heavy beam across her body. Terror welled up inside her. She lifted her head and felt something warm and sticky flow into her eyes.

"Oh, Lord," she moaned and swiped at her face. The faint but unmistakable odor of blood wafted around her nose, but was soon lost amid the dank, musty smell of the mine. Her right leg throbbed painfully. She wondered if she had broken it, but pushed the horrible thought away.

"I'll be fine...somebody will find me," She said aloud. The echo of her own voice bounced back at her from deep below, and icy, paralyzing fear began to seep into her body. She was lying on a rough shelf of rock with murky darkness above her. While she lay there in the smothering darkness, she began to perceive that the bottom of the mine was far beneath her in the pitch-black hole.

Abigail felt around until her fingers closed on a small stone. She held it away from her body, then she opened her cold fingers and let the pebble fall. She held her breath while she waited for it to strike bottom. She felt light-headed and her lungs were nearly bursting before she heard the muffled click and the splash of water.

The stone had hit bottom far, far below her.

"Oh, dear God. I am going to die."

Abigail felt her own hot tears turn cold where they cut a trail down her cheek and settled into the hollow of her throat. She let her aching head fall back against the hard surface and sobbed uncontrollably. She was scared and she was utterly alone.

She thought of Matthew and of Willem.

A bit of dirt and small stones from above pelted Abigail in the face. She took in a breath and held it, afraid to move. Abigail saw herself falling, crushed to death, buried in a mine the way Carl had been. Then the dirt stopped falling, and Abigail tentatively let out the breath she'd been holding. She wanted to move, to bring the blood flow back into her cold limbs, but she was too terrified. If she made one small mistake, moved one inch too far right or left, she would plummet like a stone to the bottom of the deep mine shaft.

She felt a scream building in the back of her throat and squeezed her eyes and lips closed against it. After a minute of focusing on Matthew's image in her mind, she managed to breathe more or less normally. She bit her lip and started to pray.

She saw images of Carl swirling in her memory. He had died so young, but she realized he had died while he was following his dream. Abigail rubbed her hand under her nose and sniffed. It occurred to her that dying didn't frighten her nearly as much as the knowledge she was leaving so much *undone* in her life.

She thought of Matthew. He would be left alone, just as she had been. Without a permanent home, without anyone to care for him.

No. That wasn't true.

Now that Willem had found him, she knew he would care for Matthew. She smiled inwardly and realized with a sobering jolt that Willem would walk over hot coals to see the child happy and well cared for. It gave her a measure of peace, but it also made her realize how harshly she had judged Will Tremain.

And on what evidence?

Rumors, innuendo, a dark name from his past.

The thought raked along her skin like a blacksmith's rasp. Her stomach wrenched painfully. She tasted something sour in her mouth. It was guilt.

Abigail gulped in a great long breath and thought about Willem. For the first time she felt she was seeing the man clearly. Here in the darkness with her life clinging precariously to a ledge of abandoned stone, she finally saw the truth. In the black pit she could see him for himself—not through her own fears, or other men's jealousy—but the man he truly was.

Abigail saw a man who had been shaped by the tragedies of his life. A man who had lived with the stigma of past mistakes, a man who never gave up searching for his family.

A man she cared for.

Her husband.

She felt the cold deepen around her bones. She cared more than she had ever admitted. It was the most bittersweet revelation of her life.

Abigail knew when she died she would be leaving the most important thing in her life undone. She would die with Willem's name on her lips, and the regret of never having told him how much she cared about him locked in her heart. It brought a hot lump to her throat and the sting of salty tears to the back of her eyes.

"Please, God, give me another chance."

Willem grabbed hold of the shattered timber and jerked, but it would not budge. The opening to the shaft was narrow and each move he made sent handfuls of dirt tumbling down. He stood and stared at the sky. The clouds were darker and the thready light of the sun was growing more dim each moment. He looked at the shivering dog and raked his hand through his wet hair.

"I need lanterns and rope," he muttered into the swirling flakes. The dog whined and made a halfhearted attempt to dig the timber out.

"No, girl. That won't help." Willem stuck his numb fingers in his armpits and tried to think. He couldn't leave Abigail, but he had to have equipment to reach her. He turned his face heavenward and prayed for a miracle.

"Please, Lord, please don't take her from me." His voice cracked with emotion in the silence of the meadow.

The dog growled low in her chest. Will looked down and saw her ears perking up and her tail wagging. Willem turned his head and squinted into the gray, swirling haze of snow. A clink of metal against rock halted his breath in his chest.

He saw Lars's snow-covered head appear over the pile of boulders. A flood of relief swelled inside him.

"Lars. I'm glad to see you." He rushed over and helped the old man over the cold, slick rocks. "Abigail has fallen down an old mine shaft." The words woke the cold terror lurking at the edge of his mind. He fought to keep his demons at bay. Abigail needed him and he was going to be there for her—even if it killed him.

"You heard her?" Lars asked.

"No, but she's down there—I can feel it." Will felt the clammy constriction around his heart and knew it was true. She was in there and the only way to save her was for him to go inside—inside the belly of the earth where he'd sworn he'd never go again.

"I brought a shovel and some rope, but it won't be enough. We need help." Lars surveyed the opening and the rotten timbers.

"Will you go back for help? I can't leave." Willem felt his heart thudding in his chest.

"Have you heard anything?" Lars's brows were nearly invisible in the snowy gloom.

"Not a sound." Willem flinched at the thought he had been trying to avoid—that perhaps she was dead—but he shoved it aside. If Abigail was not alive he would surely know it. "I have to get her out."

"I understand. I'll go back to town and see who I can round up." Lars turned away.

"Lars, where is Matthew?" Willem felt the responsibility of fatherhood more strongly at this moment than he ever had before. He visualized the clear blue eyes rimmed with worry, and his gut twisted.

"He's at Hans Gustafson's. He'll be all right as soon as we bring his mama home."

"Lars—" Willem swallowed hard. He had never openly spoken to the old man about Moira and what had happened that night. It seemed important that he do so now, just in case. "I want to thank you for saving my son's life and for giving him to the finest woman I've ever known, to be his mother."

Lars's mouth twisted on one side. His eyes became milky with tears. "Thanks, Willem. I've been waitin' a lot of years to hear somebody tell me that."

Without another word Lars turned and made his way slowly over the stones and out of Will's sight.

"Go with him, Brighty." Willem gestured with his hand. The dog looked at him with soulful brown eyes. "Go ahead." She hesitated for a moment then bounded over the boulders and disappeared into the murk.

Willem turned back toward the yawning black pit and felt a shiver of fear snake up his back. He picked up the shovel and coil of rope and took a deep breath. No matter what, he was going into that hole and bringing Abigail out.

* * *

Abigail closed her eyes and tried to rest. She wasn't sure how long she had been down here, but there was a big lump on the back of her head and she could feel what she thought was dried blood around it. She forced herself to breathe slowly and think of something that would take her mind off the pain in her leg.

Willem's dark, brooding features took shape in her mind. She felt the tight constriction in her chest, but was determined not to cry again. Abigail tried to be strong, but the more she thought about Willem Tremain—the Black Irish—the more she hated herself for the way she had treated him.

Another hot tear managed to escape and slide down her cheek. Again, she felt the cold trail it left behind on her face. Why hadn't she realized before now how she felt about Will?

Abigail forced herself to be brutally honest. In the stygian darkness she remembered the day he'd arrived...how angry and alone he'd seemed. Even then she had felt something unique for him. A tiny smile curved her lips when she remembered his growling stomach.

Willem had been stern and brusque, but she realized now it was because of his frustration about Moira and not knowing where his child was. Matthew had warmed to Will right away. From the very first there had been a connection between them.

"I should've known him...I should've seen it," Abigail whispered. A tiny pebble moved beneath her shoulder. She heard it skitter over the edge of the rock and waited for ten heartbeats before it hit the bottom with a faint splash.

She tried not to move a muscle for fear she would topple over the edge and fall to her death. Memories of Willem came unbidden now, like a flood too powerful to hold back any longer. From the very first she had feared him, now she realized what she had really feared was herself.

Abigail drew in a shuddering breath and the beam across her chest shifted and put more weight along her ribs. For a moment the panic rose uncontrolled within her. Slowly, with the greatest amount of restraint, she forced herself to be calm. She made herself examine her fears closely, and finally faced the bitter truth.

She had been a fool. She had been so afraid of being hurt that she had chosen to live half of a life, a life without love. She had used Willem's dark reputation as an excuse. Now that she saw her own mortality looming before her, she knew she had cheated herself and Willem.

He had never done anything cruel to her. Even when he found out about Matthew he had never made a move to take the child from her, yet she had assumed the worst of him without cause. Even if he had done what people accused him of—*murder*—it was in the past. He was a changed man. She didn't care what he had been, he was her husband now.

He had shown her his kindness and his compassion. Why couldn't she have been brave enough to accept it and forget what other people said? She could have known what it was like to love him completely—and to be loved—if only for a little while. She had always thought it would be better not to love at all than to risk losing it. Now she knew she was wrong. Abigail tasted the truth on her tongue and flinched.

Dear God, if I had only known. She sobbed. She would give her heart completely if she had it all to do over again. She would give of herself and win her husband's regard. Abigail knew if she had it to do over, there would be no bartered marriage. She would allow passion to consume her body and her heart until Will could not stand against it.

She turned her head to the side and moaned her grief into the cold, rough stone.

Chapter Twenty-Six

Willem heard the sound, it was a tiny muffled moan. He leaned closer to the dark cavity and held his breath. A wave of nausea gripped him, but he ground his teeth together and ignored it. He had to help Abigail—his own fears could burn in hell for all he cared. She was the only important thing right now.

A bit of loose rock moved under his boot and he slipped forward. Willem realized he would need to tie the rope off if he was going to go any deeper into the shaft. He pushed himself up off the snow-covered ground and formed a loop around his waist. Then he found a slim aspen growing on the east side of the shaft and tied the rope to the slender trunk. The tree was so little, but it was his only hope. With a deep sigh he turned and forced himself to look at the cavern.

"I can do this—for Abigail." He strode forward and forced himself to squirm into the narrow opening of the mine shaft.

As soon as he was inside it began. Voices from the pas pummeled him. He smelled the dank, musty odor and hi own thick fears in the confined space. Waves of gut wrenching nausea engulfed him. He paused for a momen with his fists tight on the rope and forced himself to face it

For the first time in seven years Willem looked his terror in the eye.

He saw the aging dynamite in his own hand. He saw Sen-nen and the others, working side by side in the cramped, ill-it shaft. He saw the explosion and felt the tons of rock rashing down upon them. He tasted the suffocating, dusty ir. He saw the dead bodies of his friends, littered about him ike so much broken wood and timber.

The tear sliced through his memory like a sharp-edged nife. Willem heard the sound of his own soul-rending sob.

"I killed them . . . I was reckless and foolish and I killed hem all." His voice was harsh with guilt and long-buried ain. He hung on to the rope, suspended over the deep dark ole, and he cried openly for the long-dead men and for imself.

Abigail heard the sound. It sounded like a sob, but she as sure she had not been crying. She wiped at her tear-tained face with fingers that felt like wood. Abigail forced er shoulders up a fraction of an inch and peered into the nrelenting darkness.

Above her in the column of the ebony crater there ap-eared to be a shape. She blinked and tried to keep her eyes om blurring with more tears.

The murky shadow moved, and she heard the sound gain. It sent a shiver coursing through her. It was the sound f pure misery and desolation. Her skin prickled when the oise echoed off the stone walls and back to her ears.

"Is—is—is anybody there?" she called tentatively, afraid hope, afraid to be disappointed. Then she remembered e lost moments with Willem and plucked up her strength d spoke a little louder. "Is someone there?" Her cramped ngs would not allow her to breathe deeply enough to yell.

A stillness settled over the mine shaft. Abigail felt fool-ı for allowing herself to grasp at nothing.

"Abigail? Is that you? Are you hurt?" Willem's deep voice penetrated the gloom. It washed over her like warm sunshine. She felt her heart beat a little more rapidly and she moved. The beam across her chest shifted again and she felt more of the ledge crumble away beneath her left knee. Abigail's ankle and her hip were still supported by something but her calf, her heavy skirt and her knee were suspended over nothing but cold, musty air.

"Willem?" She held her body in tight restraint. Each time she spoke she sent a small avalanche of rock falling towar the bottom of the mine. She felt the ledge beneath he shoulder shift and become less substantial.

He was so near.

"Thank God. Abigail, where are you?" Willem's voic filled her with hope and longing. She wanted to touch hin to have an opportunity to tell him all the things she had kep locked inside her.

A large rock sailed past her head. She felt the distu bance of air when it narrowly missed hitting her cheek.

"Willem, the rocks are falling," she warned. Then sh heard him groan in frustration above her.

"Abigail, can you move?" He had lowered his voice to controlled low timbre.

"No. There is something across my chest. I think it's beam." She felt another section of the ledge fall from b neath her thigh and skirt.

"It will be all right. I'll work my way down to you. Do move." Willem lowered himself hand over hand towa Abigail. He tried to keep clear of the loose sides so he wou not send any more rocks down upon her. Time hung like sword over his head while he crept lower, inch by inch.

Finally he reached a point where the shaft narrowed ev more. He could feel the constriction in his lungs. It broug the sickening waves of memory plunging over him. He called the strangling feeling of suffocating. Of running out of air and seeing his friends dying of their wounds and lack of oxygen as the hours ticked on.

"Willem, I think I can see you."

Her voice came to him like the song of an angel and wrenched his soul free from the demons in his mind. He sighed and shifted the rope to one hand. He hung on tight and reached out.

His fingers touched Abigail. Her life force traveled up his hand to his heart and lit a torch there in the darkness.

"Oh, honey. I was so afraid I wouldn't be able to reach you."

Abigail heard the affection in his words, and it sent strength darting through her. She felt the words building in ıer throat. She had to hurry—to tell him—before the ledge crumbled away. "I was so scared, Will."

"It'll be all right, honey, I promise." He heard her call ıim by name and it brought a lancet of poignant need shooting through him.

She closed her eyes and tried to stay calm. Willem was ıere and she could tell him what was in her heart.

"Willem, I have to tell you—"

The sound of creaking wood sent a frisson of terror up Villem's spine. "Shh. Don't talk. Don't even breathe ard."

He knew what that sound was—he'd heard it before when ıe mine had collapsed in on him and Sennen and the other ıen.

Willem shifted his position in the loop of rope and quinted toward the sound of Abigail's voice. He could just arely make out her silhouette. The broken section of beam y across her chest and below her...

He blinked once and looked again. She was resting on the ther, shattered end of the beam. It was broken in half, and only the small section that was embedded in the dirt and debris prevented Abigail from plummeting to the bottom of the shaft.

"Abigail, do you trust me?" Willem swallowed hard. Everything he held dear hinged on her answer.

Abigail smiled. A few hours ago even she didn't have the answer to that question, but now she knew she trusted Willem Tremain with her life and her heart. "Yes, Will, I trust you."

He let out a great rush of breath. "Good. I'm going to swing over near you. You grab hold of me and don't let go. No matter what you hear or think you hear don't let go."

"All right." Abigail closed her eyes and tried to calm her thudding heart. She wanted to feel Willem near her more than anything else in the world. There was no chance of her ever letting him go again.

Willem braced his feet against the side of the shaft and shoved as hard as he could. He swung away from the wall. A shower of loose rock and stone tumbled down from the edge of the shaft above him when the rope moved. He ducked his head and tried to focus on Abigail's position. When he reached a point that he hoped put him near her, he reached out. His fingers closed around the splintered end of the beam on her chest.

"Abigail, grab hold of me—now!"

She grasped the damp fabric of his thick wool coat at one shoulder. He felt her fingers dig into his biceps through the cloth. Then he uttered one last prayer and shoved the beam as hard as he could.

Abigail's added weight caused the rope to sear into his flesh at his waist. He heard the beam fall free and the roar of the dirt and rocks tumbling into the pit below them.

"Oh, Willem!" she whimpered while she buried her face into his neck.

He held her there—too grateful to move, too terrified of losing her to let her go. He kissed her cheek and tasted his own tears and blood.

"Abigail." He nuzzled her and clung to her with his one free arm. The rope made it hard for him to take a deep breath but he didn't care. He had Abigail in his arms and that was all that mattered.

"Are you hurt?" Will gasped and tried to brace his muscles against the increasing pressure of the rope.

"N-no, I don't think so. I'm cold and my leg feels awful. There's a big bump on my head." Abigail leaned her cheek against his chest and he felt a burst of happiness inside him.

"Hang on, honey, I'm going to get us out of here." Willem shifted Abigail to the center of his body and grabbed hold of the rope with both hands. They swung there, like a child's toy, suspended above the yawning pit.

Willem closed his eyes and fought off the feeling of nausea. When he felt he had it under control, he opened his eyes and squinted into the unrelenting blackness.

"It feels like it's getting colder," Abigail whispered against his chest.

"There's a storm. I was afraid I wouldn't find you." His voice was low with emotion.

"Will, there's something I need to tell you."

"Later, just hang on." Willem wondered if she realized how serious their situation was. It almost seemed as if she had no fear at all since he had found her—but surely that was his imagination.

"No. It can't wait. I need to tell you now." Abigail summoned her courage. "I'm sorry I blackmailed you into marriage."

Willem stopped looking upward and held his breath. When he let it out in a slow, controlled hiss it seemed to echo off the sides of the mine shaft. "You think you blackmailed me into marrying you?"

"Of course. I was determined to hold on to my place in Matthew's—in your son's—life. I never should've asked you to do it." One tear cleared a clean trail down her cheek.

"Listen, Abigail, I did exactly what I wanted to do." Willem fought to ignore the sense of loss ripping through him. He had known it would come to this—that he would have to let Abigail and Matthew go for their happiness—but hearing her say it was a hundred times more painful than he'd thought it would be.

"You did?" She sniffed and squeezed the damp wool more tightly in her fists.

"Yes. I wanted you and Matthew. I was more than willing to do what you asked."

"Oh, Will. If only I hadn't been such a fool. I was afraid."

"Why?" Will knew the answer. It was his past. The sinister ghosts of his past had tainted what he and Abigail might have had together.

"I—" Abigail had the sensation of falling. Suddenly she and Will were slipping downward. A cold wind made her damp skirt billow out around her chilled legs. She squeaked and clung more tightly to his shoulders.

"Dear Lord." Willem visualized the aspen. In his mind's eye he knew that the bank around the roots was crumbling away. He felt the pressure around his body ease into nothing while they fell deeper into the shaft. He expected the sharp boulders to crash against them any moment.

Suddenly he felt as if he were being cleaved in half. His weight and Abigail's hit the end of the taut loop of rope. Will grabbed Abigail with both hands and crushed her hard against him for fear she would be wrenched away with the force of the abrupt halt.

The sound of the cord snapping tight sent a *twang* of sound echoing all around them. The air was painfully squeezed from Willem's chest. He saw a cascade of stars inside his head and felt the nauseating sickness of tunnel vision while his brain was denied oxygen. It took every ounce of strength he could find to reach above his head and grab the rope. He grasped the rope and jerked, allowing a tiny bit of give in the line around her middle. Air flooded into his starved lungs. He gasped and clung more tightly to Abigail.

"Is the rope breaking?" Her words were thready with fear.

"No, I don't think so, but the bank is giving way around the tree. It won't hold for long. We've got to get to the top."

"How?"

"I'll pull us up."

Slowly, laboriously, he began to climb. Hand over hand Willem pulled himself, and Abigail, toward the colder air at the opening of the shaft. Willem clasped his jaw shut and tried to ignore the rope cutting into his palms and the fear nipping at his mind.

He would see to it that Abigail was safe—that was all he could allow himself to think about. No matter what lay ahead of him he would keep Abigail safe and get her home o Matthew.

For what seemed like hours Willem tugged his body, with Abigail's additional weight, up the shaft. For a moment he ancied he could smell cool fresh air instead of the dank, musty shaft, but he told himself it was wishful thinking. At times he thought he could hear the murmur of voices, but that, too, he dismissed as a trick of his mind.

Willem grated his teeth together and continued putting ne raw palm above the other on the rough hemp rope, until at last he felt the cold sting of wind and tasted snow on his tongue.

"We've made it, Abigail." He told himself the worst was over, but he had no idea how he was going to get her out of the mouth of the shaft and onto solid ground.

"Look, I can see them!" Lars moved the lantern closer to the mine shaft. The dirt beneath his feet crumbled and he jumped back before the entire side caved in. The roots of the slender aspen were exposed and clinging tenaciously to the sifting soil around them. It was all that was holding the rope, and the two people clinging to it.

"Watch out—that edge is going to go," Brawley barked, and elbowed his way up beside Lars.

"I can see that. We've got to lift her out," Lars told the group of men gathered around the depression in the snow-covered ground.

"We'll have to cut some saplings and shore up the edge first," a deep voice announced from the back of the crowd "I'll go get started."

"There's no time for that," Brawley said. He threw hi body down and leaned near the crumbling edge. "Tre main? Can you hear me?"

"I hear you." Will's voice drifted up from the dank pit.

"Can you lift Mrs. Cooprel out?"

Cooprel, was it? Willem felt the cold stab in his heart Nobody considered his marriage to Abigail valid—not eve her, it seemed. "I'll find a way."

He let go with one hand and grabbed a handful of Ab gail's clothing.

"What are you doing?" Her voice was faint and slight slurred.

"I'm going to help you climb up, over me, so they can li you out, Abigail."

"No. I'm afraid." He felt her tremble against him. A ribbon of bittersweet longing and regret tied itself around his heart. "I don't want to leave you."

"You have to, Abigail, for Matthew."

"For Matthew?"

"Yes. He is worried about you and I promised I'd get you home safe."

"Will—before I go I have to tell you—"

"There'll be time enough later. Now climb, Abigail." He jerked her upward and felt his shoulder take the additional strain. She began to move toward safety—toward life. Willem had the strangest sensation of being deserted, abandoned, with each inch Abigail progressed toward the top.

The rope jerked taut and Willem felt a moment of panic when Abigail's weight left his body. For a gut-wrenching minute he saw in his mind the tangle of bodies and stone of long ago. He nearly crushed her to him, but then he forced himself to remember that this was another time and place.

Slowly Abigail was raised out of the dark pit. Willem glanced up and caught sight of her in the slender shaft of light from someone's lantern.

He sighed. She was safe. It was all that mattered to him.

"Will—I—I love you...." Her words trailed off when suddenly several pairs of hands grasped her shoulders and her arms to wrench her up into the biting cold snow. She felt the warm protection of Willem vanish when she emerged from the musky pit.

Willem was alone.

He let his body sag against the rope and wondered if he had truly heard what he thought. Could Abigail have said she loved him? He heard voices above him and felt the sprinkle of loose rocks falling on his head.

"Abigail? Are you all right?" Lars moved forward and caught her when she stumbled against him.

"Lars, we have to get Will out of there!"

A sudden sharp crack drew every pair of eyes to the little aspen. The feeder roots came free with a snap and the tree moved several feet before the solitary taproot halted its progress toward the yawning hole. The leafless limbs vibrated with the force.

"That tree is getting ready to go. Somebody grab another rope," the deep, faceless voice yelled into the flurry.

Abigail shuddered when she saw the tree slipping closer to the edge of the pit. If it was not stopped, Willem would surely plummet to his death.

Will felt the rope sag, and the weight of his body slipped two feet before it was yanked up short again. A loud groan escaped his lips when the rope tightened around his aching ribs. He was sure one of them had cracked earlier.

He thanked God for getting Abigail out. He had no doubt that he would never come out of this hole alive.

"He's a goner." Grady Dawson's voice drifted down the mine shaft.

The blood in Willem's veins congealed. He hung there on the rope and wished for all the world that the past would finally be put to rest. Abigail had trusted him, for a little while, at least. It was something to take to his grave. He thought of Matthew and what a fine boy he was.

"Abigail..." Willem had only one real regret. He wished he had told her how much he loved her.

"There's no way to get him out of there," Brawley said, and stuck out his chest.

Abigail sobbed and clung to Lars. Surely they did not mean to leave Will down there. Then a stranger appeared carrying three long, slim aspen saplings.

"Lay these over the shaft." The deep voice now had a face. "We can anchor them on either side and run another rope over the top for support."

Abigail didn't know who the man was, but he seemed to know what he was doing. She clung to the hope that he did. Lars patted her hand and moved away. He nodded to the man and began to help him position the saplings across the pit like latticework. Soon the trees were laced over the gaping hole in the snow.

Abigail sniffed and stuck her fingers in her mouth. That was when the slim aspen's taproot snapped and it went sailing toward the opening.

Chapter Twenty-Seven

Abigail held her breath and prayed. The aspen hit the lattice of trees with a crash and the ground beneath her own feet vibrated with the force—but it held fast.

"My God." The man crossed himself and wiped his sleeve across his forehead. Abigail could see he had been unsure if it would hold Will's weight.

"That would've torn him in two," Brawley said without emotion.

Abigail felt the hot tears stinging the back of her eyes. She felt nothing but contempt for these men, who stood like a pack of wolves while Willem clung to his life. She did not care what he had done in the past. He was her husband and a human being and he did not deserve this.

Lars held the lantern up near the aspen. The heat created a tiny cloud of vapor around the glass chimney.

"We'll have to pull him up." He looked at the stranger with milky blue eyes and Abigail read his thoughts.

"Do you think he is...dead?" The word caught in her throat.

"Good riddance," Grady said before he spit into the snow.

Abigail hated the man with a white-hot intensity that shocked her. She had never hated anyone in her life, but she hated this man, and all the other men who had gossiped about Will. She turned to the stranger, the only man except for Lars who seemed to give a damn about Willem.

"Can you do it alone?" She sniffed and hobbled nearer. She had forgotten about the cold and the pain in her leg. She only wanted to see Will brought out of that hole.

"Aye, I can do it alone. I'd not expect help from the likes of these vultures." The man's eyes were aglow with determination. He began to work his way forward to the latticework of tree trunks. Inch by inch he tested each spot until finally he was positioned near the hole. Then he crouched and braced his boots against a tiny outcrop of rocks. More loose stone tumbled down the hole while he grasped the rope and maneuvered it around his body. Finally he had the rope around his shoulders and threaded through both hands. Then he began to pull.

"You're crazy if you think you can pull up a man's dead weight alone," Grady snorted.

Abigail heard the word *dead* and felt a cold shiver run hrough her. Could she have finally recognized her own need and her own feelings just in time to lose Willem? She hobbled nearer and knelt in the snow beside the stranger.

"Tell me what to do to help."

He turned and looked at her. Tiny beads of sweat had ormed across his forehead. She watched the cords and tenons in his neck pop up with each measure of rope he ulled.

"Cut the rope from the aspen and when there is enough, ake the end and tie it good and fast to another strong tree."

Abigail nodded. Lars was beside her in a heartbeat. Beveen the two of them they finally hacked the rope from the attered little aspen.

Abigail watched while slowly the coil of rope grew in size. hen it was long enough, she and Lars located another tree—a juniper with its roots firmly cleaving into stone—and tied the rope off. Then she turned back to look at the man straining to pull Willem from the pit.

"He's dead, he has to be," Brawley exclaimed. "Nobody could survive that kind of jerking around. 'Sides, the way the rocks have been falling in he probably got hit in the head and killed." Brawley tucked his fingers inside his armpits and rocked back on his heels.

"Why don't you shut up, Brawley," Lars snarled.

Abigail looked at the man and saw no trace of pity or remorse in his eyes. She realized he would be glad if they pulled Willem from the shaft dead.

"Why don't you just leave, Brawley?" she asked.

He frowned and looked up at her. "You don't mean to tell me that you care about him?"

"Of course I care. He's my husband." She turned away and tried to ignore the shocked look on Brawley's face.

"What happened?" Lars's voice cut through the fog o pain surrounding Abigail. "What were you doing out here Abbie girl?"

"I slipped and fell. I didn't know there was an old min shaft here." The feeling was returning to her limbs. Fir burned along one leg and sent a dull, throbbing ache cours ing through her body. She sank to the ground, and Lars sa beside her.

"You gave us quite a scare." Lars patted her arm. "Wi and Matthew were worried sick."

"Where is Matthew?" Abigail felt herself torn in hal She worried for Matthew but she felt anchored here wit Will.

"He's with Gustafson's daughter. He'll be all right soon as we get you both home."

"Both—yes—he has to be all right."

"We ought to leave him down there, damned Black Irish."

Abigail recognized Grady Dawson's voice. She turned her head and looked at him. His eyes were ringed in dark circles and his nose was swollen twice its normal size from his "conversation" with Willem.

"Mr. Dawson, that's my husband down there." It took every ounce of breath she had to speak, but she would not let him malign Willem anymore.

"Damned murderer, that's what he is." The man hissed and moved from her line of vision. She heard the sound of wood creaking and the singing of rope being strained to its limits. Fear shot through her.

"Lord, help him, please."

Lars slowly got to his feet. She couldn't see beyond the small circle of light provided by the lanterns but she could hear. He was speaking with the man who doggedly pulled the rope and fed the extra line into the pile behind him. She saw Lars take one of the lanterns and go to the juniper tree. He found a large branch and rigged the rope to create a makeshift pulley.

Now each time the man gained purchase at the pit, Lars took up the slack. More rope was being hoisted upward with each pull. Abigail leaned forward and strained with every sinew in her body for the sound of Willem's voice.

"I tell you that son of a bitch is a black-hearted murderer. Do you want to be next?" Dawson spoke again. He stared down on Abigail while he waited for her response.

"I don't care what he's done or what he's been. He's my husband and the father of my child. I love him." Abigail felt the salty sting of tears in her eyes. She wished she could get to her feet and slap the man across the face, but her leg was throbbing with an intensity that sapped her strength.

"Just exactly what is it you are accusing Willem Tremain of doing?" asked the stranger who had his body braced to pull Willem from the dark pit.

"I guess you ain't heard. In Leadville, 'bout seven years ago, he killed an entire crew." A murmur of agreement came from Brawley.

The man scowled and opened his mouth to speak, but a commotion froze the words inside his throat.

"Look—it's him!" Lars's voice cut through the night.

Abigail gasped and turned to look. Willem's head lolled to the side and there was blood running from a deep gash near his temple.

"Oh, dear God. Is he alive?" Abigail waited while the man struggled to pull Willem's limp body to the safety of the aspen lattice.

"I—I can't quite reach him," Lars said.

Finally the man leaned out to a point where Abigail was sure he, too, would plummet through the limbs and down the shaft. When she was sure all was lost, his fingers closed around the wool collar of Will's coat. He yanked him hard and soon had Willem's body stretched out safely across a frozen snowbank.

"Will? Will?" she sobbed while the man cut the rope from around Will's middle. A groan and gasp for air was the sweetest sound she'd ever heard. Willem tossed his head from side to side in obvious pain.

"Will, where are you hurt?" She touched him on the face, the shoulders, anywhere she might lay her hands, more to assure herself he was alive than for any other reason.

"Abigail?" His words were thick and slurred. "Abigail, are you all right?"

His eyes opened and she felt the tears freezing to her face again. He was haggard and pale but he was alive. Her heart leapt inside her chest at the sight of him. She loved him so much.

"I want to hear more about this murder." The man who had saved Will's life got to his feet and walked toward Grady Dawson. "In Leadville, you say? You were there?" The man took another step closer.

Abigail saw lantern light flicker across his cold gray eyes and she was afraid for Willem.

"Not exactly, but I heard." Dawson backed up in the face of the stranger's curiosity.

"You heard? I wonder how much you heard and how much you made up."

Abigail felt Will's fingers tighten on her own. She saw the pain written across his face and in his eyes.

"It doesn't matter what you did, Will, not to me. I love you for the man you are—not what you used to be," she whispered.

He smiled at her and she felt something hot flow over her cold body.

"I love you, too, Abigail." He tried to raise his head off the ground but she saw him grit his teeth and sag back in pain. "Who is that man talking?" Willem asked when he let his breath out in a painful groan.

"I don't know, but he saved your life, Will."

"I like it when you call me Will." He shifted his body and tried to smile.

The man's voice was familiar, and Willem wished he could see better, but the lanterns cast eerie shadows over the man's face. He wiggled around and tried to hear what was being said.

"Let me tell you something. That cave-in in Leadville was an accident. Willem Tremain had no more to do with it than having the misfortune of being supplied with old dynamite."

"You expect me or anybody else to believe that? I suppose that's why he was the only one who came out alive. And how do you know so damned much about it, anyway?" Grady challenged.

Abigail listened in mute fascination. Something about Willem's changing expression told her this man spoke from firsthand knowledge.

"Willem Tremain wasn't the only man to come out." The man's voice was hard.

"That's true. I heard there was one other man." Brawley Cummins frowned and narrowed his gaze on the stranger "Who are you?"

"Sennen Mulgrew."

Abigail remembered the name. Sennen Mulgrew had been with Willem. She found herself holding her breath, hoping he would continue. The pressure from Will's hand kept increasing with each passing minute.

"Everybody seems to be real curious about what happened. Maybe it's time somebody did talk about it. Afte three days of being buried alive in that hellhole, they fi nally dug us out. Willem and I were the only ones left alive Do you have any idea what it's like? Do you know what thing like that does to a man's mind?"

Sennen moved, and Abigail saw the haunted look in h face. She was beginning to understand more about her hus band.

"Sennen—don't." Willem spoke, and Abigail saw him wince in pain. She wondered how seriously he was hurt.

"No, Will. It's time these buzzards heard the truth." H spun around and faced the men.

"They brought us out—two shells of the men we ha been—barely alive and more than half out of our mind with grief and fear. I tried to explain to Moira that Wille had been through hell, but she wouldn't listen. Then wh the nightmares started coming she ran like a frightened rabbit from the responsibility of having a husband who needed her. By the time Will realized what had happened she was long gone and the rumors got worse."

Willem coughed and shuddered. Abigail wondered if he was letting the ghosts of his past go, she hoped he was.

"Willem has felt guilty for that accident for years—thanks to the waggin' tongues and some damn idiot hangin' the name of Black Irish on him. I'm telling you now, it was no more his fault than it was any other man jack in that hole. It just happened."

"Sennen, it's all right. I don't care anymore—it's in the past." Willem reached out and touched Abigail's face. She realized it was in the past for them both.

"What about us now, Will?" Abigail's voice was full of emotion.

"Don't you worry about me. I'm tougher than you think. The only thing we need to do is get you back home. Mathew must be worried about his mama." Willem kissed the back of her hand.

"Oh, Will, I do love him like he's my own."

"I know you do, Abbie girl, and he is your own. He is the hild of your heart." He took in a painful breath and closed is eyes. Abigail caught sight of blood in his raw palms and er heart twisted with love.

"Oh, Will, you're hurt."

"Abigail, I never felt better in my life." He smiled and ressed her cold knuckles to his cheek.

He reached out and brushed one wayward strand of hair ack from her face. She was bruised and her face was coved with dirt but she had never looked prettier.

"Will, I want to go see that judge in Silverton again."

Willem frowned and tried to make sense of her words. I'll do whatever you think is best, Abigail." He had told himself that he would let her and Matthew go if it meant their happiness. Now he would have to be man enough to keep the vow.

She leaned over and kissed his forehead. Her lips were warm and soft in the cold, crisp air. "Do you know why I want to see the judge again?"

"No."

"I want you to marry me again."

"Marry...you...again?" He heard the happiness and doubt in his whispered words. "Why? Wasn't marrying me once more than enough?"

"No. I want to do it again, because this time I want yo to know it's not just for Matthew. I want you to believe tha I love you, completely—I want to be your wife in ever way."

"Are you sure, Abbie? Even with my dark past and hars temper? Do you really want to remain bound to me?" Wil lem raised his throbbing hand and stroked the side of he face. The falling snow had wet her hair and stuck severa strands to her red cheeks.

"I have been a fool, Will. I tried to hold back, to insulat myself—and Matthew—from life. But I see now that is n way to live."

"You are an angel sent to bring light into my gloom life." He kissed her knuckles. "I love you."

"Willem, I think it's time Matthew learned about his fa ther."

"Abbie, if you do that you'll have to tell him abo Moira. I wouldn't ever ask it of you. You have been the on mother he has ever known. You've earned that place."

She smiled and touched his lips, as if to silence his pr test. "He will always be the child of my heart, if not n flesh. I believe our love is strong enough to withstand th test."

"All right, Abigail, whatever you want." Willem pulled her close and felt the warmth of her tears on his face. He gently touched his lips to hers and let their warmth mingle. The cool snowflakes began to gather on their faces.

"Come on, you two, let's get you home before we all freeze," Lars's voice interrupted.

Will looked up and chuckled. Sennen Mulgrew and Lars were grinning at him and Abigail, and he realized what a sight they must make, huddled in the snow.

Will realized he had never felt better, even with his throbbing hands and aching ribcage. He felt like the king of the mountain, lying in the snow with Abigail in his arms and the future before them like a bright, shining nugget. He had finally been freed from his past and the ghosts that haunted him and Abigail.

"Let's go home, honey, home to our son," he said softly, before he kissed the snowflakes from her lips.

* * * * *

Author Note

Today Guston is a ghost town. Gone is the little church, so unique, with both bell and whistle to satisfy the Cornish miners. There are no more boardinghouses, bordellos or billiard halls.

Silverton, however, survives. The plucky town has endured the boom and busts of the mining era since 1874. In the last century fortunes were made and lost around the small community. The town motto is The Mining Town That Never Quits.

Still in operation almost a century later is the Grand Imperial Hotel. There is no more haberdashery, San Juan County now has their own offices, and the dining room is no longer in the basement, but the hotel looks, sounds and *feels* the same. When climbing the beautiful, steep stairs to the rooms above, you almost expect to see a rough miner, or lady in silk and satin.

At the Silverton museum, you can see a "single-jack,' eighteen-pound sledges, peacock copper and gold. There is even a display in honor of Otto Mears, the determined gen tleman who built the first road—"The Million Dolla Highway"—through the lofty peaks of southern Colorado

As you probably already know, it was all true—except o course the story of Abbie and Will. Then again, if you stan on the edge of town, there is a whisper of voices from long ago that winds through the quaking aspens. Maybe it was all true.

Readers just can't seem to get enough of
New York Times bestselling author

Sandra Brown

This May, a mother searches for

A Secret Splendor

(previously published under the pseudonym Erin St. Claire)

Arden Gentry is searching for the son she was forced to give up. But finding him could resurrect all the half-truths, secrets and unspeakable lies that surrounded his birth. Because it means finding the man who fathered her baby....

Find out how it all turns out, this May at your favorite retail outlet.

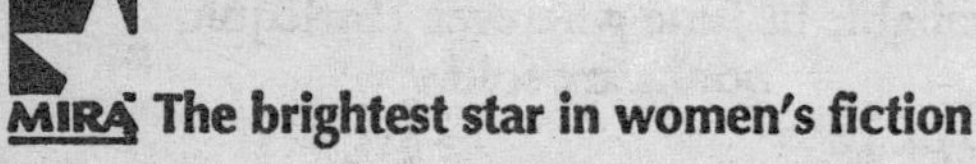

MSBASS